2/9 800
1⁰⁰

BANTAM BOOKS

New York   Toronto

London   Sydney

Auckland

WITH THIS PUZZLE, I THEE KILL

Parnell Hall

WITH THIS PUZZLE, I THEE KILL

A Bantam Book / December 2003

Published by
Bantam Dell
A Division of Random House, Inc.
New York, New York

Book design by Glen Edelstein

Library of Congress Cataloging-in-Publication Data
Hall, Parnell.
With this puzzle, I thee kill / Parnell Hall.
p. cm.
ISBN 0-553-80241-0
1. Felton, Cora (Fictitious character)—Fiction. 2. Crossword puzzle
makers—Fiction. 3. Women detectives—Fiction. 4. Connecticut—Fiction.
5. Aged women—Fiction. 6. Weddings—Fiction. I. Title.

PS3558.A37327W57 2003
813'.54—dc21
2003052404

Manufactured in the United States of America
Published simultaneously in Canada

BVG   10 9 8 7 6 5 4 3 2 1

For Lynn,
who said yes.

A CRYPTOGRAM FOR THE PUZZLE LADY

A cryptogram is a coded message. There are many types. In a common cryptogram, each letter of the alphabet has been replaced by another letter of the alphabet. This is rather easy to solve.

Other codes are harder. Letters are not substituted but rearranged. To solve the code, it is necessary to figure out the method by which this was accomplished.

It took the Allies ten months to crack the Enigma code in World War II. . . .

The Puzzle Lady doesn't have that long, and would appreciate all the help she can get.

WITH THIS PUZZLE, I THEE KILL

Prologue

"Are you going to wear white?" Sherry Carter asked.

Cora Felton flailed her way through the profusion of material the seamstress had managed to drape about her body, then shot her niece a reproving look. "Of course I'm going to wear white. I always wear white when I get married. Except what's-his-name, who wanted me to wear the frou-frou thing." She grimaced at the memory. "That really should have given me the hint."

"It certainly should have," Sherry agreed, a little too quickly. In Sherry's opinion, *all* of Cora's husbands had been undesirable, and she marveled at the fact it had taken marrying them to get Cora to see that.

Cora Felton, though quite aware of her niece's views, was not at all sympathetic to them. After all, Sherry's marriage had been an absolute disaster.

"Is that right?" Cora said. "I bet you don't even know which one I'm talking about."

"Do you?" Sherry shot back.

Cora frowned: Which damn husband was it who had wanted the unorthodox ceremony? *Unorthodox.* Was it the Jewish one? No, he'd gone along with the church wedding.

"Could you keep your arms up?" the seamstress asked, a trifle too sweetly. Cora had been squirming like an octopus ever since the fitting began, and the woman's nerves were getting frayed.

"Not if you're gonna poke me," Cora grumbled defensively. "If you're gonna poke me, I'm gonna move."

"I'm not going to poke you," the seamstress said, edgily. She was a lean woman in work shirt and jeans, with her hair cut in bangs, and a kerchief around her neck. To Cora, the scissors stuck in the woman's belt began to look like a weapon.

The bridal shop where Cora was being fitted for a wedding gown was in New York City. Had it been in her hometown of Bakerhaven, Connecticut, Cora would undoubtedly have been recognized instantly as the Puzzle Lady, famous for both her crossword puzzle column and her TV commercials, but the seamstress here in the big city didn't seem to have a clue. Not that Cora expected special treatment. Still, it would have been nice not to merit contempt.

"I didn't think you could remember," Sherry told Cora.

"A lot of them tend to blend together," Cora admitted. "You've only been married once. Any memories you have are apt to be right."

"You make that sound like a bad thing."

"Well, your marriage was."

"I was talking about quantity, not quality."

"Please," Cora protested. "No wordplay, or I'll go nuts."

The seamstress gasped. "Oh, my God, you're the Puzzle Lady! Here I am working on you, and you're the Puzzle Lady! Goodness, how extraordinary!"

Cora didn't feel obliged to point out just how ordinary it was for her to get married. Nevertheless, some self-deprecating gesture was indicated. Cora resented that. The woman abuses her for an hour, then makes her apologize.

"It's really nothing," Cora told her. "But this wedding is important to me. Even if it's not important to my niece."

The seamstress, not five minutes from flinging Cora around like a rag doll, now sprang to her defense. "How can you say that?" she demanded of Sherry. "Of course the wedding must be just right."

Sherry groaned. Here she was, getting the worst of it on all fronts. And maddeningly so. The accusations were unfair, unjust, and dead wrong. In point of fact, Sherry Carter wrote the crossword puzzle column her aunt took credit for. If the truth be known, Cora Felton couldn't construct a puzzle if her life depended on it. Not that she wanted to. Cora Felton didn't even *like* crossword puzzles. She liked solving crimes, and was unusually adept at it. Puzzles, on the other hand, left her cold.

The seamstress, writhing in the death throes of the terminally starstruck, simpered, "You're going to need some more lace. The grander the wedding, the grander the lace, that's what I always say. You would not *believe* the way I can streamline a gown." She flushed. "Not that you *need* streamlining, mind. But the lines do make a difference, dear."

Cora was beginning to miss the acerbic seamstress who thought she was a pain. "Just don't squeeze me into it like a sausage. If I gotta wear the damn thing all day, I gotta be comfortable."

The seamstress raised both eyebrows at the word *damn*. Could this *really* be the same woman who sold breakfast cereal to children on TV? "I promise you'll be comfortable. Of course, many brides drop five to ten pounds just before walking down the aisle. We have to take that into consideration."

"If you do, you'll bleed from the nose," Cora informed her. "If I lose weight, you can take the dress in. If I gain weight, you can let it out. Make it fit me *now*."

"Yes, of course, dear."

The seamstress, much chastened, looped some more fabric.

Cora fingered the silk. "Oh, this is nice! You think he'll like it?"

"He hasn't even proposed yet," Sherry pointed out.

Cora waved it away. "That's a mere formality. Trust me, I've been married often enough to know. When it happens, you've gotta be ready. I mean, what if the guy proposed, and before you could get the dress made he changed his mind?"

"I would think you'd count yourself lucky you didn't marry such a fickle man."

"Oh, yeah? I'll have you know just such a fickle man paid for my apartment. Men agree to anything when they want to be free."

The seamstress could not have looked more shocked had Cora just revealed herself to be a phone-sex operator. Cora stuck one finger under the woman's chin, closed her mouth.

"I don't care what you say, this is tight. Let's go one size larger. If you need to, you can take it in. *Dear*."

"Yes, ma'am."

"You do have it in a larger size, don't you?"

"Yes, of course. Just let me go look."

"Good. When you find it, bring it to me. I'm getting out of this straitjacket."

Cora thrust the veil at Sherry, and stomped off in the direction of the changing rooms.

"Oh, dear," the seamstress said. "Is she . . . I mean . . . is she really going to buy a dress?"

Sherry smiled. "I don't think there's anything I could say that would stop her. Yes, she's worth waiting on. You can count on the sale."

The seamstress flushed again. She hurried off to the back of the store to look for a larger wedding gown.

Sherry sat, turning the veil over in her hands. She smiled wistfully. Her own wedding had been an elopement. No gown, no veil, no church service, no guests.

If only that had been the worst of it.

She shrugged off the thought. This was about Cora, not her. This was Cora's chance for happiness. Just because she couldn't remember how many chances she'd had shouldn't diminish its importance. And, assuming it took place, this would be the first of Cora's weddings Sherry had attended. Cora had asked her to be the maid of honor. Sherry couldn't disappoint her. She needed to get in the spirit.

Out on the sidewalk, a scraggly young man in black jeans and a sleeveless black T-shirt stood peering in the window of the bridal shop. Razor, as the lead guitarist for the rock band Tune Freaks liked to be called, pushed the matted hair off his forehead, rubbed his bleary eyes. To a casual observer, Razor might have appeared stoned out of his mind, but that was just the way Razor always looked. In point of fact, the guitarist could seldom afford drugs, and had long since run out of young women willing to give them to him.

Of late, Razor had been in a particularly foul mood due to the fact the Tune Freaks' lead singer, Dennis Pride, had quit the band, leaving the singing chores up for grabs. Razor didn't want to sing, but he didn't want anyone *else* in the band to sing, and possibly rival him. So Razor was singing *and* playing lead guitar. His voice was adequate at best, his guitar playing suffered, and no one in the band was happy.

At the moment, however, Razor appeared to be having either an epiphany or an acid flashback. He stood mesmerized, gazing in the window at the beautiful young woman sitting alone in the Fifth Avenue bridal shop, a beautiful young woman who smiled wistfully and held a bridal veil.

1

CORA FELTON WAS RADIANT. CORA ALWAYS LOOKED GOOD, WHICH was one of the reasons Sherry had chosen Cora's picture to grace the Puzzle Lady column. But tonight, in the presence of Raymond Harstein III, Cora was positively glowing. She blossomed in his notice, she basked in his gaze.

Sherry Carter was amazed. She had met some of Cora's husbands, but always after Cora had married them. This was the first time she'd witnessed a courtship, and it was an eye-opening experience. Cora was totally gaga. Seeing her aunt in love helped Sherry understand how Cora had fallen for some of the despicable men she'd managed to wed. The woman was giddy as a schoolgirl.

And on her finger was a ring with a diamond as big as the Ritz.

Cora and Raymond had just gotten engaged.

Much to Sherry's dismay.

"You are the most gorgeous girl in the world," Raymond assured Cora.

Sherry Carter shuddered. Her aunt was all decked out in a red satin number that was just a little too young on the one hand, and a little too narrow in the waist on the other. Cora looked perfectly respectable. But the most gorgeous girl in the world? Really.

If the truth be known, Sherry was not as upset with the assessment as with the assessor. Raymond Harstein III was, in Sherry's humble opinion, one of the most pretentious human beings she'd ever met. She didn't care for the way he talked, the way he moved, the way he tilted his nose, the way he carried his chin. She even resented the III in his name, although, presumably, that was Raymond Harstein Jr.'s fault, and not his. Be that as it may, Sherry Carter was not smitten, and it took only a single effusive, hyperbolic compliment to set her teeth on edge. Although, as a wordsmith, Sherry had to admit "the most gorgeous girl in the world" was not really hyperbole, just a gross exaggeration.

Cora, however, seemed to take the praise at face value. "Oh, Raymond," she simpered. "You spoil me."

It was all Sherry could do to keep from gagging.

"Not at all, my dear," Raymond declared, patting Cora on the hand, another gesture that Sherry deplored. Good lord, couldn't Cora see through this man? A lovesick schoolgirl of *sixteen* could see through this man. Surely her aunt had learned *something* in her umpteen previous marriages. How could she be so blind? When Raymond favored her with "Of course, *you* look lovely too," it was all Sherry could do to keep from leaping across the table and strangling him.

Raymond Harstein III was a slender man of indeterminate age, the difficulty of that estimation a testament Sherry ascribed to the effectiveness of Just For Men hair coloring. Raymond's dark brown hair was gray at the temples, which didn't fool

Sherry one bit. She suspected him of having snow-white hair, dyeing it brown, and then touching it up with gray highlights.

As to the rest of it, Raymond Harstein III had blue eyes and a nose both pointed and rounded at the same time, as if the scurrilous gentleman was unwilling to commit to anything. A trim mustache, brown from the bottle, topped thin lips that never ceased to smile. He was dressed in a blue suit, white shirt, red patterned tie. Raymond always wore suits, ranging in Sherry's opinion from the cheap to the inexpensive, or in Cora's, from the practical to the thrifty.

"Thank you," Sherry told him now. "You're looking quite distinguished yourself."

Raymond made a self-deprecating gesture. "Please. I am a weed amongst blossoms, happy to be growing. So sorry your young beau couldn't join us. I should really get to know him if I'm marrying into the family now, shouldn't I?"

"Aaron's not really family," Sherry said.

"Ah, but he could be." Raymond's eyes twinkled. "If your aunt wouldn't mind sharing the spotlight. What do you think, Cora? How would a double wedding suit you?"

Sherry stiffened at the suggestion.

Cora threw back her head and laughed. "Fine by me, Raymond, but I'm afraid you don't know my niece very well. I don't think Sherry's inclined to accept a wedding proposal unless it's the bridegroom making it."

"Yes, yes, of course. Wouldn't want to usurp the young man's prerogative."

"Of course," Cora agreed. "But you should snap him up, Sherry, before that Becky Baldwin gets her claws into him."

For Sherry, that comment marked the point at which she knew her aunt really was out of control. Under normal circumstances, Cora never would have teased Sherry about her rival, Becky Baldwin, in front of a third person. The idea that Cora was treating Raymond as family didn't cut it with Sherry. As far as she was concerned, her aunt had gone completely round the bend.

A waitress with a notepad swooped down on their table. "Can I get y'all something to drink?"

Raymond immediately took charge, proceeded to relay all orders through himself—another habit Sherry detested. "And what would you like, my dear?" he asked her.

"I'll have a white wine," Sherry said directly to the waitress.

Raymond went on as if he hadn't noticed. "Excellent," he said. "A white wine for the young lady. Now, my dear, what would you like this evening?"

Cora hesitated just a moment before saying, "I'll have a Shirley Temple."

Raymond nodded his approval, relayed those instructions, and ordered a seltzer and lime for himself.

Sherry watched with growing horror. Raymond had taken exception to Cora's drinking, counseled moderation. For one who imbibed as heavily as Cora was in the habit of doing, this was a major step, and one of which Sherry would have ordinarily approved. The thought Cora was doing it for *him* rankled. Sherry sighed, glanced around.

They were dining in the Country Kitchen, Bakerhaven's homey, inexpensive, and popular restaurant, which featured a well-stocked salad bar and standard American cuisine. As usual, the tables and booths were quite full. Most of the customers were local, and many seemed to have taken an interest in their table. Bakerhaven was the type of town where most everybody knew everybody. A stranger such as Raymond Harstein III was indeed cause for comment.

"What do you think, Sherry?" Raymond asked.

As she hadn't heard a word, Sherry was hard-pressed to offer an opinion.

Luckily, Cora swooped to the rescue. "Oh, what does Sherry know about weddings? The poor girl's only had one, and that was an elopement. Trust me, this is not a big deal. The TV people probably won't even come."

Raymond frowned. "TV people?"

"Yes, the Channel 8 news team. They cover this town."

Raymond seemed amused, but Sherry could have sworn he was putting it on. "You expect your wedding to rate TV coverage?" he asked Cora.

"*Our* wedding," Cora corrected demurely. "No, I don't. I was just saying I don't expect them to come. Even though that reporter seems to have it in for me."

"A TV reporter? Why?"

"No reason. Just every time Rick Reed tries to cover me he winds up looking stupid."

Raymond's blue eyes twinkled. "You mean you make a fool of him?"

"No. I think he's just naturally stupid."

Aaron Grant came in the door. The young newspaper reporter looked around, spotted their table. He strolled over just in time to have his way blocked by the waitress with her tray of drinks.

"Hi, gang," Aaron told them. "Don't let me interfere with your dinner. Just dropped by to say hello."

"Would you care to join us?" Raymond invited. "We're just about to order."

"Thanks, but I'm working," Aaron replied. "I'm doing an interview."

"Having dinner with someone?" Sherry asked him.

"Just a drink. I'm interviewing an ambulance driver. I checked the bar, he's not there yet."

"Interviewing an ambulance driver in the bar?" Sherry said. "I would think that's a story in itself."

Aaron frowned. "I hadn't thought of that."

"Your readers won't either, unless you start off with a folksy, 'I caught up with so-and-so in the bar, and over a few pints of ale he told me,'" Sherry pointed out.

"You're very good with words," Raymond observed.

Sherry grimaced. "Runs in the family."

"That it does," Aaron said, with a knowing smile. Aaron was one of the few people in town who knew that Sherry, not Cora, was the real Puzzle Lady and composed the crossword puzzle column.

"Say, nice ring, Cora!" Aaron whistled. "Do I gather there is to be an announcement in the near future?"

Cora shot a glance at Raymond. "Yes, but don't put it in the paper. We haven't even set the wedding date yet."

"Really? Well, congratulations! This is wonderful."

"Thank you," Raymond said. He added tentatively, "You will sit on the announcement?"

"Sure thing. As long as it's just me. If my editor finds out and tells me to write it, that's another story."

"Just hold off as long as you can," Cora said. "Once it's published it's tabloid material. I don't really want to read about it in the *National Enquirer*."

Becky Baldwin came in, looked around.

Sherry Carter caught her breath. Sherry often did on seeing Becky Baldwin. Stunning as usual, in a purple pants suit which could have served the young lawyer quite well had she had to appear in court, and could easily double as evening wear, Becky looked so good that had Raymond Harstein III pronounced her the most beautiful girl in the world, Sherry would have found it hard to refute.

Becky swooped down on their table, hooked her arm through Aaron Grant's, and said, "Well, here I am. Where do you want to do the interview?"

Sherry Carter arched her eyebrows at Aaron.

Cora Felton, boundlessly amused by Becky's announcement, pretended to cough into her napkin.

"Do you drive an ambulance, Becky?" Sherry inquired politely.

"Not that I am aware of."

"No, that's my other interview," Aaron said. "You're early, Becky. The ambulance driver's actually scheduled first."

"Yes, of course," Becky said. She turned her eyes to Raymond Harstein III. "I don't believe we've met. I'm Becky Baldwin. I'm the town lawyer."

Raymond Harstein III rose to his feet, crossed around the table to take her hand. He didn't shake it, however. Instead, he clasped it in both of his as if it were a precious thing. "Raymond Harstein III. Very pleased to meet you. You say you're the town lawyer? You mean you're the only one?"

"No," Becky told him. "Just the only one worth mentioning."

"I'll say." Raymond smiled. "I bet the young men invent excuses to hire you."

"Oh, please," Becky demurred. "What do you say, Aaron? If the ambulance driver's not here, why don't we go first?"

Aaron smiled sheepishly. He clearly wasn't comfortable walking off with Becky, but there didn't seem to be any alternative, short of sitting down to eat dinner.

"Run along, you two," Sherry said. "I'm sure you have lots to talk about."

"Do we?" Becky said archly to Aaron. "What *did* you want to interview me about, anyway?"

"Oh, we'll think of something," Aaron said breezily. In point of fact he was doing a piece on single career women, but he was damned if he was going to start explaining. Anything he said would only sound defensive.

"You better," Becky purred. "If you don't write an article, the paper won't pay for the drinks."

"The paper won't anyway," Aaron said. "What, did you think I had an expense account?"

Sherry's smile was becoming more and more frozen. Any more cute banter and she was going to scream.

"Sherry!" came a voice from across the room.

Sherry looked up, and was amazed to see Brenda Wallenstein, her college roommate, hurtling across the dining room floor.

Brenda was what the boys called pleasingly plump, a short, cute, comfortable dynamo, with a sense of humor to boot. Brenda and Sherry had been close and stayed in touch even after college. When Sherry had been going through rough times with her husband, there were many nights she had crashed on Brenda's couch.

Sherry's face lit up. She hadn't seen Brenda since she'd moved to Connecticut, but the sight of her old college chum always cheered her. She leaped to her feet, gave Brenda a hug.

"Oh, my goodness, it's good to see you. Brenda, it's been too long. It's nice in the country, but I miss my friends from New York. Not lumping you with my friends in general, I mean I miss you in particular. Oh, my goodness. Everyone, this is Brenda, my roommate from Dartmouth. You know my aunt Cora. This is my friend, Aaron Grant. He's a reporter. And Becky Baldwin, she's a lawyer. Aaron's about to interview her for the paper." Sherry flushed slightly. That was more information than she needed to give. "Brenda's a nurse at Mount Sinai Hospital," she appended, as if to make up for it.

Raymond had stood up again.

"Oh, and Raymond Harstein III." Sherry looked at Cora. "Can I tell her?"

"If you can do it quietly."

"Yes, of course." Sherry lowered her voice. "Raymond and Cora are engaged."

"Oh, my God!" Brenda shrieked in excitement, then lowered her voice and hissed congratulations. Brenda had round cheeks,

big eyes, long lashes. Her curly brown hair added to her perpetu-
ally bubbly look. "This is *so* amazing! And what a *coincidence*."

"Coincidence?" Sherry's mouth dropped open. But of course.
How could she have missed it? Her friend was radiant, glowing,
giddy—just like her aunt. "Brenda, are you kidding me? Do you
mean it?"

Brenda nodded. "It's true. Can you believe it? Me. It finally
happened to me."

Sherry shrieked, hugged Brenda again, and they were off,
chattering like crows on amphetamines.

"Well, who is he?" Sherry demanded. "Do I know him?"

This time Brenda's laugh sounded somewhat forced. "Yes,
you do. . . ."

And in from the bar walked Sherry's ex-husband, Dennis
Pride.

2

SHERRY'S HEART STOPPED. A COLD, ICY FEELING GRIPPED HER from head to toe.

Dennis.

Good God.

Dennis.

It was too much to take in all at once.

The last time Sherry had seen Dennis he'd beaten her up. He'd defied a court order to do it. He still called her now and then, when he was on a binge. On such occasions Sherry would simply let the answering machine pick up.

Now here he was, standing in front of her, for the first time since her bruises had healed. Long enough ago that the only reminder was a faint trace of a scar remaining from her split lip.

"Dennis," Sherry said. "You shouldn't be here."

He winced, then smiled deprecatingly as if she'd committed a social faux pas. "Times have changed, Sherry. Things are different now. I'm different."

Dennis certainly *looked* different. The Dennis of old had hair to his shoulders, wore dirty T-shirts and ratty jeans, as befitted the lead singer of a rock group. Today, his hair was razor cut and styled, slightly long by normal standards, but practically a crew cut for him. He wore a navy blue sports jacket, a white shirt, open at the neck, and tan pants. His black hair glistened, his blue eyes sparkled, his white teeth gleamed. It was a shock to see him standing next to Aaron Grant. Aaron looked good. Dennis looked like a movie star.

As Sherry hesitated, Brenda grabbed her hands. "Sherry. Sweetheart. Get with the picture. It's ancient history. This has nothing to do with you. Dennis is here to marry me."

Sherry took a deep breath. "I'm happy for you," she managed grudgingly. "But why are you here?"

"You're my best friend. I need you. You have to be my maid of honor."

Sherry's mouth fell open.

"I know, I know, it's all so sudden. You haven't had time to think it over. But, Sherry, sweetheart. It's good for you, and it's good for me, and it's good for Dennis. Is it all right?"

"Of course it's all right," Dennis agreed with a charming smile. "And all you people will come too. Cora and her friend. And this young couple here. You're welcome too."

"Oh, we're not a couple," Becky laughed. "I'm Becky Baldwin. I'm quite single myself, thank you very much."

Under other circumstances, Sherry might have rolled her eyes at her aunt. Becky's behavior was so typical, flirting with the handsome newcomer even as he announced his engagement.

"Oh, is that right?" Dennis said, favoring Becky with a smile.

"Yes, it is," Becky answered. "This is Aaron Grant. Aaron happens to be the object of Sherry's affections."

A cloud passed over Dennis's face. It was momentary, but for a second his facade slipped. For a second he was the same old

Dennis Sherry had always known. The same old Dennis he always would be.

Then he was smiling and extending his hand. "Very pleased to meet you, Aaron. I'm glad someone's taking care of that little girl of mine."

Aaron, usually so glib, was at a loss for a rejoinder. Nothing seemed appropriate. After all, Dennis *was* her ex-husband. There was no denying that. And somehow any comment seemed wrong.

It didn't help when Dennis said, "You're engaged to my Sherry, are you?"

"I'm going with Sherry. We're not engaged."

"Going with?" Dennis was tremendously tickled. "You mean like high school? You hear that, Brenda? They're going together."

"Yes, I know."

"Oh?"

"Sherry's my best friend. We tell each other things."

"We *used* to," Sherry said.

"Sherry, don't be like that. This is a *good* thing. It's the answer to all our prayers. Unless it hurts our friendship. That's why it's so important that you be my maid of honor."

"Brenda, I can't."

"Sure you can."

"I'm his ex-wife. It would be wholly inappropriate."

"No, it would be a wonderful gesture, healing the rift, and making amends."

Sherry's eyes blazed. "Making amends?"

Cora leaped to Sherry's rescue. "Well, she can't do it. She can't be your maid of honor. She's gonna be mine."

"I don't think it's an exclusive position," Dennis observed with a grin.

"Of course it isn't," Brenda said. "Come on, Sherry. I need your blessing."

"What's your wedding date, Brenda?" Cora asked.

"Saturday!" Brenda bubbled. "I'm to be a June bride! We're getting married next Saturday! June 12!"

Cora shook her head. "Same as mine. You see, it won't work. You'll just have to get someone else."

Raymond Harstein's mouth fell open at this announcement. Aaron and Sherry looked at each other.

Dennis frowned. "You're getting married next Saturday?"

"Yes, we are," Cora cooed. She squeezed Raymond's cheeks, partly as a gesture of affection, and partly to make sure he didn't protest. "So I'm afraid Sherry's going to be busy."

"But we need Sherry, don't we, honey?" Brenda urged her intended bridegroom.

Dennis ignored Brenda completely, having zeroed in on Cora as his biggest obstacle. "Okay. So here's what we do. We make it a double wedding. That way Sherry can be there." He turned to Raymond Harstein III. "You wouldn't mind sharing, would you?"

Raymond, still reeling from the news his wedding was to take place the very next weekend, said, "Not at all. Ow," he added, as Cora kicked him in the shin.

Dennis took no notice. "Perfect. Then it's settled. We'll have a double wedding, and Sherry can be maid of honor for both."

"Where's your wedding going to be, Brenda?" Cora asked.

"St. Patrick's Cathedral." Brenda's eyes were bright.

"In Manhattan?"

"Of course."

"What a shame." Cora tried not to look smug, but she was practically beaming with mendacious glee. "Our wedding's going to be here in Bakerhaven. Too bad. A double wedding is a wonderful idea, and we'd have been delighted to do it, but it simply won't work. But do give us the address, and we'll be sure to send a gift."

"You're getting married *here?*" Dennis made it sound like slumming.

"We *like* it here," Cora told him. To her chagrin, she realized she was making a conscious effort not to sound defensive.

"Well, why not?" Dennis said airily. "If you can, we can. Whaddya say, Brenda? You wouldn't mind getting married in the country, would you? Let's move our wedding here."

"Do you mean it?" Brenda's mouth was open.

"If your folks can stand the shock. I know it's short notice, but what the hell. We're not that far from the city. The wedding party can drive up."

"Yeah, but we'll have to notify them," Brenda said. "You know how many people my mom invited?"

As Brenda and Dennis discussed the logistics of moving their wedding, Sherry's heart sank. This was the last thing in the world she wanted. But what could she do about it? She could refuse to be maid of honor, but she really couldn't tell Brenda and Dennis where and when they could get married. And if it was the same time as Cora's wedding, how could she not be there?

Dennis grabbed Brenda, gave her a squeeze. "Oh, boy," he declared. "This is going to be great."

Cora knew better.

As far as her niece was concerned, it was the worst thing that could have happened.

3

RAYMOND HARSTEIN III PATTED THE COUCH BESIDE HIM. "COME and sit down."

"I don't want to sit down," Cora snapped. "Sorry, sorry," she instantly amended. "I'm touchy, I'm irritable, I want a cigarette."

"Chew the gum."

"I hate the gum. I hate the patch. I hate pills, psychotherapy, twelve-step programs, support groups. I want to suck smoke into my lungs. That's what I like, that's what I want, that's what I crave. A huge puff of foul, noxious, carcinogenic smoke. Is that too much to ask?"

"You're doing quite well."

"I'm jumping out of my skin. Did you see me at dinner? I thought I was going to throttle that damn Brenda."

"Her? I thought the ex-husband was the problem."

"Yeah, but we *know* he's a schmuck. She's the real stab in the back."

"Why? Sherry wants him out of her life. He's getting married again. Why isn't that a good thing?"

"He's marrying her best friend. That puts him back *in* her life. It's creepy. Hell, it's damn near incestuous."

"It can't be all that bad."

"Raymond, you have to either stop contradicting me, or let me have a cigarette," Cora snarled.

"Now, now, dear, you're doing absolutely great."

Cora shuddered, told herself for the umpteenth time that giving up drinking and smoking was good for her. After all, she'd done worse things for former husbands. She couldn't recall exactly what, but surely she had. "Raymond, sweetheart," she said as she sat next to him on the couch, "could you be a dear and make me a nice cup of tea?"

"With honey and lemon?"

"Yes, with honey and lemon."

"Of course. You just relax, my love, and I'll bring it to you."

Cora relaxed on the couch until Raymond went into the kitchen. Then she jumped up, grabbed her floppy drawstring purse, scurried on little cat feet to the front door, eased it open, and slipped out.

Raymond Harstein III's modest rental house was in what in Bakerhaven passed for a housing development. The houses were small and close together. The couple on the porch swing next door smiled and waved.

Cora's wave back was perfunctory. The neighbors were an old hippie couple, he bald-headed and bearded, with a fringe of long hair, and she a tie-dyed waif in wire-rimmed glasses and fat braids. Either or both often sported love beads. The VW microbus in their driveway had a roof rack on top, a bicycle on the back, and was painted in colors so psychedelic it set your teeth on edge.

Cora fished her cigarettes from her purse, whipped out a

lighter, and fired one up. She puffed on it anxiously, inhaling huge clouds of smoke into her lungs, then expelling them almost violently, so as to suck in more. In approximately thirty seconds she had consumed half the cigarette. She stamped it out, hurled the butt into the bushes, swept the tobacco and ash off the porch with her foot.

Cora pulled out a small plastic bottle of Listerine, took a huge gulp, gargled, and spat into the bushes. She whipped out a breath spray, and squirted it into her mouth. Jamming it back in her purse, she noticed the hippie couple rocking up and down in ill-suppressed glee at her antics. The thin cigarette they had been passing back and forth must not have been tobacco. She had clearly blown their minds.

Cora muttered something she hoped the hippie couple wouldn't hear, opened the door, eased it shut, tiptoed across the room, and flung herself down on the couch just as Raymond Harstein III glided through the kitchen door bearing a cup of tea.

"Here you are, my dear. This will fix you right up. My, you look a little flushed. Are you sure you're feeling well?"

"I'm *not* feeling well," Cora said. "I *told* you I wasn't feeling well."

Raymond's nose twitched, and he frowned ever so slightly.

Cora couldn't tell if he was smelling tobacco or Listerine. "Would you like a breath mint?" she ad-libbed, fumbling in her purse. "Not that you need one, mind. They're just so refreshing. Here, have one and let me sip my tea."

Raymond accepted the mint. "You were saying, dear? About your niece?"

Cora slurped tea. "Ow. Hot. I was saying this wedding is a kick in the face. I was saying it shouldn't be happening at all, but if it is happening, it certainly shouldn't be happening in Bakerhaven. You really have to be more aware of my signals, dear."

"You were trying to signal me?"

"Did you think I was trying to kick a hole in your shin?"

"No, but the message wasn't entirely clear. We should agree on some sort of code, like one kick means invite them to join us, two kicks means get rid of them."

"Couldn't you tell from Sherry's body language?"

"Frankly, I was desperately trying to read yours. Unfortunately, it was in Swahili."

Cora giggled in spite of herself. "Stop humoring me."

"I'm not humoring you, my love."

"See that you don't. This is a serious matter. This guy Dennis is dangerous. The problem is, he *seems* so nice nobody really believes it."

"If you tell me, I believe it."

"That's *exactly* what I mean by humoring me. I don't want you to believe it just because I tell you. I want you to consider the facts and come to an independent conclusion."

"Did I really agree to marry you?"

"That's not exactly the best phrasing."

Raymond's eyes twinkled. "That one was deliberate."

"I know, dear. I'm just distracted. What are we going to do about this damn wedding?"

"That's not how I would have phrased that, either."

"Not ours. Theirs. Raymond, we gotta do something."

"You want me to stop their wedding?"

"No, but we could at least divorce it from ours."

"How? Tell 'em we thought it over and we wanna have our own ceremony?"

"I don't think so."

"I was sure you wouldn't. It's way too straightforward."

Cora looked at him sharply, but his eyes were still twinkling. "You're a wicked man," she scolded, melting. "A wicked, wicked man."

"And you love it," Raymond told her, enfolding her in his arms. "That's amazing."

"What?"

"With a smoker. Even when you quit, the smell of tobacco still lingers."

"I suppose it does take time," Cora murmured. "Raymond, what are we going to do about this other wedding?"

"Think we should try to bust them up?"

"Sherry's fragile. That jerk beat her. Repeatedly. Not that she was a doormat. She fought back. But he was stronger. And, yes, she asked for help. She called the police, they'd come arrest him, he'd get out, come after her again. Dennis is a very sick man. And Brenda is Sherry's best friend."

Cora sighed. "Poor Sherry. This has to be tearing her apart."

4

BRENDA RAN HER FINGER AROUND THE EDGE OF THE BUTCHER-block table in the center of the kitchen, and side-spied up at her best friend.

"Sherry, I swear I never fooled around with Dennis when you were married. Or in college. I barely knew him in college. I don't know how it happened. The band would crash in my loft when they came through town. We just . . . clicked."

"Sit down. I'll make you some coffee."

"I don't need coffee," Brenda said.

"I don't, either," Sherry agreed. "I just like making it. Gives me something to do. Keeps me calm."

"Coffee makes you jittery."

"It's decaf. And you don't have to drink it."

Brenda frowned, but sat at the kitchen table. The large, eat-in kitchen was one of the prime selling points of the modest prefab house, and Sherry was more comfortable entertaining visitors there than in the living room.

"Can't you just be happy for me?" Brenda asked.

"I'm happy for you. At least, I'd like to be happy for you. Brenda, you know what that man did to me."

"He's changed."

Sherry began measuring coffee into the filter of her automatic-drip coffeemaker. She didn't say a word.

"Sherry, don't be like that. Just look at him. Can't you see he's changed?"

"I see he's changed his shirt."

"Sherry . . ."

Sherry slammed the coffeemaker shut, switched it on. She turned to her friend. "Brenda. I'm trying to cut you as much slack as I can. If there's any way this works for you, fine. I'm happy for you. And I understand you needed to come here and tell me about it. You didn't need to bring him, but what's done is done. But there are limits. You want me to stand up and smile at your wedding like I think it's a good thing. How can you ask me that?"

"I know. It seemed a little much to me too."

Sherry's eyes widened. "It's *his* idea?"

"Don't say it like that." Brenda sounded defensive in spite of herself. "Dennis knows how close we are, and he knows what he did to you. Don't you think he wants to make amends?"

Sherry sat at the table across from her friend, took hold of her hands. "Brenda, I would never do anything to hurt you, and I don't want to hurt you now. I'm your friend, and I have to talk to you as a friend. Dennis is a sweet-talking guy. He could charm the birds down from the trees. He could sell ice to the Eskimos. He could even make a foolish girl believe he wasn't going to hit her anymore."

"Sherry—"

"No. Don't argue with me. I'm not arguing with you. I'm just telling you something. I know it won't do any good, but I couldn't live with myself if I didn't say it."

"Fine. You've said it. You're off the hook."

"That's not what I meant."

"Sherry, Dennis only hit you when he was drunk."

"That makes it better?"

"He's stopped drinking."

"He's in AA?"

"No. He just stopped."

"Since when?"

"Since a while."

"How long's a while?"

"Sherry, look at him. It's not just the drinking. He cleaned up his act. He quit the band. He got himself straight."

"What's he doing for cash?"

"My father offered him a job."

"In the textile industry? What does Dennis know about textiles?"

"Dad's gonna train him as a salesman. You said yourself, it's the one thing Dennis can do."

"And Dennis agreed to give up the band and sell sheets and towels?"

"I think years of earning no money wore him down."

"Brenda, you wanna marry Dennis, I can't stop you. But staying here, having the wedding here, that's cuckoo stuff."

"I know," Brenda said. "What about Cora? What's happening there?"

Sherry paused a moment before giving in to the change of subject. "I don't know. This guy moved into town and swept her right off her feet."

"Who is he?"

"Raymond Harstein III."

"Who's Raymond Harstein II?"

"That's the question. According to Raymond, he comes from

San Diego, but I can't find any record of any Raymond Harstein living there."

"You investigated him?"

"I don't want Cora getting in over her head."

"You think she would?"

"It's all she ever does."

Sherry and Brenda laughed.

Sherry shook her head. "I was thinking back to some of Cora's past disasters, trying to figure out which husband I liked the best. All things considered, I think it was Larry."

"Larry? Who's Larry?"

"One of Cora's husbands. Though I'm not sure if she counts him. She married him in a drunken stupor. The marriage was annulled the next day."

"On what grounds?"

"He had another wife living. Something trivial like that. Anyway, he wasn't around long enough to become annoying."

"So you haven't been able to find out anything about this Harstein guy?"

"Not a thing."

"Why don't you let that cute reporter do it? Give him a reason to talk to you instead of that Playmate of the Month."

"Who?"

"Miss Calendar Girl posing as an attorney. Where'd she come from?"

"Local girl."

"Really? They grow 'em big around here."

"Yeah." Sherry grimaced. "Brenda, you can't stay."

"Sherry . . ."

"And you don't *wanna* stay. And neither does Dennis. It's just a whim. He saw me, he saw Cora, he said, 'Gee, isn't it like old times, why don't we all get married together?' But it's a stupid idea. As soon as he has time to think it over, he'll realize that."

Brenda's smile faltered. "I suppose."

"No supposing about it. He'll come to his senses, and if he doesn't, you'll straighten him out."

"*I'll* straighten *Dennis* out?"

Sherry leaned in. "Brenda. If you're afraid to do that, doesn't it tell you something?"

"I'm not afraid to do that," Brenda snapped. "My God, you can twist everything around!"

"Twist everything?" Sherry was offended. "I wasn't aware I was twisting anything."

"That's not what I mean, of course," Brenda relented. "But you have to admit you're not exactly rational where Dennis is concerned."

Sherry was stunned. "Excuse *me*?"

"What he did was wrong. I'm not denying that. But people can change. And you just won't accept that. You're the one in denial."

"I'm in denial? Brenda, you can sit there and tell me I'm in denial?"

"Sherry . . ."

"No. I do not need some two-bit psychological analysis culled from *Vogue* to tell me how I feel. It took a court order to get rid of Dennis. It took moving and leaving no forwarding address to get rid of him. He still calls me up when he gets drunk."

"He's not drinking."

"He will."

Brenda sprang to her feet. "Well, isn't that great? Isn't that how you back me up? You wish me well, but how do you *really* feel?"

"I feel hurt. I feel betrayed."

"Betrayed? Now you're saying I betrayed you?"

"Not you. Him."

"Oh, come on. Dennis is betraying you by marrying me?"

"That's not what I mean."

"It sure sounds like it."

"I just don't want you getting hurt."

"I won't get hurt."

"I don't mean emotionally. I know you can cope with that."

"Sherry, Dennis would never hurt me. I know that's hard for you to accept. The idea it would be different with me. But I swear, he's never laid a finger on me."

"Yeah."

"You don't believe me?"

"I do believe you."

"Then what's your problem?"

"Dennis never hit me until after we were married, either."

"Either?"

"Sorry, I forgot. He hasn't hit you yet."

"Yet? Damn it, Sherry. That's not fair."

"Not fair? Brenda, this is not a game. I got a restraining order against the guy. As far as I know, it's still in effect. If so, he's in violation of it. I could call the cops and have him taken in."

"You'd do that to me?"

"I'm not doing anything to you. Jesus Christ, get it through your thick head! You think he's back at the bed-and-breakfast waiting for you? More likely he's out back trying to listen in at the window."

"Oh, for pity's sake!"

"He's sick, Brenda. It's a disease. He's a sick son of a bitch. He needs help. Psychiatric help."

"Oh, please . . ."

"You think it's normal to come here, shove his wedding in my face?"

"That's the problem," Brenda raged. "That's what's eating

you. You're taking this whole thing personally. It's not something Dennis is doing, or something I'm doing, it's something the two of us are doing to *you*! Well, guess what? You're not that damn important! If Dennis wants to have the wedding here, it's because he thought it would be nice. A fun thing to do. But I guess you've spoiled that, haven't you?"

"Is that how you see it? Good God, he's got you so brainwashed."

Brenda hurled the coffee cup. It shattered against the wall.

"Oh, my God! Look what I did. . . ."

Sherry nodded grimly. "Maybe you're what he needs. Beat him the hell up."

"Sherry—"

"You know what, Brenda? This is all too sudden. That's the problem. It's all too sudden. And I'm not dealing with it well. I'm not sure I ever *will* deal with it well, but right now I *know* I'm not."

Brenda was picking up pieces of the broken cup. "I'm sorry. I don't know what got into me."

"Brenda, I don't care about the damn cup. I care about you."

Sherry held out the kitchen garbage can.

Brenda dumped in the shards of glass.

"So tell me, how do you get on with his parents?"

"I haven't met his parents."

A cold chill ran down Sherry's spine. "You're getting married next weekend, and you haven't met his parents?"

"They aren't coming to the wedding. They all but disowned him since he joined the band."

"Brenda. I married Dennis without meeting his parents. When I finally did, they disapproved. That's what set him off."

"Things have changed, Sherry. Dennis isn't looking for their approval anymore."

"Uh-huh."

"You sound like you don't believe me."

"I believe you. It's Dennis I don't believe."

"He's changed, Sherry. He's really changed."

Sherry sighed.

"Oh, for your sake, Bren, I really hope so."

5

BECKY BALDWIN CAME OUT THE FRONT DOOR OF THE COUNTRY Kitchen and skipped down the steps, as the youthful attorney was wont to do when walking by herself and having no client she needed to impress. She reached the bottom, turned toward the parking lot, and stopped.

Dennis Pride was perched on the top rail of the fence. When he saw her, he grinned and waved. "Howdy, Miss Lawyer Lady. You have some business in this corral? Perhaps one of these fine steeds is yours?"

"Nice try, cowboy." Becky jerked her thumb at the country restaurant, fashioned to look like a huge log cabin. "But the motif's not Wild West, it's New England Early American."

"What, they didn't have horses?" Dennis said. "Come on. Which stallion here is yours?"

"That would be the gelding," Becky said. "You will be, too, if you don't get out of my way."

"Oh, tough stuff. If I ever need a lawyer, I'm calling you."

"Do that." Becky headed for her car.

"Can I have your number?"

"I'm in the book."

Dennis trotted after her. "I didn't catch your name."

"I guess I'm not memorable."

"I was looking at your eyes and missed the introduction. All I know is you're the town lawyer, and you're not going with what's-his-face."

"Right." Becky jerked her car door open. "Because he's going with your ex-wife."

Dennis frowned.

"Bothers you, doesn't it?"

"Hey, you're close to somebody, of course it leaves a scar."

"Interesting choice of words."

"Why do you say that?"

"Sherry told me about the divorce."

"Don't believe everything you hear."

"I try not to," Becky said serenely. "Listen, why are you hanging out in the parking lot, preying on unsuspecting women? Aren't you engaged to be married?"

"Yes, I am. And my bride-to-be ran off with my ex-wife. I'm not sure where they went, but she's driving the rental car."

"Oh. Your fiancée left you here."

"That she did."

"Do you need a ride?"

"I'd like one."

"Where are you staying?"

"Bed-and-breakfast. I'm not too clear on the address, but I could find it."

"Then why didn't they drop you off?"

Dennis shrugged. "You're asking me why women do things? I gave up trying to figure that out long ago. Can you give me a ride?"

"Sure. Hop in."

Becky and Dennis drove out of the lot, headed back toward town.

"All right, where is it?" Becky asked.

"Just down here," Dennis replied casually. "But, tell me something. Is there anyplace I could get a cup of coffee first?"

"Coffee? You have got to be kidding. We were just at the Country Kitchen."

"Yeah, but I'm a recovering alcoholic. It bothers me to sit in the bar."

"Is that so?"

"This town doesn't have someplace to get coffee?"

Becky hesitated. She had a coffeepot in her office, but she wasn't about to take Dennis there. "There's a diner just outside of town. One cup of coffee and that's it."

"Fantastic. You're too kind."

Becky drove to the diner, an all-night greasy spoon on the edge of Bakerhaven. They went in, got a booth, ordered coffee.

The waitress who brought it raised her eyebrows at the handsome young man Becky was dining with.

As the waitress moved off, Becky frowned. "You have a sponsor?"

"No."

"You should have a sponsor."

"I'm doing this myself."

"Ever try to quit before?"

Dennis dismissed this with a smile. "Let's not talk about me. Let's talk about you. You're a native, right? You grew up here, know everybody?"

"You make it sound like I spent my life here. Actually, I just got back."

"Oh? Where were you?"

"Harvard."

"Impressive." Dennis regarded his coffee as if it were castor oil. He took a sip, made a face. "God, that's vile. So, anyway, how's your love life? You got a steady boyfriend?"

"I wouldn't exactly say that. I've got a TV guy who's interested."

"TV guy? That's not the guy tonight?"

"No, he's a newspaper reporter."

"What's his name?"

"Aaron Grant."

"That's the newspaper reporter?"

"Yeah."

"Funny. You two look like a couple. Did you ever date?"

"We went out in high school."

"Went out? My, my, what a lovely euphemism."

"Now, look here—" Becky began.

"And you're not still involved?"

"No. Like I said, Aaron's involved with Sherry."

"Oh, really. Is that serious?"

"I wouldn't know."

"Yes, you would."

The timbre of Dennis's voice had altered ever so slightly, but it was enough that Becky noticed. She looked up sharply.

"You women always know," Dennis told her. "It's your business to know."

Becky pursed her lips. With her finger, she absently twirled her coffee cup around in the saucer. "Drink up. I'll drive you home."

"No offense meant." Dennis kept his best smile on.

"Sure," Becky said. "So you were in a band?"

"Yeah. Tune Freaks. We weren't all that bad."

"You cut a record?"

"There's the thing. That's what needed to happen. We were this close."

"Uh-huh." Becky imagined Dennis with long hair, strumming his guitar, blasting music through an amp. Distorting the features of his pleasant-looking face to belt out the raw angst of his tortured soul. It was a troubling image, both repellent and attractive. For the first time, she could empathize with Sherry's plight.

"Come on, let's go." Becky's voice was firm and steady. She hoped Dennis wouldn't sense the nervousness she actually felt.

They got in the car, drove to the bed-and-breakfast.

"That's it right there." Dennis pointed to a three-story wood-frame house, white with green shutters, set back from the road.

Becky pulled up in front to let him out. Was glad he didn't try to kiss her. She didn't really think he would, but she wasn't sure quite what to expect from this volatile young man.

As she drove off, it occurred to Becky she had never been so relieved to get someone so handsome out of her car.

Dennis watched her go, then strolled up the walk and in the front door.

Mrs. Ramsey, the elderly owner of the B&B, met him in the foyer. "You're back early," she observed.

"Yes, ma'am, but I have to go out again. May I use your phone?"

"Is it a local call?"

"Yes, of course."

Dennis called a car service, had them come pick him up, drive him to the Country Kitchen.

He didn't go in, however. Instead, he walked out into the parking lot. He took his keys from his pocket, unlocked his rental car.

Dennis smiled as he drove out of the parking lot.

6

CHIEF DALE HARPER PULLED HIS CRUISER TO A STOP IN FRONT of the police station, set the brake, and killed the motor. He got out, yawned, stretched, and squinted into the early-morning sun. A cool breeze was blowing down the street, and as Chief Harper stepped up on the sidewalk his nose twitched.

Damn.

He could smell the coffee brewing in Cushman's Bake Shop just down the street. The shop was a terrible lure. Mrs. Cushman couldn't bake a lick, but the muffins she had trucked in every morning from New York were fantastic. The chief was particularly partial to the orange cranberry.

Chief Harper exhaled in exasperation.

The problem was that he had just had breakfast at home with his wife and daughter, just as he did every morning. He didn't *need* a muffin. Particularly since his pants were starting to get a little snug in the waist. More than a little snug, if truth be told. He really didn't need any more breakfast.

The ideal thing would be to have a muffin for lunch. Of course, there wouldn't *be* any muffins by lunchtime. The muffins sold out quickly, and if he didn't buy one now they'd be gone.

He could get a muffin and keep it for lunch, but that wouldn't work. The longest one had sat on his desk was an excruciating thirty minutes—actually closer to twenty-three—before he had succumbed to its allure.

The other theory, that he would have one now and skip lunch, didn't seem to work, either. Even though no muffin would present itself at lunchtime, something else would. And who could work from nine to five on nothing? It was totally unrealistic.

Chief Harper hesitated in front of the police station, shifting his weight from one foot to the other, as indecisive as Hamlet.

Another waft of bakery air tipped the scale, helped with his decision. He would have a muffin today, and tomorrow he would begin doing without.

Chief Harper had been making that decision for months.

He hurried down the sidewalk to the bakeshop, queued up in the line of townspeople waiting to be served. Which did not take long. Mrs. Cushman, the plump, robust, good-natured proprietor of Cushman's Bake Shop, had the chief's muffin in the bag before he even reached the counter. A shrewd businesswoman, Mrs. Cushman kept the early-morning line moving by anticipating the regulars' requests.

"Here you go, Chief," she said, handing him the bag.

The fact he was so predictable didn't trouble Chief Harper. His step was light as he approached the station. Now, to wash out the pot and make the coffee. It was a beautiful summer day, there was no immediate work to be done. He might even sit outside and drink it. Chief Harper skipped up the front steps rather lightly for a solid policeman whose pants had become a bit tight.

The Bakerhaven police station was a former antiques shop, and not too much work had gone into its transformation, aside from installing holding cells in the back, and hanging up a decorous sign in front that said POLICE. It was still a white, wood-frame building just like all the rest on Main Street.

Chief Harper fished his keys out of his pocket, unlocked the door.

The letter was lying just inside. A white envelope, business size, address side up. The name had been typed on the envelope in capital letters. Chief Harper picked it up and read it.

IMBBOP OFXQ

Great. Absolute gibberish.

It occurred to Chief Harper that his young officer, Dan Finley, loved word games, so the letter was presumably to Dan. Harper wondered if it was from a young lady. He grinned at the thought. Dan was eager, earnest, and easily embarrassed. He had sandy hair and freckles. The idea of him getting a mash note at the police station was delightful. It would be delicious if he shared it, but it would be almost better if he refused to.

Chief Harper flipped the letter onto Dan Finley's desk, went into the pantry, and washed out the coffeepot. He filled it, switched it on to perk. Checked the minifridge to make sure there was milk.

Great.

All systems were go for Operation Orange Cranberry.

Dan Finley came in carrying a brown paper bag.

"What you got there?" Chief Harper asked.

"Muffin."

"What kind?"

"Blueberry. You make coffee?"

"It's perking now. How do you stay so thin?"

"Don't know. Just do."

Dan Finley set his bag on his desk, picked up the envelope. "What's this?"

"I don't know," Chief Harper replied innocently. "What is it?"

"Beats me. How did it get on my desk?"

Harper hesitated a second. This wasn't the way it was supposed to be going. "I put it there."

"Oh?"

"Someone slipped it under the door. I figured it must be yours."

"IMBBOP OFXQ? Why would it be mine?"

"Well, it sure isn't mine."

"Maybe it's Sam's," Dan suggested.

They both laughed. Sam Brogan was a particularly cranky police officer. The thought of anyone sending such a letter to Sam was ludicrous.

"Well, should I open it?" Dan asked.

"I guess we have to. Otherwise we won't know who it's to."

"Guess you're right."

Dan Finley picked up the letter opener, slid it in the slot, slit the envelope open. He pulled out the letter, looked at it, and frowned.

"Well, what does it say?" Chief Harper asked.

"I don't know."

"What do you mean, you don't know? Just read it."

"Here, you read it," Dan said. He handed the letter to Chief Harper.

Harper looked at the letter.

His mouth fell open.

It read:

XPFU IMBBOP OFXQ,
QVM'UP GFAJWS F CJS GJZEFAP. ENJZ JZ F CFX GFEKN. JR
QVM'UP ZGFUE, QVM'OO CUPFA JE VRR, CPRVUP ZVGPENJWS
NFIIPWZ. CPRVUP ZVGPVWP SPEZ NMUE. OPFHP NJG. LFOA
FLFQ, FWX XVW'E OVVA CFKA. JE'Z WVE EVV OFEP EV UPKEJRQ
ENP PUUVUZ ENFE QVM'HP GFXP. LFOA FLFQ LNJOP ENPUP'Z
ZEJOO EJGP. LFOA FLFQ.

7

SHERRY CARTER WAS BEHIND ON HER PUZZLE LADY COLUMN. It wasn't like Sherry to fall behind, but what with her aunt's nuptials and the arrival of Brenda and Dennis, she hadn't been able to work last night, and hadn't finished the column she was supposed to fax this morning.

Sherry was working on it now. She was sitting at her computer creating the crossword puzzle. She was using Crossword Compiler, a handy program that allowed her to type right into a crossword grid, search for words and definitions, and even fill in parts of the puzzle if she was pressed for time. Sherry never went so far as to turn in an electronically generated puzzle, but the resources helped.

Sherry had almost finished the grid when she heard gravel crunch in the drive. She went to the window, expecting to see her aunt. Instead, Chief Harper was climbing out of his cruiser. Sherry frowned, opened the front door.

"Hi, Chief. What's up?"

"Hello, Miss Carter. Is your aunt home?"

"No, she's not."

"Oh? Her car's here."

"Yes. She's out with Raymond."

Sherry hesitated only slightly when coming up with this ob-
fuscation. While quite true, it was also a deliberate piece of misdi-
rection, aimed at preserving Aunt Cora's reputation, if any
remained. Cora had in fact been out all night with Raymond, instead of the early-morning after-breakfast drive Sherry's light-
hearted remark implied.

"Well, I hate to leave this," Chief Harper said. "Should have
made a copy."

"Leave what?"

"You don't have a copy machine, do you?"

"No. But our fax machine makes copies."

"Really? I wonder if ours does. I'll have to ask Dan."

"What do you need to copy?"

"Oh. This."

Chief Harper whipped out the envelope, showed her the message.

"Oh, my goodness," Sherry said.

"Yeah, it's a puzzle," Chief Harper said. "You think your aunt
can solve it?"

"Oh."

"Not to disparage her ability. But this is another type of puzzle
entirely. I don't even know what you call it."

"It's a simple cryptogram," Sherry said. "A basic code. Letters
are substituted for other letters."

"How do you go about solving it?"

"Find letters that are obvious. Apostrophes help a lot. An
apostrophe and a letter, it's gonna be *S* or *T.* You notice here
you've got an apostrophe and *two* letters. There are not many
contractions of that nature. *VE* or *RE* or *LL.* Plus the letters are

the same in every word throughout the message, so if you get one letter here, you replace it all the way through. And—" Sherry broke off, blushing.

"What is it?"

"Nothing," Sherry said. Actually, she'd just realized she was revealing far too much expertise. "I guess I was speaking out of turn. I know a lot from helping Cora."

"Let me copy it, and I'll leave it for her."

"Yes, of course. Come on in, Chief."

Sherry led Chief Harper into the office, realized belatedly that her crossword puzzle was still on the screen. She flushed again, murmured, "Oh, just let me save this puzzle Cora was working on."

She saved the puzzle, closed the program. "You know, these machines are all interrelated. Sometimes when you print on one, you screw up the other. Modern technology run amok. You gotta be careful."

Sherry realized she was chattering on. She took the paper from Chief Harper, fed it through the fax machine. "Now, if I just press PRINT instead of dialing a number, it'll go through and make a copy. See? Watch."

Sherry ran off a copy, handed the original back to Chief Harper. She took her copy, wrote on it.

"What's that?" Harper asked.

Sherry showed him. "Just writing what was on the envelope. No need to copy it, but Cora should see what it was."

Chief Harper stuck the letter back in his pocket. "Have her call me as soon as she gets in."

"Yes, of course."

Sherry walked Chief Harper out just as Cora and Raymond drove up in Raymond's rental car. Cora was wearing the same dress she'd worn at dinner. Sherry wondered if Chief Harper knew that. Had he seen her yesterday? Would he notice even if he had?

Raymond Harstein III seemed to flinch at the sight of the police officer. If so, he immediately covered it with hearty goodwill. "Oh, no, the authorities!" he cried. "Don't tell me, let me guess. We're busted! Some local ordinance no one ever knew about, and damned if we didn't break it."

Chief Harper smiled. "Nothing so serious. We received some sort of cryptic message and I need Miss Felton to decipher it."

Raymond's nose twitched, making his mustache dance. "Well, that's mighty interesting. Some kind of puzzle?"

"So it seems. Miss Carter, here, thinks it's some sort of code."

Cora, whose fingers had turned to putty at the sight of a puzzle, grabbed at this lifeline. "Then I'm sure it is. Sherry does all my research and is invaluable in my work. She is invariably right."

"Here, take a look," Chief Harper said.

Cora tried to hide her reluctance by snatching the puzzle.

Sherry and Raymond crowded around and looked over her shoulder.

"Aha," Cora said, not having the faintest idea what she was aha-ing at. She pointed to the handwriting. "What's this here?"

"That was typed on the envelope," Sherry said. "I wrote it there so I wouldn't have to make a separate copy. You'll notice," she went on, "that these two words on the envelope are exactly the same as the two words in the *salutation*. Which will make this very easy to solve. This will be the name of the person the letter is to. This word in front of it will undoubtedly be *dear*. Knowing four very common letters will go a long way toward solving this thing."

"Yes, it certainly will," Cora said. She hadn't the faintest idea what Sherry was talking about.

"Too bad there aren't any blanks for you to fill in, like a crossword," Sherry said. "But I have fairly good handwriting. Maybe I can fill in the letters for you, just above the ones they replace."

"That would be very helpful," Cora said.

"Come on, everybody, let's go inside, sit down, and Cora will solve this for you."

Like a fast-talking master of ceremonies, Sherry managed to shepherd everyone into the living room and install the two men in easy chairs. She and Cora sat on the couch.

Sherry picked up a magazine to lean the letter against, and, still talking fast, said, "I'm going to fill in all the *D*'s, *E*'s, *A*'s, and *R*'s in the puzzle. That will give us something to work with, then Cora can tell us what comes next."

Sherry's pen flew over the letter, writing a *D* over every *X,* an *E* over every *P,* an *A* over every *F,* and an *R* over every *U,* all the time keeping up a running commentary.

"Well, this seems to be a simple cryptogram, which you might recall from childhood. Every letter stands for another letter. It's just a question of figuring out what."

Sherry's chattering allowed her to fill in all of the four letters.

Cora watched, hypnotized, hoping for a clue.

She got one.

In what Sherry had referred to as the salutation, she had written *DEAR* over *XPFU.* Over the third word, *OFXQ,* where Sherry had written an *A* over the *F* and a *D* over the *X,* she added an *L* over the *O,* and a *Y* over the *Q,* to spell *LADY.* Over the *B*'s in the second word, *IMBBOP,* she wrote two *Z*'s:

```
Dear    zz   Lady,
XPFU IMBBOP OFXQ,
```

Waves of relief poured over Cora. She beamed. "Well, I guess this letter is to me."

"What?" Chief Harper said.

"Sure," Cora told him. "The salutation, 'Dear gobbledygook' is going to be 'Dear Blank Lady.' The *B*'s in *IMBBOP* will be *Z*'s, and *IMBBOP* will be *PUZZLE*. Puzzle Lady. That's what's on the envelope, and that's who the letter is to. Fill that in, Sherry, and we'll take it from there."

"Good work, Cora," Sherry said. "Here, let me see what that looks like."

Sherry swiftly filled in the letters:

```
Dear Puzzle Lady,
XPFU IMBBOP OFXQ,


Y u're a    a       a e.       a ad a    .
QVM'UP GFAJWS F CJS GJZEFAP. ENJZ JZ F CFX GFEKN. JR


y u're   ar , y u'll  rea        ,  e re   e
QVM'UP ZGFUE, QVM'OO CUPFA JE VRR, CPRVUP ZVGPENJWS


  appe  .  e re   e e e     ur . Lea e   . al  a ay,
NFIIPWZ. CPRVUP ZVGPVWP SPEZ NMUE. OPFHP NJG. LFOA FLFQ,


a d d  ' 1    a .  '        la e    re   y   e
FWX XVW' E OVVA CFKA. JE'Z WVE EVV OFEP EV UPKEJRQ ENP


err r   a y u' e ade. al  a ay   le  ere'     11
PUUVUZ ENFE QVM'HP GFXP. LFOA FLFQ LNJOP ENPUP'Z ZEJOO


  e. al  a ay.
EJGP. LFOA FLFQ.
```

"Looks like *you're* in luck, Cora," Sherry said, managing to point at the word *Y u're* as her pen flew over the paper.

"I sure am," Cora said. "The first word is *You're*. Which gives us the letter *O*. Add that in, Sherry."

"Sure thing. And you've got apostrophe *Z* and apostrophe *E*. That can only be *S* and *T*. I'll add them in too."

```
Dear Puzzle Lady,
XPFU IMBBOP OFXQ,


You're a    a       sta e. T s  s a  ad  at  .
QVM'UP GFAJWS F CJS GJZEFAP. ENJZ JZ F CFX GFEKN. JR


you're s art, you'll  rea  t o  ,  e ore so et
QVM'UP ZGFUE, QVM'OO CUPFA JE VRR, CPRVUP ZVGPENJWS


 appe s.  e ore so eo e  ets  urt. Lea e    .  al  a ay,
NFIIPWZ. CPRVUP ZVGPVWP SPEZ NMUE. OPFHP NJG. LFOA FLFQ,


a d do 't loo  a . t's  ot too late to re t  y t e
FWX XVW'E OVVA CFKA. JE'Z WVE EVV OFEP EV UPKEJRQ ENP


errors t at you' e ade.  al  a ay    le t ere's st ll
PUUVUZ ENFE QVM'HP GFXP. LFOA FLFQ LNJOP ENPUP'Z ZEJOO


t e.  al  a ay.
EJGP. LFOA FLFQ.
```

Cora's eyes widened with excitement as she realized she could actually see words emerging. "Look! *Do 't* is going to be *don't*. So *W* is *N!* And *_t's* has to be *It's.* So *J* is *I!* Fill them in, Sherry! Fill them in!"

Sherry was writing as fast as she could, but it was hard to keep up with Cora, now that she was on the scent.

"Look! *T_e* is *The,* so *N* is *H!*"

Sherry filled it in.

```
Dear Puzzle Lady,
XPFU IMBBOP OFXQ,


You're a in a i  ista e. This is a  ad  at h. I
QVM'UP GFAJWS F CJS GJZEFAP. ENJZ JZ F CFX GFEKN. JR
```

```
you're s art, you'll rea  it o  ,  e ore so ethin
QVM'UP ZGFUE, QVM'OO CUPFA JE VRR, CPRVUP ZVGPENJWS
```

```
happens.  e ore so eone  ets hurt. Lea e hi . al a ay,
NFIIPWZ. CPRVUP ZVGPVWP SPEZ NMUE. OPFHP NJG. LFOA FLFQ,
```

```
and don't loo   a . It's not too late to re ti y the
FWX XVW'E OVVA CFKA. JE'Z WVE EVV OFEP EV UPKEJRQ ENP
```

```
errors that you' e ade.  al a ay  hile there's still
PUUVUZ ENFE QVM'HP GFXP. LFOA FLFQ LNJOP ENPUP'Z ZEJOO
```

```
ti e. al a ay.
EJGP. LFOA FLFQ.
```

"And look!" Cora cried. "_hile there's still ti_e is while there's still time! So G is M! And L is W! So the second word is going to be making! So A is K and S is G! So it's You're making a big mistake. So C is B! And that gives you, you'll break it off. So R is F! Fill it in, Sherry! We got it!"

The puzzle was finally done:

```
Dear Puzzle Lady,
XPFU IMBBOP OFXQ,
```

```
You're making a big mistake. This is a bad match. If
QVM'UP GFAJWS F CJS GJZEFAP. ENJZ JZ F CFX GFEKN. JR
```

```
you're smart, you'll break it off, before something
QVM'UP ZGFUE, QVM'OO CUPFA JE VRR, CPRVUP ZVGPENJWS
```

```
happens. Before someone gets hurt. Leave him. Walk away,
NFIIPWZ. CPRVUP ZVGPVWP SPEZ NMUE. OPFHP NJG. LFOA FLFQ,
```

```
and don't look back. It's not too late to rectify the
FWX XVW'E OVVA CFKA. JE'Z WVE EVV OFEP EV UPKEJRQ ENP
```

```
errors that you've made. Walk away while there's still
PUUVUZ ENFE QVM'HP GFXP. LFOA FLFQ LNJOP ENPUP'Z ZEJOO

time. Walk away.
EJGP. LFOA FLFQ.
```

"Okay," Sherry said. "Here it is:

```
" 'Dear Puzzle Lady,
You're making a big mistake. This is a bad match. If
you're smart, you'll break it off, before something
happens. Before someone gets hurt. Leave him. Walk
away, and don't look back. It's not too late to rectify
the errors that you've made. Walk away while there's
still time. Walk away.' "
```

Sherry looked up. "There's no signature. Of course, you wouldn't expect one."

Raymond Harstein's brow was knit in angry lines. "What the hell is this?" he demanded. "It sounds like a personal attack against me. That's what it is, isn't it? A letter addressed to Cora telling her to dump me. Who could have done such a thing?"

"Who *would* have done such a thing?" Cora said. "Raymond, don't be silly. This is just a sick joke. I don't know who would do such a thing, or why. But it doesn't mean a thing. Just ignore it."

"Ignore it? Someone tells you I'm a wicked man and you shouldn't marry me, and you want me to just ignore it?"

"Marry you?" Chief Harper said.

Cora flashed her ring as coyly as a schoolgirl who'd just been asked to the prom. "We're engaged."

"Well, congratulations!" Chief Harper smiled at Cora. Then he frowned. "You realize that makes this a little more serious.

It's probably just a prank, but it isn't funny, and I intend to get to the bottom of it." He chuckled, shook his head. "So you're really getting married. Isn't that something. Have you set the date yet?"

Cora smiled. "As a matter of fact, we have."

8

"What's bugging you?" Cora demanded.

Sherry was on the couch, lost in thought. She didn't even hear the question. Cora had to ask it again.

"Huh?" Sherry said. "Oh, nothing."

Cora snorted in exasperation. "Don't 'Oh, nothing' me. I know a something from a nothing. Now, what's this nothing all about?"

"The warning letter."

"Sherry, sweetheart. I'm not worried. Raymond's not worried. And if you noticed, Chief Harper's not really worried. Who the hell *cares* if I get married to Raymond? Who the hell even knows? I mean, people may have seen us around town, but I doubt if it's upsetting anyone."

"I doubt it too," Sherry said.

"So what's the problem?"

"Dennis."

"Sherry, you're not making sense. I thought we were talking about the letter."

"I *am* talking about the letter."

"What?"

"The letter wasn't addressed to you. It was addressed to the Puzzle Lady."

"So?"

"You're not the Puzzle Lady. I am."

"Yeah, but no one knows it."

"Dennis does."

Cora's mouth fell open. She closed it. Then she grimaced, shook her head. "Sherry, I gotta stop you right here. You're not thinking clearly. I know you're upset to see Dennis. But you're projecting. Just because you're obsessed with Dennis doesn't mean everything that happens has something to do with Dennis. You really think after he got here last night and met Aaron Grant, he rushed back to his hotel, made up a threatening puzzle, and dropped it off at the police station in the hope it would get to you? I feel it only fair to point out if the answer to that question is yes, you are in serious need of therapy."

Sherry sighed. "No, I don't think that happened. At least not the way you lay it out. I don't know if Dennis is involved, I just wish he weren't around."

"You and me both." Cora shook her head. "No, the letter is warning me about Raymond. Why, I have no idea. A nicer man you wouldn't want to meet."

"Didn't you say that about Melvin?" Sherry invoked the name of one of Cora's least favorite husbands.

"Please." Cora shuddered. "There's no comparison. None. Raymond's a brick."

"Where's he come from?"

"San Diego."

"What's he do there?"

"Sherry, what are you trying to pull?"

"I'm not trying to pull anything. But if someone is warning you not to marry Raymond, don't you think it would be advisable to know who Raymond is?"

"Raymond's in hotel management."

"He's a concierge?"

Cora made a face. "No, he's an owner."

"So what does he do?"

"He doesn't do anything. He's independently wealthy."

"From owning hotels?"

"Yes."

"Which hotels?"

"Stop it! Stop it right there. Don't you see? This is just what the person who wrote that letter wants."

Cora pulled her cigarettes out of her purse and lit one up.

"I thought you quit smoking."

"I *have* quit smoking. I never smoke when I'm with Raymond. I never smoke in public. You're family, you don't count."

"Aunt Cora—"

"How can I stop drinking and smoking at the same time? It's unnatural."

"Does Raymond know you're smoking?"

"Sherry, you're such a stickler for details. Raymond knows I'm making an effort. Raymond appreciates the effort I'm making. Why should I depress him?"

"Why, indeed?"

Cora took a greedy drag. "Oh, that's good. I can almost think straight. See, even in the middle of a nicotine fit I can tell you Dennis didn't send that letter."

"Then you're still not thinking straight, Cora. We finished that subject. We were talking about Raymond."

"Talking? No. You were cross-examining me about Raymond, and I won't have it. He's the first man to come along for years—"

"And how many years would that be?"

"Never mind. He's the first decent man to come along—"

"I don't understand. If you knew the other men were indecent, why did you marry them?"

"You're getting on my nerves, Sherry."

"Something needs to make an impression on you. You just got a letter warning you off your marriage. Yet you refuse to discuss the man you're going to marry next Saturday. Talk about love being blind."

"Oh, give it a rest," Cora snapped. "You're just freaking out because Dennis is marrying your best friend."

Sherry's angry retort froze on her lips. She sighed. "You're right, I am. I absolutely am. But can you blame me? It's bad news, Cora. It's the worst. My best friend making the same mistake I did. And she won't even listen to me when I try to warn her off."

Cora stubbed her cigarette out. She sat on the couch, took Sherry by the hands. "Exactly. That's why you're upset about Dennis being here. It has nothing to do with the stupid message."

"So the stupid letter isn't about Dennis, it's about Raymond?"

Cora let go of Sherry's hands, fingered her engagement ring. "The stupid message has nothing to do with anyone. Hell, I'm not even sure we solved it right. I mean, all we're doing is substituting letters. Maybe we fill in a different set and it says, 'Mail in this entry and win a free DVD player.'"

"I can assure you it doesn't."

"The point is, you wanna get freaked out about Dennis, fine, I don't blame you. If there's any way I can help you convince Brenda he's a schmuck, let me know." Cora leveled her finger at

Sherry. "But Raymond's a good man, I'm marrying him next Saturday, and that's all there is to it. And nothing you can do or say is going to change my mind."

Sherry watched Cora stalk off toward her room.

Maybe not, Sherry thought, but she was sure gonna try.

9

AARON GRANT TIPPED BACK IN HIS CHAIR AND FROWNED UP AT Sherry Carter, who was perched on the edge of his desk. "I am not a private eye."

"No, but you're an investigative reporter."

"For the *Bakerhaven Gazette.*" Aaron gestured around the newsroom. Aside from his cubicle, only three other desks were occupied, and that included the one in the managing editor's office. "This is not exactly a national news organization. What do you expect me to do?"

"Come on, give me a break. If it were a story, you'd know how to handle it."

"That's what I've been trying to tell you. If it were a story, I could."

"Then pretend it's a story. Is that so hard?"

"Sherry—"

"Aaron, this is Cora we're talking about. You want her to wind up marrying some creep?"

"You don't know Raymond's a creep."

"Yeah, because you won't make a phone call."

Aaron winced at her tone. "Sherry, I've never seen you like this."

"What, utterly frustrated at every turn? That's how I feel. Why won't you help me?"

"What do you want me to do?"

"Look this guy up. Find out who he is. Give me something I can show to Cora."

"Sherry, I've got no authority to do that."

"Can't you bluff, for God's sake?"

"Who would you like me to bluff?" When she started to erupt, he pointed out, "You tried to trace this guy on the Internet, and you couldn't find him. There was no Raymond Harstein III. So, even if I contact the San Diego police and ask 'em to look him up, they're just gonna come back and tell me they have no record of him. Now, what good will that do?"

"It'll give me something to hit him with. 'Gee, Mr. Harstein, how come no one's ever heard of you?' "

"He'll just have some suave answer, and all you'll do is tick Cora off."

"Yeah, I know," Sherry said. "All right, look. He rented a car. So he must have a driver's license. If he does, we can trace it. If it's in the name of Raymond Harstein III, we can find out how come he doesn't live anywhere."

"So how do we get a look at his license? Have Dan Finley pull him over?"

"That's not a bad idea."

"That's a *terrible* idea. It means we have to let Dan in on what we're doing. Then he has to let Chief Harper in on it, or do it without his knowledge. If Dan tells Harper, what do you think Harper's gonna say?"

Sherry was silent.

"Look, I'll do what I can. If it were a crime, and it were a real story, I could call the San Diego cops. 'Hey, can you run this down for me.' But to check out a prospective bridegroom?" Aaron shook his head. "Reporters deal in credibility. You know how high mine would be after that?"

"Just do the best you can. I'll try to think of something."

Sherry smiled at the managing editor on her way out. He did not smile back. A hard-nosed newspaperman, Aaron's boss didn't believe in social visits on company time.

Sherry went downstairs and through the room with the big printing presses, silent now until the evening, when tomorrow's paper would be run. She came out the front door, climbed into Cora's car, and drove off.

Across the street, Dennis stepped from behind a tree. He watched Sherry's car turn the corner. As soon as she was out of sight he crossed the street, and went in the door of the *Bakerhaven Gazette.*

On the second floor, the managing editor popped out of his office and said, "Can I help you?"

"Looking for Aaron Grant."

The editor gnawed his lip. What was this, a frat house? He jerked his thumb in the direction of Aaron's cubicle.

Dennis wove his way through the newsroom, and found Aaron sitting at his desk.

"Aaron Grant?" he asked.

Aaron turned, spotted Dennis. His eyes grew cold. "Yes?"

"I saw you last night in the restaurant. With the lawyer lady."

"Yes?" Aaron said again, an edge in his voice.

"I'm Dennis Pride. Sherry's husband. I hear you used to date the lawyer lady."

"Where'd you hear that?"

"It's a small town."

"Yes, it is. What do you want?"

"It's not what I want, it's what Sherry wants. Sherry deserves a chance to be happy. No one should screw that up for her."

"That's one thing we agree on."

"Really? Then why are you doing it?"

Aaron's jaw tightened. "I beg your pardon?"

Dennis grinned. "Oh, yeah, like you don't know what I'm talking about. You and the lawyer lady. A blind man could see the chemistry there. That girl wants you bad."

Aaron stood up. "Now, look here—"

"What, are you threatening me? Please, just tell me you are. Make my day." Dennis leaned in close enough that Aaron could smell the whiskey on his breath. "You're young. You're human. You got this gorgeous, high-powered woman throwing herself at you. Sooner or later you're gonna give in. And what's gonna happen to poor little Sherry then?"

"Poor little Sherry's been doing just fine without your help."

"Oh, is that so? I guess she just doesn't know she's bein' two-timed. She and the lawyer lady are probably great friends, am I right?"

"You're way off base. For your information, Becky Baldwin is hung up on a TV reporter."

"I heard that. If I hear it one more time I might even start to believe it. So there's a TV station in town?"

"No."

"I didn't think so. So this guy's not local. He's just around when there's a story."

Aaron said nothing.

Dennis's grin widened. "Yeah. And the rest of the time she's free. To make a play for you."

"Oh, for God's sake."

"Hey, no skin off my nose. But if you're hurtin' my little girl, that's something you shouldn't do. I would get very angry if I thought you were hurtin' my little girl. Trust me, it's better to leave her alone than hurt her like that."

"Thanks for the tip."

"You bein' sarcastic with me?"

"Now, why would I wanna go and do a thing like that?"

Before Dennis could retort, the managing editor stuck his head in the door. "Hey, guys, this is a newsroom. You wanna gab, take it outside. Got it, bub?"

Dennis smiled as if the editor were his long-lost brother. "Am I glad to see you! I'm just giving your boy here a story, but he doesn't seem to want it. I'm Sherry Carter's ex-husband. Her aunt's getting married this weekend. You know, Cora Felton. The Puzzle Lady. Sherry's going to be her maid of honor."

The managing editor's eyebrows rose. He looked at Aaron. "Is that right?"

"Well . . ."

"Is Cora Felton getting married? Yes or no."

"That's what she told me last night in the Country Kitchen." Dennis jerked his thumb at Aaron. "Hell, he was there when she said it."

The editor glared at Aaron. "And you didn't write it up? You did that puff piece on Becky Baldwin. And that damn EMS guy. I thought you knew better than that. Cora Felton is the biggest celebrity in town. If she gets married, it's news. If we break it before everybody else, it's good. If we break it the same time as everybody else, it's bad. If we break it *after* everybody else, someone gets fired."

"Aw, gee, Bill . . ."

The editor ignored Aaron, turned to Dennis. "I guess I owe you an apology. I saw you in here gabbin', I thought it was more of the same. But, no, you got a corroborated news scoop we can substantiate. Thanks a lot."

Dennis smiled smugly, happy to be sticking it to Aaron Grant. "Don't mention it," he said, and walked off.

The editor stabbed his finger at Aaron. "You write this up."

Aaron hunched over the computer, began banging on the keys. He was not happy. The nerve of that damn Dennis, pretending he'd come by to bring them a wedding announcement. Aaron wondered if Dennis had had that excuse in his hip pocket, or if he'd made it up on the spur of the moment. Dennis didn't strike him as very smart, but Aaron realized he was probably biased in his assessment. He had to remind himself Dennis had been clever enough to trick Sherry into marrying him.

It was not a pleasant thought.

As soon as the editor was out of earshot, Aaron snatched up his phone and punched in the number. He was not surprised when the answering machine picked up.

"Sherry, it's Aaron. Guess who just dropped by?"

10

DENNIS CAME OUT OF THE *GAZETTE* OFFICE TO FIND BRENDA Wallenstein looking for him. "Yoo-hoo," she called, waving from down the street. "There you are. I had no idea where you were. Your car's parked down there."

"Yeah. I was gonna get a coffee. You want one?"

"Coffee?" Brenda was baffled. "But that's back there. Where you're parked. What are you doing down here?"

Dennis grimaced. "Oh, I guess you caught me."

Brenda's face fell. "Why? What is it?"

Dennis smiled ruefully. "I wasn't gonna tell you. It was gonna be a surprise. But I gotta tell you now. That's the *Bakerhaven Gazette*. The daily paper. I told them about our wedding."

"You what?"

"Well, sure. Don't you want everyone to know?"

"Of course I do! But why would they care? We're not from Bakerhaven."

"No, but Cora is."

"You told them about Cora?"

"It's a double wedding. How can you have a double wedding with just one couple?"

"Yes, but—"

"Brenda." Dennis turned on all his boyish charm. "What could it matter? I love you. I want everyone to know."

He swept her up in his arms, gave her a big hug.

For a moment she smiled contentedly in his arms. Then she sniffed and pulled back.

"Dennis. Have you been drinking?"

"Of course not."

"I can smell it."

"Smell what?"

"Dennis. You've got whiskey on your breath."

"No, I don't."

"Yes, you do. Look at me. Now breathe out."

"Brenda."

"Breathe out."

"Damn it, Brenda."

"You do! Dennis, how could you? You promised. You were doing so well."

"I *am* doing well."

"No, you're not. You had a drink and then you lied about it."

"I didn't."

"Dennis, you just told me you didn't have a drink."

"I didn't."

"You've got whiskey on your breath."

"Oh, for Christ's sake!" Dennis said irritably. He took her by both hands. "All right, look. I went by the paper to tell them we were getting married. The managing editor got all excited, said, 'Wow, that's terrific.' He reaches in his desk, pulls out a bottle, pours two shot glasses, says, 'Let's drink to your bride.' What am

I gonna do, say, 'No, I don't think I wanna drink to the woman I'm nuts about'?"

"You could explain."

"To the newspaper? I'm announcing my engagement. You want it written up, 'the prospective bridegroom, a recovering alcoholic'?"

Brenda bit her lip. "Gee. That doesn't sound so great. And how'd you refer to me?"

"How do you mean?"

"As an artist or a nurse?"

"Oh. Jeez, I hope I didn't do the wrong thing."

"What do you mean?"

"I said artist. I know you're a nurse, but I think of you as an artist. You got a loft. You paint. Your nursing's like a job-job, you know? Like me waitin' tables when the band didn't have a gig. I mean, am I goin' to tell people I'm a waiter?"

"So what'd you tell 'em?"

"Huh?"

"The newspaper. What did you tell 'em you were?"

"Oh." Dennis thought fast, having to invent not just an answer, but a reason for his reaction to the question. "Well, now I hope I didn't do the wrong thing again. I should have talked this over with you, but I couldn't, if it was gonna be a surprise. I don't have a job with your father yet—that's all he needs, to pick up the paper and see I told the press I was working for him. So I just referred to myself as 'former lead singer of the Tune Freaks.'"

"Former lead singer?"

"Yeah. Was that wrong? I mean, doesn't 'former lead singer' sound better than 'unemployed musician'?"

Brenda's face warmed into a smile. "Oh, you're too good. You really said 'former'?"

"Well, that's what I am."

"You didn't have to say 'former.' "

"Well, I didn't want you getting upset, talking like I was still in the band." Dennis chucked her under the chin. "Come on, kid. Let's get that coffee."

They went down the street to Cushman's Bake Shop, where the morning rush had abated. Only a few straggling housewives with baby strollers were hanging out. Dennis ordered a coffee and dumped in milk and sugar. Brenda had hers black.

"How do you stay so thin?" she asked him.

"Dunno. You want a muffin?"

"Not if I wanna fit into my wedding gown."

A toddler in overalls teetered up to Brenda, plunked down on his bottom, and squealed in delight at the accomplishment.

"Oh, what a cutie!" Brenda cried.

The baby gurgled in delight at the compliment.

"Dennis, look how cute!"

Brenda glanced up to see Dennis munching on his muffin, and looking out the bakeshop window. There was nothing out there so far as Brenda could see, just their car parked in front of the town library, and a police cruiser driving by. She wondered if, in a town of this size, that was *the* police car, and the cops all took turns driving it.

Brenda looked down to find the toddler had abandoned her for greener pastures, lured by a baby girl with a doughnut.

Did Dennis think kids were cute? *He* was cute. He'd be a terrific father. Brenda joined him at the window, sipped her coffee. Looked out at the car.

Frowned.

"Why'd you drive?" she asked suddenly.

"What?"

"We're only three blocks away. I walked it. Why did you drive here?"

"Oh. Had to get gas. Town like this closes up after dark, you can't get a thing."

"Yeah, it's not like New York," Brenda agreed. "Come on. It's a nice day. Let's drink our coffee outside."

The bench under the bakeshop window had been taken over by a woman with two small white dogs. She was drinking coffee and feeding them pieces of bagel.

Brenda stood on the sidewalk, sipped her coffee, looked around. Down the street to the left was the newspaper office, where Dennis had announced their engagement. To the right was the police station. The cruiser she'd seen going by the window was parked out front. Across the street was the library, where their car was parked.

Brenda frowned. She threw her coffee in the trash can next to the bench. "Come on," she told Dennis. "Let's go back to the B&B. I want to wash up."

"Okay."

Brenda started across the street.

"Where are you going?" Dennis asked.

"To the car."

"Why don't we walk?"

"No, I wanna drive."

"Why? Like you say, it's just a few blocks."

"You can't leave the car in front of the library all day. That's not for guest parking. It's for the library."

"There's no sign."

"Even so, Dennis. We're getting married here. You want to make a bad impression?"

"Who's gonna care?"

"The police station's right there. Cops go in and out all day, see the car parked there. Even if they don't ticket it, whaddya wanna bet they note the license number?"

"It's a rental."

"Even so."

Brenda crossed the street, stood next to the car.

"Oh, for goodness' sakes," Dennis said irritably. "What's the big deal?" He fished the keys out of his pocket, pressed the zapper that unlocked the doors. "Come on. Get in. We'll drive a whopping three blocks home. Talk about the decadent, idle rich."

Brenda got in the passenger seat, looked over at the dashboard.

The gas gauge read three-quarters full.

It seemed to Brenda it had been that full when they had parked the car. Of course, she'd had no particular reason to notice. Maybe she was wrong. Maybe it had been only a quarter full, and Dennis had filled it up to where it was now. It wasn't conceivable he had filled it full and then used a quarter of a tank of gas. You could drive every road in this town and not use a quarter of a tank of gas. So maybe he hadn't filled it full. Maybe the pump had shut off automatically at three-quarters full. Those automatic shut-offs made mistakes all the time, stopping before the tank was full. Or maybe Dennis bought ten bucks' worth of gas, and this was how much it took. There were lots of explanations.

Brenda wondered if she should ask for one. Dennis wouldn't like it, not after having to explain about the newspaper. Toasting their marriage—that stupid editor—why in the world did some people force you to drink? Dennis was doing great, he really was, seeing his ex-wife again, putting his demons behind him, as he called it. His therapist had even suggested the idea. And Dennis had agreed, even though he admitted it would be painful. With all the sacrifices he was making, why should she be a nag?

Dennis started the engine.

Brenda watched the needle on the gas gauge. Some gauges didn't register until you turned on the car. But, no, the needle stayed right at three-quarters.

But so what? What did it matter? What difference did it make?

They were here, weren't they? They were going to have a wedding. A real church wedding. With a bridal gown and everything. She'd have to call her parents, tell them to come. Wouldn't they be surprised!

It was just too wonderful.

By the time they got back to the B&B, Brenda had completely forgotten about the gas tank being three-quarters full.

11

THE MANAGING EDITOR JERKED A SOGGY CIGAR AT AARON'S COPY. "That's bland."

"Hey, it's a wedding announcement," Aaron protested.

"I *know* it's a wedding announcement. And the Bible is a book. There are books and there are books. And there are wedding announcements and there are wedding announcements. I'd like *this* wedding announcement to be one people care to read about. I would like *this* wedding announcement to be the type that sells papers, the type people say, 'It says so in the *Gazette,*' and they buy it to see for themselves. Do you see the point I'm trying to make?"

"You would like me to elevate this from wedding announcement to feature news?"

"Now, there's a thought." The managing editor waved his cigar at the sheet of paper again. "Is there anything in here that would do that?"

"No."

"Why not?"

"I wrote it as a wedding announcement."

"Let's not do this again. Would you like to write it as a feature news story?"

"If that's what you'd like."

"I would. So, what's the first thing you do?"

"Throw this out?"

"Aside from that."

"Find an angle. 'Puzzle Lady Comes *Across* Suitor, Walks *Down* Aisle.' "

"No, I mean— Actually, that's not bad. Hold on to that. What I was gonna say is, this guy she's marrying—this Raymond whatever—who the hell is he?"

"He's just a guy."

"Wrong. No one's just a guy. This is a special guy who swept the famous Puzzle Lady off her feet. Who is he, and how'd he do it?"

"I have no idea."

"Well, there you are. I wouldn't presume to tell you your job, but you ever think of going out and interviewing the groom?"

"Actually, I asked him, and he didn't want to be interviewed."

"Really? That's good. That means anything we get, we're the only ones who have it. Why don't you look the guy up?"

"I would, but he's from San Diego."

"So?"

"There's nothing I can find on the computer."

"No, I suppose not. San Diego, huh? There's a reporter on the *San Diego Union*. Name of Hines. Give him a call, use my name, ask him for a favor."

"What should I offer in return?"

"It's not a trade, it's a favor. Oh, all right. Tell him if anything comes of it, I'll leak it to him before we break it."

"You'd do that?"

"Of course not. Nothing's gonna come of it. I just said that to shut you up. Get out of here, go make the call."

Aaron Grant went back to his cubicle, smiling to himself. He'd wondered if he'd overplayed his hand, writing such a bad piece, and acting so dumb. Apparently not.

Aaron grinned, and picked up the phone.

12

THERE WERE BELLS IN THE STEEPLE OF THE CHURCH. WEDDING bells. Cora smiled at them as she walked across the village green. Cora had never noticed them before, but now they were all she saw. Bright, silver, wedding bells. Poised in the white, wooden church steeple, waiting to toll on her wedding day, waiting to ring out the news.

Of course, this was all in Cora's head. The bells were not silver, but some metal alloy or other. Nor were they bright. Indeed, dirt and corrosion had rendered them a dull green.

Cora couldn't have cared less. She skipped across the street, took the steps two at a time.

The Reverend Kimble was somewhat surprised to see her, since her attendance at his Sunday sermons had been spotty at best. In fact, it occurred to Cora, unless she had stumbled in some morning from a particularly wild Saturday-night party and simply couldn't remember, it was entirely possible she had never gone to church at all. In short, Cora wasn't sure whether the Reverend did not know her, or knew her all too well.

The Reverend frowned and scratched his head. A gaunt man, with a hawk nose, an unfortunate Adam's apple, and graying hair, the minister of the Bakerhaven Congregational Church usually managed to look distinguished. At the moment he looked befuddled. "You want me to perform a wedding next weekend? That is awfully short notice."

"Yes," Cora explained. "We were going to be married in August, but we had to move it up."

The Reverend looked shocked and astonished. "Oh?"

"No, no," Cora said. "Nothing like that. We changed the date to coincide with another wedding."

"I see. You and the other couple wish to be married together."

"Actually, no," Cora said. "We were hoping to promote a conflict."

"I beg your pardon?"

Cora waved it away. "It's complicated. Anyway, it didn't work."

"I'm terribly sorry. Is there anything I can do?"

"I tend to doubt it."

"Still, if I could know the circumstances . . ."

The Reverend Kimble might have wanted to help, but he was merely confirming Cora's suspicions that clergymen were as nosy as charwomen. She took a breath. "My niece, Sherry, has been married once before."

"Sherry's marrying young Aaron Grant? Congratulations. I couldn't be happier."

"No, she's not. At least, if she is, it's the first I've heard of it. No, it's her husband who's remarrying."

"I see," the Reverend Kimble said. It was clear that he didn't.

"Sherry's supposed to be the maid of honor."

"At her ex-husband's wedding?"

"He's marrying her best friend."

"My God, it's like a soap opera," the Reverend Kimble said, then flushed violently at her look. Cora was wondering which soap opera he watched.

"Anyway, she's also maid of honor at my wedding."

"I see," the Reverend said. "So you decided to combine the two weddings."

"No. I decided to have them on the same day so Sherry could only go to one. Her ex-husband decided to combine them. Do you do double weddings, Reverend?"

"Yes, of course."

"I don't suppose you could *say* you don't?" The Reverend gave her a reproving look. "No, I don't suppose you could. I guess we're stuck unless you have a conflict. Could you *say* you have a conflict?"

"Now, see here," the Reverend protested. "I don't want to butt in." It was all Cora could do not to harrumph. She considered that statement no less a lie than his saying he had a conflict would have been. "Since this other marriage is causing grief and anxiety, surely something should be done. Perhaps if I were to have a talk with the young man, I could make him see the error of his ways. . . ."

"I doubt if it would do much good in Dennis's case."

"You'd be surprised. There's good in all of us."

"Uh-huh." Cora said it without enthusiasm.

"Ask him to come see me."

"He won't."

The Reverend Kimble smiled. "Don't be absurd. He has to arrange a wedding."

Cora was pleasantly surprised. "That's somewhat devious, Reverend."

The Reverend's eyes twinkled. "The good Lord," he assured her, "works in mysterious ways."

13

SHERRY HAD ALMOST GOTTEN THE LOWER LEFT CORNER OF THE puzzle she was creating licked when the doorbell rang. She saved her work and closed the program. It was most likely Aaron, in which case she could have left the program open, but if she did, it would turn out to be Chief Harper, and he'd have some pressing reason to lead her straight into her office. Actually, closing the program was Sherry's way of guaranteeing the caller would be Aaron. She smiled at the thought, went to the front door.

It was Dennis.

His shirt was open at the neck. The collar of his jacket was up. His hair was mussed, and his eyes were wide.

"Hi," he said.

Sherry's instinctive reaction was to take a step back. With an effort she held her ground. "You shouldn't be here."

Dennis laughed. "Now, there's an understatement. I'm about to get hitched. I really shouldn't be calling on my first wife."

"I'm glad we're in agreement."

Sherry started to close the door.

Dennis put his arm up, blocked it. Not violently, but with force. There was no way Sherry could close that door, and they both knew it.

She felt an icy rush of fear.

"Why don't you ask me in?" he said. "That would be the neighborly thing."

Sherry could think of nothing to say. She stood there, confused.

Dennis grinned, and pushed on by. He strode into the room, flopped down on the couch. "Ah, this is the life. Give me a remote control, I could be right at home here."

"You went by the newspaper today," Sherry said.

"So, that whiz-kid reporter ratted me out? I'd have thought he had more guts than that." Dennis patted the couch beside him. "Come on, sit down."

Sherry sat in a chair opposite the couch. "Why did you go by the paper?"

"Why did you?" Dennis retorted.

"Who says I went by the paper?"

"I do."

"You're following me?"

"Hey, don't get paranoid. Maybe I saw you coming out of there."

"And didn't speak to me?"

"You told me not to. You said to stay away."

"Yeah, like that ever stopped you."

"Ah, good one," Dennis said. "So why'd you go by the paper?"

"To talk to Aaron."

"There you go." Dennis nodded enthusiastically. "That's why I went too. To talk to Aaron."

"You don't know Aaron."

"Not well, but I'm getting to know him. Sort of a dweeb, don't you think?"

"That's no business of yours."

"Of course it is. I know you. I want the best for you."

"What you want doesn't matter anymore."

His eyes hardened. "Oh, yes, it does. It may not have any weight. It may not have any influence. It may not have any legal significance. But, believe me, it matters. It matters a lot."

"Why, Dennis, why? We're divorced. You're marrying my friend. Doesn't that matter?"

"Not really."

He said it calmly. Matter-of-factly.

It was cold. Chilling.

Sherry stared at him. "Good God, Dennis! You can't marry Brenda just to get at me."

"Why not?"

"Why not? Did you really ask me why not? Because I'll stop you."

"How?"

"I'll tell her what you said."

"She won't believe you."

In horror, Sherry realized it was true. She stared at Dennis in helpless frustration. He merely smiled.

Sherry stood up, pointed to the door. "Get out."

"Oh, I don't think so." Dennis seemed amused. "We're gonna sit here. We're gonna have a nice chat. And when I leave, you're gonna kiss me good-bye. That's the way it's gonna be with you, me, and Brenda. Just one big happy family."

"No, that's not how it's gonna be, Dennis. I'm calling the police. I'm having them come throw you out."

Sherry strode into the kitchen, picked up the receiver from the wall phone, punched in the number.

His hand clamped down on the button, breaking the connection. "I don't think you wanna do that."

"Let go of me, damn it!"

Sherry twisted away, ran to the butcher-block table in the middle of the kitchen, kept it between her and Dennis. She made a break for the door.

He caught her in the living room, grabbed her by the wrists. "You think I don't see your little game. Trying to provoke me. Get me angry. So I'll hit you. Give you a bruise Brenda can see. That's pathetic. I'm not going to hurt you, Sherry. I love you. Can't you see that?"

"Get out! Get out!"

He smiled. "Sorry. No can do."

Sherry slapped him across the face.

His eyes widened in amazement, like he couldn't believe she'd done it.

"Get out!" Sherry slapped him again.

This time he caught her arm. His face twisted in rage. He raised his fist.

Raymond Harstein III staggered in from the bedroom, rubbing the sleep from his eyes. He saw Dennis manhandling Sherry. "Hey!" he exclaimed. "What the hell!"

Dennis's face darkened murderously at this intrusion. He flung Sherry from him, turned, and stomped out the door.

"Raymond," Sherry said. "I didn't know you were here."

"I was taking a nap in Cora's room." He looked at his watch. "A rather long nap, I see. She's not back yet?"

"No." Sherry felt obliged to thank Raymond. "Good thing you woke up."

He waved it away. "What was that all about?"

"Dennis thinks he owns me. Always has, always will."

"Then he shouldn't be marrying your girlfriend."

"No kidding."

"Why don't you stop her?"

"She wouldn't listen to me."

"Maybe she'd listen to me."

"I doubt it."

"Mind if I try?"

Cora came in the front door. "Oh, good, you're awake. Was that Dennis I saw tooling out of here? He left enough rubber in the driveway to start a condom factory."

"I'll bet," Sherry said. "Aunt Cora, this double wedding isn't going to work out."

Cora looked offended. "Hey, like it was my idea? Sherry, trust me, it's not gonna happen. I just had a nice talk with the Reverend Kimble. He's on our side."

"I'm scared, Cora. I'll have to move again. Change my name."

"Nonsense," Raymond said. "Just go to the police."

"It would be my word against his."

"No it wouldn't. I saw the man grab you. I'm a witness."

"He'll talk his way out of it. He always does. Even if he couldn't, it wouldn't matter as long as he can fool Brenda."

"She seems an intelligent young woman," Raymond said. "Surely she could see through that."

Sherry grimaced. "You don't know Dennis."

14

BRENDA WAS IN BED READING A ROMANCE NOVEL. SHE WAS LYING on her stomach, propped up on her elbows, with her feet idly kicking the air. Dennis figured she'd probably seen Drew Barrymore do that in some god-awful chick-flick.

She smiled up at him. "Hi, sweetie. Where you been?"

"Out," Dennis grunted.

He glanced around the room, irritably.

His suitcase was sitting open on a wooden chest. He walked over, inspected it briefly. "What you been doing?" he demanded.

"Reading. Why?"

"You been in my suitcase?"

"No. Why would I?"

"You take anything out of my suitcase?"

"No."

"Or look for anything in my suitcase?"

"I haven't been near your suitcase."

"Damn it."

"What's the matter?"

"Someone's been through my stuff."

"Oh, come on. Why would anyone do that?"

"Some people are nosy."

"Oh, big deal. It's not like we've got anything to hide."

"We can't stay here."

Brenda's mouth fell open. She swung her legs over the side of the bed and sat up. "Are you kidding?"

"I'm not going to stay someplace where people spy on you. It's creepy. Like the Bates Motel. How do I know they don't have a peephole in the wall?"

"Oh, come on, Dennis—"

"Hey, if you didn't go through my suitcase, someone did. Pack your stuff. We're going."

"Where?"

"I suppose we could ask Sherry."

"Dennis!"

"Well, her aunt's staying with that guy, so she's got a spare room."

"Dennis, you can't ask to stay there."

"No, but you could."

"Dennis. I couldn't. It would be weird."

"Then we'll have to find a place. You pack up the room, I'll look around."

"You're serious about this?"

"If you didn't go into my suitcase. You're sure you didn't? Take your time. Let's not be hasty. You didn't go through my things?"

"Of course not."

"Then we gotta leave." Dennis nodded in agreement with himself, and went out the door.

15

RAYMOND HARSTEIN III PARKED IN FRONT OF HIS HOUSE AND came around the front of the car to open the door for Cora. He took Cora's arm, led her up on the wooden porch of the rental house. He put his key in the lock, held the door open.

Cora stepped in, said, "You've got mail."

She picked up the envelope that had been lying just inside the door. "Uh-oh."

"What is it?" Raymond asked.

Cora hesitated a moment, then passed the envelope over.

It was addressed to: KSTLQZSUUD.

Raymond frowned. He closed the front door, walked into the living room, snapped on the light. He tore the envelope open, pulled out the paper, and whistled.

"What is it?" Cora said.

"Here, take a look."

LQXS KSTLQZSUUD,
RUJ FGTPO RUJ'SQ VU VDXSF KJF RUJ'SQ PUF. KJFF UJF UB DR
KJVTPQVV, US FGTV AQLLTPZ TVP'F ZUTPZ FU GXHHQP. FGTV TV
X AXSPTPZ. T'D ZQFFTPZ XPZSR.

"Well," Cora said. "What do you think we should do? Turn it over to the police?"

"You should probably solve it first," Raymond said.

"Oh, no," Cora said. "The police don't like it when you mess with evidence."

"Evidence of what? There's been no crime," Raymond persisted. "Not yet, anyway. But what if this is a death threat?"

"Then we should certainly take it to them."

"Don't you think they'll be a lot happier to know what it says? And if it turns out to be harmless, there's no reason to go rushing over there."

"Let me call Sherry," Cora said. "She'll know what to do."

"She will when this is decoded. But so will we. Come on, aren't you eager to see what it says?"

"Not if it's gonna tell me not to marry you."

Raymond chuckled. "Cora, sweetheart. It's gonna take more than an anonymous note to scare me off."

"I'm not sure I have my reading glasses," Cora protested. "I think I left them at Sherry's."

"You're wearing them."

"Of course. These *are* my reading glasses. I get so flustered around men. Raymond, could we take this over to Sherry and solve it over there? It sometimes helps to bang it up on the computer."

Raymond laughed again. "Cora, sweetheart. Sit down." He sat on the couch, patted the cushion beside him. "Come on, sit here. Everything's going to be all right."

Reluctantly, Cora sank down on the couch.

Raymond took her hands in his. "I know you can't do cross-word puzzles. It's all right. You don't have to pretend."

"Raymond?" Cora's eyes were wide.

"Not that you don't do a marvelous job of making believe. The way you and Sherry solved the first cryptogram was inge-nious. I swear Chief Harper never knew."

"But you did?" Cora murmured.

"Of course," Raymond said. "I make a point of never marry-ing anyone unless I know whether she can do crossword puzzles. I don't care whether she *can,* I just want to know. It's quite obvi-ous you can't. I therefore assume your niece is the power behind the throne, so to speak, and that she writes the Puzzle Lady col-umn. I'm not sure why, but it's fine with me. The point is, with me you don't have to pretend anymore. So, let's take a look at this puzzle, and see what it says."

"But I can't . . ."

"I know. But maybe I can. Let's tackle it together. My impres-sion was these aren't that hard. Look how it starts off."

Raymond pointed to the opening of the letter:

`LQXS KSTLQZSUUD,`

"Isn't KST-whatever the same word that's on the envelope? Then this is the salutation, and the first word will be *dear.*"

"Yeah, but the second word sure isn't *Puzzle Lady.*"

"Right. So we plug in some letters and see what it is."

Raymond wrote the letters over the salutation.

```
Dear   r de      ,
LQXS KSTLQZSUUD,
```

```
            're       ar          're    .
RUJ FGTPO RUJ'SQ VU VDXSF KJF RUJ'SQ PUF. KJFF UJF UB DR
```

```
   e  ,  r       edd          '             a  e  .
KJVTPQVV, US FGTV AQLLTPZ TVP'F ZUTPZ FU GXHHQP. FGTV TV
```

```
a  ar    .  '   e      a  r  .
X AXSPTPZ. T'D ZQFFTPZ XPZSR.
```

"That doesn't help much," Cora grumbled. "The other cryptogram we had *Puzzle Lady*. Here we just have *dear*."

"Yes, but look at the *RUJ* apostrophe *re*. It occurs twice. I bet that's the word *you're*. It was in the first cryptogram. Let's plug those letters in and see what we've got."

Raymond wrote in *Y* for *R*, *O* for *U*, and *U* for *J*.

```
Dear  r de roo ,
LQXS KSTLQZSUUD,
```

```
You       you're o  ar  u  you're o  .  u  ou o   y
RUJ FGTPO RUJ'SQ VU VDXSF KJF RUJ'SQ PUF. KJFF UJF UB DR
```

```
  u  e  ,  or       edd          '    o      o  a  e  .
KJVTPQVV, US FGTV AQLLTPZ TVP'F ZUTPZ FU GXHHQP. FGTV TV
```

```
a  ar    .  '    e    a  ry.
X AXSPTPZ. T'D ZQFFTPZ XPZSR.
```

"I still don't see it," Cora said. "Anything jump out at you?"

"Jump *out*, indeed." Raymond grinned. "*Ou_* is either *our* or *out*. And since we know *S* is *R*, *F* has to be *T*.

"We also have *DR* equals *_y*. That's either *my* or *by*. But if you look at the last sentence, we have *T* apostrophe *D*. There's no word that has an apostrophe *B*. But there is a word with apostrophe *M*. The word *I'm*. So *D* is *M* and *T* is *I*. Let's fill those in."

Raymond added the letters.

```
Dear   ride room,
LQXS KSTLQZSUUD,


You t i  you're  o  mart  ut you're  ot.  utt out o  my
RUJ FGTPO RUJ'SQ VU VDXSF KJF RUJ'SQ PUF. KJFF UJF UB DR


 u i e  , or t i  eddi   i  't  oi  to  a  e . T i  i
KJVTPQVV, US FGTV AQLLTPZ TVP'F ZUTPZ FU GXHHQP. FGTV TV


a  ar i . I'm  etti   a  ry.
X AXSPTPZ. T'D ZQFFTPZ XPZSR.
```

"Dear Bridegroom!" Cora exclaimed. "It's to you!"

"It sure is," Raymond said grimly. "And I don't think I'm going to like the message."

```
Dear Bridegroom,
LQXS KSTLQZSUUD,


You t i  you're  o  mart but you're  ot. Butt out o  my
RUJ FGTPO RUJ'SQ VU VDXSF KJF RUJ'SQ PUF. KJFF UJF UB DR


bu i e  , or t i  eddi g i  't goi g to  a  e . T i  i
KJVTPQVV, US FGTV AQLLTPZ TVP'F ZUTPZ FU GXHHQP. FGTV TV


a  ar i g. I'm getti g a gry.
X AXSPTPZ. T'D ZQFFTPZ XPZSR.
```

Raymond pointed to the cryptogram. "The last two words have to be *getting angry,* so *P* is *N.* And the first line is going to say *you're so smart,* so *V* is *S.* Then *FGTV,* which appears twice, will be *this,* so *G* is *H.* And the rest should be obvious."

It was. Raymond quickly filled in the rest of the puzzle:

```
Dear Bridegroom,
LQXS KSTLQZSUUD,
```

You think you're so smart but you're not. Butt out of my
RUJ FGTPO RUJ'SQ VU VDXSF KJF RUJ'SQ PUF. KJFF UJF UB DR

business, or this wedding isn't going to happen. This is
KJVTPQVV, US FGTV AQLLTPZ TVP'F ZUTPZ FU GXHHQP. FGTV TV

a warning. I'm getting angry.
X AXSPTPZ. T'D ZQFFTPZ XPZSR.

"So," Raymond said. "Not exactly a death threat."

"Not exactly a valentine, either."

"No. The interesting thing is he's talking to me directly. The other message he was talking to me through you."

"Yeah." Cora looked up into his eyes. "Raymond, I'm scared."

"It's nothing to be afraid of, dear. It'll take more than anonymous threats to make me go away."

"That's what I'm afraid of."

"What?"

"That this creep will do more than just threaten."

Raymond chuckled. He put his arms around her, pulled her to him. Tucked her head on his shoulder, patted her hair. "Sweetheart, I promise you. I can take care of myself."

Cora pulled away. "We should take this to the police," she insisted.

"No reason to involve the authorities."

"They brought us the first letter."

"Which is good, or we wouldn't have it. But there's no reason to reciprocate."

Cora snuggled up against him. "Reciprocate? What's with the big words? I'm not the Puzzle Lady, you know."

"I know. And I don't care."

Raymond held her close. And Cora was at peace. She had a man, and with him she didn't have to pretend she was the darned Puzzle Lady. It was the best of all possible worlds.

Except for the letters.

16

CORA FELTON WOKE UP IN THE DEPTHS OF THE NIGHT WITH the feeling something was wrong. She rolled over and discovered the first thing that was wrong was that she wasn't in her own bed. Ah, yes. She was at Raymond's. Instead of getting out of bed she had rolled onto his side. If she wanted to get out, she had to roll back the other way.

Cora's bleary mind had scarcely managed to untangle all that information when another thought struck her. If she was on Raymond's side of the bed, where was Raymond?

Cora struggled to her feet, stumbled into the bathroom. Cold water on her face did not really wake her up. She grabbed a towel, dried her hands and face, switched off the light. Padded out into the living room to see if Raymond was sleeping on the couch. The moonlight through the window was enough to show the room was empty.

The digital readout on the VCR under the TV said 2:15.

Cora frowned.

This wasn't right. Men usually ran out on her *after* the wedding.

Cora smiled at the thought that she was jaded enough to make such a joke.

Then another thought struck her. If Raymond wasn't here, she could smoke.

Cora tiptoed to the window, peered out. The car was there. So he couldn't be far. Could she risk it? Hell, yes.

Cora's drawstring purse was on the coffee table. She snatched it up, started out.

The door to the study clicked open, and Raymond came out. He was dressed in his pajamas and robe. He saw Cora, reached for the light. "What are you doing up?"

"What am *I* doing up? What am *I* doing up?" she blustered. "I wake up in the middle of the night and you're gone."

"Where were you going?"

"Out to look for you."

"In your nightgown?"

"At two in the morning you expect me to get dressed?"

"You took your purse. Why did you take your purse?"

Cora blinked. "Wait a minute, wait just one minute. Why am I answering all the questions? You're the one wide-awake at two in the morning. What were you doing in the study?"

"I couldn't sleep."

"Is this a chronic problem, or only when you're faced with a wedding?"

"It's not that."

"Then what is it?"

"Cora, Cora. I have business problems that I've let slide because I'm here with you."

"You're attending to business at two in the morning?"

"I was typing some things on my laptop, yes."

"What sort of things?"

"Just business notes," Raymond answered airily. "I was also thinking about our honeymoon."

Cora blinked. "You never mentioned a honeymoon."

He smiled and chucked her under the chin. "I didn't know I was getting married next weekend. Have you ever been to France?"

"Actually, yes. My second husband, Henry, loved to travel. First with me, then without. When he started traveling in different circles we called it quits."

"Well, I've never been to France. But if you don't wanna go . . ."

"I'd love to go!"

Cora became acutely self-conscious of the fact she was still holding her handbag. She shrugged it off her shoulder and dropped it on the coffee table, hoping to remove it from the conversation. Unfortunately, this merely called attention to it.

"So, why'd you take your handbag?" Raymond persisted. "A pretty funny image, in your nightgown with your handbag."

"My keys," Cora improvised. "I didn't want to be locked out."

Raymond frowned. "Did I give you keys to the house?"

"No, and don't you think it's about time?"

He digested this illogic.

"Of course it is," Cora went on breezily. "We're getting married, for goodness' sakes. We're going to France. You mean to tell me you've never seen the Eiffel Tower? I promise you we are going to the top of the Eiffel Tower."

With her non sequiturs and her feminine wiles, Cora was able to prevent Raymond from finding out she had been on her way to sneak a cigarette. Within minutes, she managed to maneuver him into bed. Like most men, he immediately rolled over and began snoring.

Cora was pretty pleased with herself, until it occurred to her she hadn't had that cigarette. That realization made her crave one more than ever. She resolved not to have it. She would roll over and go to sleep, just like Raymond. Only without the snoring. Yes, that's what she'd do.

Three minutes and forty-seven seconds later Cora slipped silently out of bed.

The door to the study was still ajar. Cora could see a dim light. It drew her, like a moth to a flame. She pushed the door wide, peered inside.

Raymond had left his laptop on. It sat open on his desk. The screen was angled away, so Cora couldn't see what was on it. Of course, there wasn't any reason why she should. Raymond was a good man, there was absolutely no reason to check up on him. Despite anything Sherry might say.

Except Cora had been married enough times to realize she couldn't know enough about *any* man. That was the *only* reason she was doing this. Not for any silly paranoia Sherry might have. Indeed, there was no reason to even mention this to Sherry. But just for her own peace of mind.

Cora tiptoed to the desk, peered at the screen.

There. Absolutely nothing. No open program. Just a screen full of icons, exactly like Sherry's computer always looked when you first turned it on.

That was all Cora needed to know. She wasn't about to open anything, even if she knew what the icons meant. There was no way to know which one Raymond had just used. Sherry might be able to tell, but not Cora. So there was really no point.

An icon near the bottom of the screen caught her eye. It looked like a spiral notepad. Looking closer, Cora saw that was exactly what it was.

A notepad.

Raymond had said he was writing notes.

Cora stared at the screen. Where was the cursor? There it was. But she had no idea how to move it. She only knew it was

called a cursor, because the word always made her think of a
sailor swearing a blue streak.

Cora found the mouse pad, but no mouse. She moved her fingers over it, found the pad itself moved the cursor. She moved the
cursor down to the spiral notepad, clicked it on.

A notebook page opened up on the screen.

Written on it was:

```
DADTT DIHNA NERMR OUFSH UCEGE DEORY OPOAA NBNEP IANSU
RNNNW HATED NIDOO EFVLE ISARO SASOE ATUPA RPEHZ RNETM
LIOWB WTEWN OFMNO LTOEA KTAAR
```

Cora groaned in disappointment. Raymond had typed a copy
of that darn cryptogram. The last thing in the world she wanted
to see. Just when she thought she was on to something. . . .

Cora sighed. She was still half asleep, or she'd never have been
so suspicious. Well, it served her right.

Cora moved the cursor, closed the notebook. It shrank back to
an icon again.

It occurred to her she really needed that cigarette.

Cora grabbed up her purse, and slipped out the door.

17

Brenda stirred at the sound of the door clicking shut. "Dennis?"

"Shh," he hissed as he slipped into bed.

"Where were you?" Brenda murmured drowsily.

"In the bathroom."

That woke her up. "No, you weren't. You came in the front door."

"You were dreaming."

"Maybe, but you still came in the front door. Where were you?"

"Out."

"You said you were in the bathroom."

"I was in the bathroom, then I went out."

"Why?"

"Why was I in the bathroom?"

"Don't play dumb. Why'd you go out?"

"Just to look around."

"At three in the morning?"

"I couldn't sleep."

"What's the matter?"

"Nothing's the matter."

"Why couldn't you sleep?"

"I just couldn't. No big deal. Sorry I woke you. Go back to sleep."

But Brenda was wide-awake now. After a few moments, she said, "Why'd we move?"

Dennis didn't answer.

"Dennis, why'd we move?"

"Brenda, why are you doing this at three in the morning?"

"I'm awake. You woke me up coming in. Why'd we move?"

"I told you. The nosy landlady went through our things."

"What things? It's not like we have anything to hide."

"It's the principle of the thing. I don't want anyone pawing through my stuff."

"We don't know she did that."

"Oh, no? I had my electric razor packed under my shirts. So how did it wind up on top of my shirts?"

"Maybe I took it out."

"Why would you move my electric razor?"

"I'm not saying I did."

"I don't like people going through my stuff. Bed-and-breakfasts are just a little too cozy for me."

"This is a bed-and-breakfast."

"Yes, it is. And maybe it will work out, maybe it won't."

"We could have stayed somewhere else."

"Where? You didn't wanna ask Sherry."

"Oh, come on, Dennis. You know we couldn't ask Sherry!"

"Why not? We're all friends."

"Yes. And it's important we stay that way."

Brenda got up, padded to the window.

"What are you doing?"

"Looking out."

"Why?"

"Same reason you went outside. Restless."

Dennis came to the window, put his arm around her. "You having second thoughts about the wedding?"

She snuggled against him. "Not at all."

"Then come on back to bed."

"In a minute."

"What are you doing?" There was just a hint of impatience in his voice.

"I thought I saw something."

"Where?"

"Across the street."

"It's called a house. They have them in towns. You city girls lead such sheltered lives."

Brenda batted at him playfully. "No, silly. I thought I saw someone. There. On the porch. Dennis, look!"

"Look at what?"

"See that orange glow? There's someone standing behind the pillar, smoking a cigarette."

"You've been reading too many mystery novels."

"You trying to tell me that's not a cigarette?"

"It could be a firefly." At her impatient exclamation, he said, "I admit it *looks* like a cigarette."

"It *is* a cigarette," Brenda said, "and . . . Oh! Look who that is! It's Sherry's aunt Cora!"

"It couldn't be."

"Well, it is. Didn't you see her in the moonlight?"

"I was looking at you."

"Dennis!"

"You don't want me to look at you?"

"Dennis, did you know Cora and Raymond were staying right across the street?"

"No. What a shock."

"I don't like the idea of being so close."

"Oh, what does it matter? Come on back to bed."

Brenda allowed Dennis to walk her across the room, but she wasn't happy. It was quite a coincidence, Cora and Raymond living right across the street.

Brenda didn't like it.

18

CORA STOPPED IN FOR HER MORNING DANISH TO FIND THE bakeshop buzzing with the news.

"Congratulations!" First Selectman Iris Cooper cried. "I can't believe it. What am I saying, of course I can believe it. I'm so happy for you. What a thrill."

"Yes, it's terrific," Amy Cox agreed. "We'll have to have a shower. Oh, wait. That's babies, isn't it? You're not having a baby, are you, Cora?" The young housewife had a habit of sticking her foot in it.

Iris Cooper jabbed Amy painfully in the ribs, said, "Oh, for goodness' sakes, no. Cora's just getting married. In our very own church. Isn't that something?"

"Isn't it, indeed?" Cora replied dryly. Her first thought was the Reverend Kimble couldn't be trusted with a secret.

"So," Iris gushed, "I assume he's that distinguished-looking man you've been seen around town with. Of course, they didn't run his picture."

"His picture?"

"Yes. There was a nice picture of you, but none of him."

"You mean in the *Gazette*?"

"Yes, of course. Didn't you see it? Here, take a look. Amy, where's the paper?"

Mrs. Cox pulled the *Gazette* out from under her arm and flipped it open. "Here you go. 'Puzzle Lady to Wed.' Right on page 5."

Cora took the paper, read:

> Cora Felton, of Bakerhaven, Connecticut, is engaged to be wed to Raymond Harstein III, of San Diego, California. The wedding is to take place Saturday, June 12, in Bakerhaven, at the Congregational church. Miss Felton has been married before. It is not known if this is the first marriage for Mr. Harstein.

Cora harrumphed. " 'Married before.' That makes me sound like used goods."

"Not as much as if they'd said how many times," Amy Cox pointed out, then tittered at her own wit.

"Maybe not," Cora said. "But remind me to give Aaron Grant a rap upside the head."

"Why?" Iris asked. "Surely you intended to announce your own wedding."

"Yes, but *I* intended to announce it. Not have it announced for me." Cora scowled, buried her head in the paper.

A portly, balding man in a brown suit scuttled through the bakeshop door. He wore no tie, and his white shirt was open at the collar.

"Is it true?" he cried.

Cora knew that voice. She looked up into the anxious little eyes of Harvey Beerbaum. Harvey was Cora's rival, nemesis, and major pain in the fanny, always suggesting they solve or construct puzzles together, which of course she could not do. And she was running out of excuses. Cora stifled an involuntary curse at the sight of him. What did that annoying man want now?

Harvey, like Cora, held a copy of the *Bakerhaven Gazette*. "Is it true?" he repeated, holding it up. "Are you really getting wed? I saw you around town with the gentleman. And of course I heard the talk."

"The talk?"

"I, I, I don't mean the talk," Harvey floundered. "I mean I'd heard there was a possibility there might be nuptials in your future, but I'd dismissed it. But now I perceive it's true. That is to say if it *is* true. Is it true?"

"Yes, it is," Cora told him.

Harvey seemed taken aback. "I see. Well, my goodness. Congratulations, of course. I must say I'm astonished. I always thought if you married again it would be to one of us. You know, a cruciverbalist. A constructor, perhaps."

Cora noticed Harvey's shirt was buttoned wrong, and what little hair he had was uncombed. She stifled a smile. Cora had long suspected Harvey of wanting to either expose her as a fraud or marry her. Apparently, it was the latter.

"The paper doesn't say what the gentleman does," Harvey persisted. "He's not a puzzle maker, is he?"

"Not at all."

"So what does he do?"

"He owns hotels. In San Diego."

"Oh. So does that mean you'll be relocating?"

"No, we'll be staying here. Of course, Raymond may have to travel some."

"You'll be getting an abode."

Cora frowned. Her compassion for Harvey's disappointment in love was rapidly eroding in the face of his annoying, pedantic questions.

Iris Cooper came to her rescue. "Oh, for pity's sake, Harvey. Don't be a nudge. Of course she hasn't thought of that yet. But really, Cora, sweetie, if you want to go house hunting, I am best friends with Judy Knauer of Judy Douglas Knauer Realty. She happens to owe me one. I'd be delighted to call in the favor. Do you know Judy?"

"No, I don't. Sherry rented our house. I think it was through Kemper."

"Kemper's fine for rentals. Of course you'll want to buy. Judy's the best."

Harvey Beerbaum, left standing with romantic egg on his face, excused himself and bought a cup of coffee, as if that were what he'd really come into town for.

Cora watched, but her mind was elsewhere. She and Raymond hadn't discussed buying a house. As opposed to renting a house. As opposed to staying in the house he was renting now. If the truth be known, Cora hadn't thought much beyond the honeymoon, and before Raymond had mentioned that, she hadn't thought much beyond the wedding ceremony. Cora had a problem when she fell in love of not thinking of much of anything. Except that this time it was different and this time it would work. And what a wonderful man she had found.

It didn't occur to her she had felt that way about Melvin.

Or Henry.

Or Frank.

A shriek from Mrs. Cushman roused Cora from her musing.

She glanced up to see Harvey Beerbaum had spilled his coffee all over the counter. The poor man was clearly distressed.

Cora's smile was maternal. She was surprised to find herself thinking almost fondly of Harvey.

At a table in the far corner of the bakery, Brenda Wallenstein snapped her newspaper shut, picked up her coffee, and stalked out the door.

Dennis was sitting in the rental car with the motor running.

"What kept you?" he asked.

Brenda thrust his coffee through the open window, stomped around the car, and got in. She slammed the door just as Dennis was prying the plastic lid off the cardboard cup. Steaming coffee sloshed in his lap.

"Hey, watch it," he snarled irritably. He looked over, caught her expression, scowled. "What's the matter now?"

"I thought you went down to the paper to announce our engagement."

"I did."

"They didn't print it."

"Oh?"

"There's a big piece about Cora getting married, but nothing about us."

"That's hardly my fault. Why are you getting torqued off?"

"How could that happen?"

"How should I know? Probably that kid reporter. You can tell he can't stand me."

"Is that who you talked to? I thought you talked to the editor."

"I talked to both of them. But the kid must have written the piece."

"And you told him it was a double wedding?"

"Of course."

"Then why would he leave us out?"

Dennis took a sip of coffee, and sighed in exasperation before answering. "Brenda. Baby. What can I tell you? These are things over which I have no control. All I know is the guy's got the hots for Sherry, he doesn't like me, and I'm not at all surprised he didn't want to write about me."

"But you drank a toast with the editor. Wouldn't the editor make him write the story?"

"If the old geezer gave a damn. Frankly, I think he was just looking for an excuse to take a drink."

"But—"

Brenda was interrupted by a rapping on the window. She rolled it down, was surprised to find a man with a clerical collar peering into the car.

"Pardon me," the minister said. "Would you happen to be Brenda Wallenstein?"

"Yes," Brenda said, utterly puzzled.

"And you would be Dennis Pride?"

"That's right."

"I understand congratulations are in order. Forgive the intrusion. I'm the Reverend Kimble. I'll be performing the service. If you wouldn't mind stopping by the church a little later on, perhaps we can make some of the arrangements."

"Arrangements? What do we need to arrange?"

"Oh, heavens. Choice of music. Guests. Wedding rehearsal."

"We gotta rehearse this?"

"Of course. I'm sorry, I thought you'd been married before."

"Not in a church."

"Ah, well, then, we can treat this as a new experience, Mr. Pride. And with a double wedding, there's twice as much to plan for, isn't there? Could you come by later this morning, say between eleven and twelve?"

"Yeah, I guess so."

"Fine. I'll see you then."

The Reverend Kimble straightened up.

"Hey," Brenda said. "Hang on. How did you know we were getting married?"

The Reverend said offhandedly, "Oh. It was in the paper."

He nodded, smiled, and walked off.

Brenda and Dennis looked at each other.

"In the paper?" Dennis said.

19

SHERRY CARTER CLICKED THE SAVE BUTTON AND PICKED UP THE phone. Sherry always backed up her work before taking a phone call, because she could never be sure how long the call would last, and if the computer were to crash, it could wipe out the whole puzzle. Sherry once had to re-create an entire crossword puzzle from memory before learning that bitter lesson; she would not make that mistake again.

The only problem was, the answering machine was in the kitchen, and it picked up on the fourth ring. So, if Sherry couldn't save her work and answer the phone in three rings, the machine would beat her to it, and she'd be on the phone in the office with no way to turn the answering machine off. Sherry could talk into the phone, but her entire conversation would not only be recorded, it would also reverberate through the house as it was broadcast by the answering machine.

So, when the phone rang while Sherry was at work, it was always a race to save her data.

This time she was in luck. She snatched up the phone on the second ring, said, "Hello?"

"Sherry. It's Brenda. Have you seen the *Gazette*?"

"It's still in the mailbox. Why?"

"Your boyfriend put something in there about Cora getting married."

"Well, he's a reporter, that's his job."

"Did you know he was going to do it?"

"Did I? I don't remember."

"Damn it, Sherry. Either you did or you didn't."

"We discussed it many times. I can't remember how we left it. What difference does it make?"

"He mentioned only your aunt's wedding. He didn't mention mine."

"Oh. And he should have?"

"Of course he should have. Dennis went by the paper yesterday just to tell him about it. And he left it out. Deliberately."

"I don't think Aaron would do that."

"Deliberately," Brenda repeated firmly. "And it wasn't what his editor wanted, because he drank a toast to us."

"Brenda, why are you telling me this?"

"Well, I just think you should know that your boyfriend is not happy about this marriage, and is looking to sabotage us."

"Oh, for goodness' sakes."

"Sherry, why else would he leave us out?"

"There could be lots of reasons."

"Name one. He doesn't like Dennis. Can you deny that?"

"Brenda—"

"Which is so unfair. Because he doesn't even know Dennis."

"*I* do."

"You *did*," Brenda corrected. "Dennis has changed, Sherry. You gotta give him a chance. Anyway, the minister wants to talk to him, and what's that all about?"

"What's what all about? Brenda, you're not making sense."

"Neither was the minister. He bangs on our car window, congratulates us on our engagement, and asks to talk to Dennis."

For a moment Sherry wished the conversation *were* being recorded. Then she could play it back and hope to make sense of it. "Bren, could you give me a small hint what you're talking about?"

"How does this clergyman know we're getting married? It wasn't in the paper."

"Are you sure?"

"I can't find it. You wanna try?"

"No, I'm sure you're right. I don't know. The Reverend must have heard it somewhere. You haven't been keeping it a secret."

"No, but no one knows us here. Except you and your aunt."

"Oh."

"Has Cora been blabbing?"

"I have no idea."

"Well, she's your aunt."

"I don't own Cora, Bren. And she hasn't even been staying here."

"Yeah, I know. She's across the street from us."

"She's what?"

"We moved yesterday. Dennis thinks the landlady was going through his things. So we found another place. Turns out it's right across from Cora."

"Well, that's convenient."

"Yeah. Too convenient, if Cora's messing in our business."

"Excuse *me,*" Sherry said. "Exactly whose idea was this double wedding?"

"Well, it wasn't mine. And I'm beginning to think it's not such a hot idea," Brenda snapped, and banged down the phone.

Sherry, too, slammed the receiver down. Well, if that didn't beat all.

Her anger swiftly turned to worry, however. Brenda just didn't seem like herself. Brenda was feisty, yes, but never hostile. Not to her. Of course, a lot of her hostility could be defensive, because of Dennis, but even so. Brenda's relationship with Dennis clearly wasn't going as well as she might try to pretend. If only she'd stop deluding herself.

A bell, a spring, and a cuckoo clock, Sherry's audio equivalent of "You've got mail," announced an incoming message. Absently, she moved the mouse, retrieved the e-mail, looked at the screen.

Her mouth fell open.

```
AWIE QPVVGW GIAU,
XLPC LZY PQ, ZO UKP BDKR RLIC'X JKKA OKE UKP. Z AKD'C
LIHW CK CIBW CLZX OEKY IDUKDW.
```

Now they were coming by e-mail?
Sherry checked the return address:

Bhl.org.

That seemed familiar, but she couldn't place it.

Sherry hit NAME on the toolbar. Her e-mails, which had been sorted by date with the most recent first, were now grouped alphabetically. Sherry had three other e-mails from *Bhl.org*. The first one read:

```
Dear Puzzle Lady,
Thank you for your donation of PUZZLE LADY PUZZLES. It's
wonderful to have a signed copy. Your book will be
treasured.
Thanks again,
Emily Potter, Librarian
```

Sherry blinked.
The public library?

She scooped up the phone, called the Bakerhaven Library, but to no avail. Emily Potter told her that she had been away from her desk working in the stacks. She hadn't seen anyone near her computer, but her e-mail account had been open, and the offending message was in SENT MAIL, so someone must have used it, she just had no idea who.

Sherry hung up the phone, turned her attention to the cryptogram.

It wasn't hard. The opening pattern suggested the salutation was "Dear Puzzle Lady." Sherry plugged those letters in:

```
Dear Puzzle Lady,
AWIE QPVVGW GIAU,


  u    up,   y u     a '   d  r y u.  d '
XLPC LZY PQ, ZO UKP BDKR RLIC'X JKKA OKE UKP. Z AKD'C


  a e    a e     r   a y e.
LIHW CK CIBW CLZX OEKY IDUKDW.
```

Sherry studied the result.

So. *UKP* would be *you*. So *K* was *O*. And *AKD'C* would be *doD'C*. So *C* would be either *S* or *T*. If *C* was *T* the word would be *don't*, which would make *D* stand for *N*.

Humming to herself, Sherry attacked the puzzle.

20

CORA HUNG UP THE PHONE AND WANDERED INTO THE LIVING room, where Raymond Harstein III sat reading the newspaper.

"Is something the matter?" he asked, not looking up.

"Is it that obvious?" Cora asked. "Yeah, I guess it is. There's been another one. Another message warning you off. This time it came through e-mail on our computer."

"A coded message?"

"That's right."

"What did it say?"

"Something to the effect that if you didn't mind your own business you'd get what was coming to you."

Raymond frowned. "That's not the same as telling me not to get married."

"No," Cora agreed. "But it's not an invitation to a dance, either. This is really getting on my nerves."

Raymond seemed interested. "But if it's an e-mail, there must be a return address. Who sent it?"

"According to Sherry, it came from the Bakerhaven Library."

"Well, that's something. You can find out when the message was sent, and check who was in the library at the time."

Cora looked at him searchingly. "You're taking this seriously?"

He smiled. "This whole thing seems like a childish prank. Tell you what. Have Sherry send it to me and we'll take a look."

"Send it to you?"

"Sure. She can forward it to me. On my laptop. Call her back and tell her to send it along."

"With the solution?"

"Oh, sure. No reason to work too hard."

Cora called Sherry and gave her Raymond's e-mail address. When Cora hung up, Raymond went on-line. Minutes later, the flag on the mailbox icon announced he had mail. Raymond moved the cursor and retrieved the message.

At the top was the address, showing that the e-mail had been forwarded from *Bhl.org*.

```
AWIE QPVVGW GIAU,
XLPC LZY PQ, ZO UKP BDKR RLIC'X JKKA OKE UKP. Z AKD'C
LIHW CK CIBW CLZX OEKY IDUKDW.
```

Below, Sherry had added the solution.

```
Dear Puzzle Lady,
AWIE QPVVGW GIAU,


Shut him up, if you know what's good for you. I don't
XLPC LZY PQ, ZO UKP BDKR RLIC'X JKKA OKE UKP. Z AKD'C


have to take this from anyone.
LIHW CK CIBW CLZX OEKY IDUKDW.
```

"Well," Raymond said. "Shut me up? I wasn't aware that I'd said anything offensive."

"Of course not."

"This is clearly nothing."

"Uh-huh."

"Why do you say that?"

"I didn't say anything."

"You said *uh-huh*."

"So?"

"Cora. I know you. If you say *uh-huh* in that tone of voice, I'm in trouble. What's up?"

Cora pointed to the e-mail on the laptop. "Can you shrink that?"

"Sure."

Raymond moved the cursor, clicked on the minimize bar at the top right of the screen. The e-mail program shrank to an icon, revealing the other icons on the start-up screen.

Cora pointed to the notebook icon. "If you thought it was nothing, why did you type it up?"

Raymond frowned. "What are you talking about?"

"I know I shouldn't have looked, but I was in here last night, and there it was on your laptop."

Cora moved the cursor, clicked on the icon. The cryptogram instantly filled the screen:

```
DADTT DIHNA NERMR OUFSH UCEGE DEORY OPOAA NBNEP IANSU
RNNNW HATED NIDOO EFVLE ISARO SASOE ATUPA RPEHZ RNETM
LIOWB WTEWN OFMNO LTOEA KTAAR
```

"There. If you thought it was nothing, why did you copy it?"

Raymond seemed troubled. "Oh."

"See?" Cora said. "You *are* taking it seriously. We'd already solved this cryptogram, and you still typed it up."

"Oh." Raymond took Cora by the shoulders. He smiled. "You know, one of the dangers of having a computer is you tend to use it for everything. Yellow Pages. Maps. Weather. Notes. The thing you have to realize is, a note on a laptop isn't any more important than a note on a scrap of paper."

"Yes, but—"

Raymond tilted up her chin. "Cora. I am not really worried. All right?"

He kissed her. After a moment's resistance, she melted into his arms. All thoughts of danger, and warnings, and secret messages were swept away. She closed her eyes.

Raymond's eyes were open. He was looking not at the computer screen, but at the strip of paper on the far side of the keyboard. It was a thin white strip, inconspicuous on the sheet of notebook paper on which it lay. A column of letters was written down the paper:

G
E
D
E
O
R
Y
O
P
O
A
A
N
B
N
E
P
I
A
N

S

U

R

Behind Cora's back, Raymond's right hand reached out, pulled a sheet of paper over the column of letters, and pushed the screen of the laptop down.

21

"REHEARSAL," DENNIS DECLARED. "I WANT A REHEARSAL."

"Yes, of course," the Reverend Kimble agreed. "We'll be sure to schedule it in."

"No. Tonight," Dennis insisted. "I want a rehearsal tonight."

The Reverend leaned back in his chair, sized Dennis up. The young man's demeanor was perfectly amiable, and yet there seemed to be a challenge behind it. The Reverend wondered how many of Cora's suspicions might be true.

"A rehearsal is a good idea," he said, "although I doubt if there's any way we could do it with so little preparation. You're from out of town, aren't you? You and your bride?"

"So?"

"I assume your wedding party is not local, either. Best man. Father of the bride. How are you going to get them here on such short notice?"

"Don't worry. We'll manage."

"And I'd have to contact Cora, see who she was planning on

having. Who may or may not be available. And then there's this whole maid-of-honor thing. I'm not entirely sure how that works. Double weddings are one thing. Siamese weddings are another."

"Very clever." The groom's smile was noncommittal, neither gracious nor sarcastic.

Skilled as the Reverend was at sizing people up, he found Dennis Pride remarkably hard to read. "Thank you," he told the young man. "The point is, if we can't get the people, there's nothing much we can do."

"You can rehearse the principals. We're the ones who really need it. Go over the procedure, settle the questions you just raised. Isn't that the way to do it? I mean, you talk to me, you talk to Cora, you come back and tell me what Cora said, and I tell you what I think of that. That's what takes so long. Why not get us all together and work these things out?"

"That's hardly a wedding rehearsal."

"Call it anything you like. The point is, do you have the time? If you do, I do. Let's ask them. Run through the ceremony, see how it's going to go."

"Here again it will depend on who the other parties are."

"Why?"

"Well, if it doesn't work . . ."

"If it doesn't work, we'll do something else. That's what we want to determine."

"If you're willing to make concessions, Mr. Pride, there's no need for the rehearsal."

"Yes, but what about the maid of honor? Brenda's got her heart set on Sherry. And that Felton woman doesn't want to give her up."

"Are you sure?"

"Absolutely. That's the reason for the double wedding to begin with. So, if that's the only overlap, that's the only thing we need to rehearse. The wedding couples and Sherry."

The Reverend Kimble frowned. Changed his assessment of Dennis for the third or fourth time since their conversation had begun. "You want me to get the five of you together tonight to see how that's going to work?"

"Sure," Dennis said. "Isn't that the whole idea?"

The Reverend Kimble was beginning to think it was.

22

WHEN THE PHONE RANG, CORA AND RAYMOND WERE MAKING out on the couch like teenagers.

"Gonna get that?" he murmured.

"Me? It's your phone."

"Yeah, but you get all the calls."

"Let the machine get it."

"There's no machine."

Cora nuzzled his ear. "Let it ring."

"What if it's Sherry?"

"Aw, hell."

Cora extracted herself from Raymond's embrace, stood up, and straightened her clothing. "This better not be a crank call. If someone starts talking in code, I'm going to flip out." Cora stomped over to the phone, picked it up. "Hello?"

"Cora Felton?"

"Why, Reverend Kimble. I was sure you were a crank."

"I beg your pardon?"

"No, not you. The phone call. Never mind. What's up, Rev?"

The Reverend Kimble filled Cora in on what Dennis had in mind.

"Tonight?" Cora asked him. "You've gotta be kidding."

"I wish I were. The young man seemed most eager to rehearse with you and the maid of honor."

"Oh."

"Yes. He did seem to attach undue importance to it. Just as we feared. So, inappropriate as the whole idea is, it's probably best to grab the bull by the horns, so to speak, and try to ascertain just how deep the problem lies."

"At a certain expense to my niece," Cora said, dryly.

"I understand. And I'd like to spare Sherry as much as possible. It will be good to have the two of you there as a buffer. As well as anyone else you'd like to throw into the mix."

"Such as?"

"Bridesmaids, best men, ring bearers."

"Ring bearers?"

"You've never had ring bearers? They carry the rings on pillows. Usually small lads, prone toward mischief. I remember one actually lost a ring once, down a ventilator shaft. Claimed it fell. That may be so, but I think the boys were playing a game like marbles."

"We will *not* be having ring bearers," Cora said emphatically.

"All right, but anyone you could bring along would be appreciated. After all, we're throwing this together on the spur of the moment."

"Yes, I know," Cora said. She hung up the phone to find Raymond looking at her expectantly. "Believe it or not, we have a wedding rehearsal tonight. At eight-thirty in the church."

"You're kidding. Who agreed to that?"

"I just did," Cora admitted. "But Dennis and Brenda set it up."

"Did they? And we're just supposed to go along? Well, that's a fine howdy-do. I don't even have a tux. And you don't have your dress."

"Oh, well, actually I have one that might fit," Cora said. It was one of her typical prevarications, not exactly a lie, but not exactly the whole truth, either. In fact, the dress she was referring to was the brand-new one she'd had made for the occasion. It had arrived last week and was hanging in her closet.

"Well, that's lucky," Raymond said. "And you'll forgive me if I wear a business suit."

"I'd forgive you anything," Cora cooed, snuggling up against him. This tender moment was short-lived, as she swung right back into making plans. "Now, then, we have to put together a wedding party. I'm gonna ask the girls to be bridesmaids."

"Girls? What girls?"

"The women I'm having dinner with tonight."

"Ah, yes." Raymond did not mention that those "girls" were older than Cora. "And I'm not dining with you?"

"Of course not, goosey. It's my engagement party." Cora frowned. "Oh, dear. How is this going to work?"

"What?"

"The cars. Sherry's got my car. She'll need it to get to the church. And I'm taking your car to dinner."

"Sherry's not going to the dinner?"

"No."

"Why not?"

"Are you kidding? If you were having a bachelor party, showing stag films, would you wanna take your young nephew along?"

"You'll be showing stag films?"

"No, we're having a male stripper. At the Country Kitchen. If I wind up in jail, bail me out."

"I'm going to assume you're joking about the male stripper,

but serious about Sherry not going. So, you'll be there without her. I trust you'll be on your best behavior."

"Raymond."

"There's a lot of drinking of toasts at these affairs, isn't there?"

"There's a lot of drinking toasts *to* me, not *by* me. So, we gotta get you a ride."

"You can't pick me up?"

"You know how these things are. I'm going to have trouble getting away. I'll meet you at the church."

"And how am I getting there?"

"Let me see. Oh, of course." Cora strode to the door, opened it. "Good. His car's there."

"Whose car?"

"The other bridegroom."

Dennis's car was indeed parked at the curb in front of the big white Victorian across the street, which a hand-painted sign identified as TRUMBLE'S BED-AND-BREAKFAST. Cora crossed the street, went up on the front porch, and rang the bell. The door was opened by a middle-aged lady with bright red hair that clashed with an even brighter plaid dress. After a brief negotiation, she went and fetched Dennis.

Brenda and Dennis both came down. Brenda was merely inquisitive, but Dennis bristled at the sight of Raymond Harstein III. "What is it?" he demanded.

"The wedding rehearsal tonight," Cora said. "I understand that's your idea."

"You got a problem with that?"

"Not at all. We think it's an excellent idea, don't we, dear?"

Raymond Harstein III, prompted, chimed in with, "Yes, yes, of course."

"The only thing is, Raymond needs a ride. Sherry's got my car, I've got his car. Then it occurred to me you guys are going."

"Oh. Yeah," Dennis said, with a complete lack of enthusiasm. "Only thing is, we'll be going out to eat first."

"We'll be coming back to change," Brenda pointed out.

"We will?"

"You think I'm going out to dinner in my wedding dress?"

"You don't *have* your wedding dress."

"I know I don't have my wedding dress. I mean what I'm wearing tonight. I'm gonna change after dinner. Aren't you?"

"I hadn't thought about it."

"Men," Brenda said, affectionately. "Of course we'll take you, won't we, dear?"

Dennis, having come to the conclusion there was no way out of it, gave in with hearty good grace. "Of course we will. After all, we're getting married together. So, we gotta be there at eight-thirty, whaddya say we leave at eight-fifteen?"

"Perfect," Raymond said. "I'll be right outside."

"We'll see you then," Brenda said.

"There, that wasn't so hard," Cora said, as she and Raymond recrossed the street.

"Are you kidding, it was like pulling teeth. That boy doesn't like me."

"He's a complex kid. For Sherry's sake, we have to put up with him."

"I'd like to knock his block off for Sherry's sake," Raymond muttered, as they went up the front steps. "Someone ought to kill that kid."

"Raymond, for God's sake," Cora hissed. Brenda and Dennis had gone back inside, but Raymond's hippie neighbors were out on their porch, smoking something that might have been tobacco, but then again might not. Cora wasn't really afraid they might suspect her prospective bridegroom of plotting murder, but she didn't want them drawn into any conversation with him where they might happen to mention what they'd seen *her* smoke.

Cora followed Raymond into the living room. "You shouldn't say such things, even in jest," she chided him.

Raymond threw his hands up in the air. "I can't win. I agree to a double wedding, get kicked in the shin because the bridegroom's a schmuck. I voice the same opinion, and you blast me for it."

"Suggesting he die is hardly the same opinion."

"Well, if you're gonna pick on every little thing . . ."

Cora started to flare up, then noticed his eyes were twinkling. "Oh, you. You are such a bad boy. Now, can I count on you riding to the wedding rehearsal without killing the other bridegroom?"

Raymond raised his right hand. "You have my word."

"I know I do." Cora melted into his arms. He kissed her. She nuzzled his neck. "Now then, if you could just do something about the wedding party . . ."

"What?"

"I'm lining up bridesmaids. What are you going to do about a best man?"

"Well, that's a bit of a dilemma. I doubt if I can get any of my friends to abandon their corporate responsibilities to fly in on such short notice. And I don't really know anyone here. What about Sherry's boyfriend? The newspaper reporter?"

Cora winced. "Oh, bad move. If you think Dennis hates you, that's nothing compared to how he feels about *him*. It's bad enough having Aaron around. Start calling him the best man, and Dennis will really flip out."

"You're right. Maybe this wedding's not such a good idea."

"Raymond."

But his eyes were twinkling again. "This is one for the record books. You want a best man your niece's ex-husband won't hate. Okay, how about our next-door neighbor?"

"Who?"

"Mr. Flower Child. Mr. Love Beads could be my best man and

give me a ride in his microbus. Then I wouldn't have to go with Dennis tonight."

"On second thought," Cora said, remembering the sweet scent of their neighbors' recreational smoking, "I'm sure Aaron will be just fine."

"Yeah, that's what I figured," Raymond said. "So, how about you? Who's going to give you away, my love?"

"Oh, right," Cora said. "Thanks for reminding me."

Cora went to the phone, punched in a number. "Hi, Chief, it's Cora Felton."

"Miss Felton," Chief Harper said. "What can I do for you?"

Cora smiled. "Funny you should ask."

23

CORA FELTON, WHIRLING AROUND THE LIVING ROOM IN HER bridal veil, and belting out wedding songs from Broadway musicals with the lusty glee peculiar to the blissfully tone-deaf, was driving her niece to distraction.

"Oh, stop it," Sherry cried, covering her ears. "You are *not* getting married in the morning. You are going to a wedding rehearsal. At night. And the bells aren't going to chime. So keep it down, would you?"

"I'm also going to my engagement dinner."

"Well, I pray there's no song about *that*."

"Spoilsport. Let me have my fun."

"Have your fun. Just don't sing about it."

"You should be as happy as me. You're my maid of honor."

"I'm *everyone's* maid of honor. This is an absolute nightmare, Cora."

"I know how you feel. But I'm not putting off my wedding."

"No one's asking you to."

"And if Dennis wants to marry Brenda, well, that could be good."

"Do you believe that?"

"Well, it could."

"Oh, yeah? Trust me: If their marriage was a good idea, I wouldn't be involved in it."

"You're coming tonight?"

"Can I get out of it?"

"I told the Reverend you'd be there."

"That was presumptuous of you."

"Well, you told me you'd be there."

"Yeah, 'cause you twisted my arm. But you'd already *told* the Reverend I'd be there."

"Are you sure?"

"Sure I'm sure. You used it in your argument for why I had to go."

"If you say so."

"Which means you'd already told the Reverend."

"What's your point?"

"My point is, when I *agreed* to be there, you'd already *said* I would."

Cora patted her on the cheek. "Really, dear. You set such store on sequencing."

Humming, Cora tried on her lavender blouse, found it a trifle snug. "Damn. It's like I gain one full size per husband."

"Must be size 80," Sherry muttered.

"I *heard* that," Cora said tartly. She pulled off the blouse, rummaged through her closet, came out with a purple shirt. She held it up, eyed it critically. "And what are you going to wear tonight?"

"Does it matter?"

"Not so long as you're there. You will be there, won't you? Eight-thirty? At the church?"

"Aren't you picking me up?"

Cora gawked at Sherry over the top of a leopard-print blouse she was seriously considering wearing. "Sherry, sweetie, is your mind elsewhere? I'm leaving you the car. I'm taking Raymond's car out to my engagement-bash dinner with Iris Cooper and the girls. I'm going directly from there to the church. You just have to meet me there."

"What about Raymond?"

"Dennis is bringing him."

"You're kidding!"

"Why not? They're staying right across the street. It's a nice gesture, Sherry. It shows Dennis is trying."

"Don't tell me you asked him to drive Raymond?"

"Of course I asked him. Otherwise, how would he know Raymond needed a ride?"

Cora tugged out a white blouse with ruffles. "Oh, I hate this blouse. I hope it doesn't fit. Damn it, it does."

"Don't wear it."

"Bite your tongue. I'm not going to my engagement dinner in an outfit that makes me look like a sausage with too tight a skin."

"Precious image."

"Okay, that's a top. Now to find a skirt that goes with it . . ."

"Anything goes with white."

"Wanna bet? I can find you half a dozen things that'll clash."

"I stand corrected."

"Sherry, loosen up. Nothing's gonna happen in front of the Reverend. Maybe he can even help you work some things out."

Sherry's eyes widened. "This wedding rehearsal was *your* idea?"

"Not at all," Cora protested. "Dennis asked the Reverend for a rehearsal."

"And why was Dennis speaking to the Reverend?"

"My goodness, look at the time! I'm gonna be late. What am I gonna do for a skirt? Ah, here we are." Cora pulled down a baby-blue skirt, stepped into it. "Now then, O merciful gods of fabric. Button meet buttonhole." She buttoned the skirt around her waist. "Ta-da! We have a winner. All set; I'm off to dinner. Sherry, sweetie, pull yourself together and get out of your funk. If you need help, I've got a mantra for you. Meditate on this. Ready?" Cora cocked her head. " 'He's not marrying *me*.' "

"That's not funny."

"It's not supposed to be funny," Cora retorted. "It's supposed to be reassuring. If you think about it, you'll realize just how reassuring it is. Well, gotta go. Ah, yes, shoes. Can't get married without shoes." She stepped into a pair of black leather pumps. "Thank God my feet haven't grown too. Eight-thirty, Sherry. Set the clock."

"I don't need to set the clock."

"You do if you're working on a puzzle. You know how you lose track of time."

"I'll be there," Sherry promised grimly.

Cora reached in the back of the closet, tugged out her wedding dress, which was on a wooden hanger and carefully swathed in plastic.

"You're wearing your wedding dress for the rehearsal?" Sherry exclaimed.

"Of course I am. It's such a lovely dress. It would be a shame to only wear it once."

"You could save it for your next wedding."

"Bite your tongue."

"Assuming it still fit."

Cora refused to dignify this remark with a comment. She stuck her nose in the air, and, humming the Wedding March, waltzed out the door.

Sherry heaved a sigh, plodded into the kitchen. Cora was going out, so what should she have for dinner? It hardly seemed worth the effort to cook for one. In the city, she'd call for takeout.

But not in Bakerhaven. There was no takeout in Bakerhaven. Were there any leftovers? Ah, chicken. Perhaps a field greens salad with balsamic vinaigrette and sliced chicken breast . . .

Sherry got out the salad spinner, prepared to wash the lettuce.

The phone rang.

Sherry scooped it up, cradled the phone to her ear, as she tore romaine lettuce leaves into the spinner.

"Hi, it's me."

"Hi, Aaron."

"What's the matter?"

"Nothing, why?"

"You sound upset. Is everything all right?"

"Everything's just dandy. I have to go to a wedding rehearsal tonight. With Cora and my ex-husband."

"I know. I'm best man."

"For Raymond?"

"Well, not for Dennis."

"No. I suppose not."

"Aha. Sherry, look—"

"I don't want to talk about Dennis."

"I don't, either. That's not why I called. I'm afraid I've got some bad news."

"Oh?"

"I just heard from my man in San Diego. Raymond Harstein III doesn't own any hotels."

"You're kidding!"

"Not at all. He's a drug dealer."

"Oh, no!"

"Oh, yes. According to the reporter in California, Cora's prospective bridegroom is a notorious dope peddler, with a record as long as your arm."

24

"HE'S DREAMY-LOOKING," IRIS COOPER DECLARED. THE FACT her own husband was bald and pudgy probably had a great deal to do with her enthusiasm.

"I'll say," Lois Greely put in. A large, horsey-faced woman, Lois was the proprietor of the general store just on the other side of the covered bridge. Though Cora had never met Lois's husband, she couldn't imagine anyone marrying her except a large, horsey-faced man.

"Absolutely dreamy," Judy Douglas Knauer agreed. The real-estate agent Iris Cooper had recommended turned out to be a genial woman, eager to agree with everyone, no doubt a social carryover from her trade.

Of the diners assembled, only Amy Cox didn't chime in immediately with effusive praise. A younger woman whose husband ran an insurance company in Hartford, Amy was not so easily impressed with an aging fiancé. "You're a lucky woman, Cora," she said, raising her glass.

The ladies all clinked their glasses.

Cora took a big pull from hers.

"Hey, slow down," Judy Douglas Knauer laughed.

Cora frowned slightly. Her tall, frosted glass looked like a gin and tonic, but was actually a tonic and lime. Not being able to drink at her own engagement party was annoying. Not that Raymond wasn't right about her drinking, of course. Raymond was often right. Even so, Cora hoped someone would change the subject.

Iris Cooper did. "So, what do we do as bridesmaids?"

"I don't know," Cora said. "I've never been a bridesmaid. I've been a bride often enough, but I never paid much attention to the other women."

"Didn't you ever have a wedding rehearsal?" Lois Greely asked.

"Probably. I don't remember."

"How could you not remember?"

"Courtships are mainly a blur. I can recall the man, and not much else."

"Not surprising, if you keep slugging them back like that," Judy Douglas Knauer said.

Cora frowned. It occurred to her the woman had put away quite a few herself. As far as Cora was concerned, Judy Douglas Knauer had just lost a sale on a house.

"So, what's for dessert?" Lois Greely asked.

"Oh, my goodness, are we having dessert?" Cora said.

"Of course we're having dessert. We've had everything else, haven't we?"

They certainly had. The girls were treating Cora to dinner, and had spared no expense. In addition to the usual trips to the salad bar, they had all ordered appetizers, and spent a hilarious half hour swapping grilled shrimp, calamari, escargots, and crab cakes. They'd eaten their way through rack of lamb, pork tenderloin, salmon fillet, fettuccine Alfredo, the last consumed by the trim Judy Douglas Knauer, who seemed to pack it away but never put on a pound.

"Won't we be late?" Amy Cox protested.

"Nonsense," Lois said. "We're with the bride. How can we be late if we're with the bride?"

"*I* shouldn't be late," Cora said.

"You think they're not gonna wait for you?" Lois scoffed. "Sweetheart, you're the *bride*."

"I'm *one* of them," Cora pointed out.

"Yes, and isn't that odd?" Amy Cox said. "A double wedding with Sherry's ex."

Cora's smile was somewhat fixed. It was at least the fourth or fifth time the subject had come up. Not that she blamed the women. It certainly *was* odd.

"Now, which is it?" Lois asked. "He *was* a rock star, or he *is* a rock star?"

"He was never a rock star," Cora said. "He had a rock band. They never got anywhere."

"But they played?"

"Sure they played. You got amplifiers and you play loud enough, no one seems to care if it's just noise."

"You say Dennis doesn't get along with Raymond?" Lois asked.

"Dennis doesn't get along with most men. Sees them as rivals."

"Big deal," Lois said. "All men are like that. I remember my Herbie used to get jealous any time another man looked at me. Can you imagine that?"

Cora Felton couldn't. In fact, she found the prospect mind-boggling.

A waitress appeared with dessert menus. Over Cora's faint

protests, coffee, cognac, crème brûlée, and tiramisu were ordered.

Cora had to remind herself it wasn't a *real* wedding rehearsal. The thought did not cheer her. She didn't want Sherry confronting Dennis if she wasn't there.

"So, does Raymond ever get jealous?" Amy Cox inquired, a twinkle in her eye.

Cora, roused from her musings, realized that dessert had been ordered, and the ladies had picked up the conversation.

"I never give him cause to."

"Men don't *need* cause," Iris Cooper declared. "They'll invent the most outlandish things."

Cora couldn't help wondering what outlandish thing Iris Cooper's husband had invented. The question perked her up considerably.

"Well," Judy Douglas Knauer said, "frankly, I don't know a thing about this man you're marrying. But I must say, I'm glad to see it. I was afraid you might marry that nerdy little puzzle man."

The table conversation stopped.

Iris Cooper, sitting across from Judy Douglas Knauer, sucked in her breath. Her eyes were wide.

Lois Greely and Amy Cox looked horrified.

Even before she turned her head, Cora Felton knew what she would see.

Sure enough, right behind Judy Douglas Knauer, Harvey Beerbaum stood frozen like a deer in the headlights. On his face, an expression of hurt and humiliation was giving way to one of anger and rage. Harvey's eyes smoldered with a fury Cora had never seen before. He had clearly come to talk to Cora, but now, instead, without a word, he turned on his heel, stalked from the dining room, and slammed out the door.

"Uh-oh," Judy Douglas Knauer said.

Cora got to her feet, wove her way through the dining room, and went down the front stairs.

A car roared by from the parking lot.

Harvey Beerbaum, his face a mask of grim determination, swerved out of the driveway and peeled out like a drunken teenager, leaving rubber all over the road.

Cora shook her head.

What else could go wrong?

25

THE ROCK GROUP, TUNE FREAKS, SWARMED OVER THE CHURCH like locusts, running cables, plugging in amps, and even hanging strobe lights.

"Where the hell's the damn outlet?" screeched a scrawny young man with a tattoo of a viper on one arm, and a knife dripping blood on the other.

"I believe that would be behind the pulpit," the Reverend Kimble suggested gravely, with his most disapproving look.

The tattooed Tune Freak snuffled into his scruffy beard. "Sorry, Father, but this really is a mess. Who designed this pit?"

"It's a church, not a pit. And it is not a concert hall."

"I'll say. We'll be lucky if your fuses don't blow."

"Yes, that would be lucky," the Reverend Kimble agreed dryly. "It was not my understanding that the wedding party would be providing music. We have a church organ."

The young man made a face. "Yeah, checked it out. Doesn't

work for us. Wrong sound, plus it's way up in the loft. But don't sweat it, we got a synthesizer."

"That's nice," the Reverend Kimble said, with a gentle irony that was totally lost on the young musician. "Tell me. Would you be the best man?" He gallantly repressed a shudder at the prospect.

"Naw, that's Razor. The lead guitar. I play bass."

"Razor?"

"Yeah. As in straight razor. As in slit your throat." At the Reverend's look the bass player added helpfully, "Not that he'd do anything like that. It's just a name."

The Reverend Kimble cast a glance at the bony man dressed in black who was sprawled out over the first pew. Razor had an arrogant, insolent look. Evidently, the lead guitarist didn't have to set up, but two other dreadful-looking young men were wrestling with sound equipment. A plump, bearded drummer, in tattered low-rise jeans and a skimpy white T-shirt that revealed more hairy belly than even the most ardent groupie could surely ever wish to see, was constantly repositioning an amplifier, cursing at his work, and beginning again. A tall, shirtless, emaciated keyboard player, who looked alarmingly like a praying mantis, was dangling a cable connector in front of his face and squinting sideways at it as if considering whether to eat it.

The Reverend looked at his watch. "I'm not sure we have time for all this. . . ."

"Sure we do. Dennis ain't here yet."

The Reverend frowned. He was not accustomed to having his authority questioned, certainly not in his own church, but the man was correct: The young bridegroom definitely wasn't present. Neither was the older bridegroom. Or either of the brides. Aside from the slovenly musicians crawling around the pews, the only members of the wedding party present were Chief Harper, on hand in uniform to give Cora Felton away, Aaron Grant, the other best man, and Sherry Carter, the universal maid of honor.

Sherry, whose maid-of-honor dress was on rush order, was conservatively dressed in a blue cotton pullover and tan slacks. That didn't stop the boys in the band from hitting on her. The drummer and bass player were new, but the keyboard player and lead guitarist knew her from when she was married to Dennis, and took that as license to act familiar. So far Sherry had endured "babes" and "tootsies" and dodged pats on the behind.

"Cora's late," Sherry said irritably.

"They're all late," Aaron said.

"I don't care about the others. I wanna talk to Cora before they get here."

"I understand."

"So what do you mean, they're all late?"

"Just trying to help."

"That doesn't help." Sherry blew out a breath, said, "Sorry, Aaron. I'm a little touchy."

"Hadn't noticed."

Chief Harper came walking over. He looked ill at ease. "How do I do this?" he said. "I've never given anyone away before."

"You just trot her down the aisle, hand her off to the groom, and move out of the way," Sherry informed him.

"Where do I go?"

"How the hell should I know?"

Chief Harper raised his eyebrows.

"She's a little touchy," Aaron said.

"Hadn't noticed."

"Tell him, for goodness' sakes," Sherry snarled. "This is too much of a strain."

"Tell me what?" the bewildered chief asked.

Aaron explained succinctly about Raymond Harstein's criminal record.

"You held this back?" Chief Harper asked incredulously.

"Held what back?" Aaron protested. "The guy's not wanted for anything *now,* he's not a fugitive from justice, there's no warrant out for his arrest. He's not on the FBI's most wanted list."

"Yeah, but Cora's gonna marry him."

"And you're gonna stop that?"

"Well, I'm damned if I'm gonna give her away to him. Does the Reverend know?"

"Not yet."

"Gonna tell him?"

"I'm gonna tell her first," Sherry intervened. "We're only telling you because I knew you'd make a fuss about it."

"Thanks a lot." Harper scowled. "So, what if you tell your aunt and she still insists on marrying this creep?"

"I'm sure she will."

"But if he's scum . . . ?"

"The men she marries invariably are."

"Yeah, but did she know it? When she married them, I mean? Isn't it different to marry a creep when you *know* he's a creep?"

Sherry flushed. "I wouldn't know."

Chief Harper winced at the tone of her voice. Noticed the hard lines at the corners of her eyes.

Aaron cleared his throat.

Chief Harper didn't know what to say next.

The Wallensteins saved him. They came sweeping in with all the subtlety of a brass band. Brenda's mother, a plump dynamo in an ostentatious plum-colored evening frock that might have been more appropriate had this been the actual wedding rather than just a rehearsal, came first, all but dragging Brenda's father, an amiable if dull-looking man in a gray business suit.

"So where is she?" Wendy Wallenstein declared in a voice that sliced through the din the Tune Freaks were making. "Where's my Brenda? Does anybody know?"

The fat drummer, who was smack in Mrs. Wallenstein's path, took one look and changed course in mid-stride, choosing to lug a heavy amplifier around the other end of the row of pews rather than attempt to pass her. Mrs. Wallenstein favored him with a sniff of disapproval, glanced around, spotted Sherry Carter.

"Ah, Sherry, there you are! Have you seen my Brenda? She called this afternoon, said she was having her wedding rehearsal tonight. What a shock. I had to cancel a hairdresser's appointment, and Norman had to leave work. I mean, it's not like we were prepared, or anything. I had to run out and buy this dress. And if they hadn't sewed it for me on the spot, I don't know what I would have done. Norman, of course, doesn't care, and what kind of an attitude is that?"

It occurred to Sherry that Norman might have cared if he'd been able to get a word in edgewise. Sherry couldn't recall a time when Brenda's father had ever said anything in the presence of Brenda's mother.

"So, where are they? Why aren't they here?" Wendy demanded. "And who are *they*?" she added, distastefully, pointing to a Tune Freak. "That better not be his band. Brenda said he left the band. He better not be thinking of going back. Norman won't have it, will you, dear?"

This, like most of Wendy's asides to her husband, was most likely a rhetorical question, but whether or not she had any intention of letting the poor man answer was never to be known, for at that moment Cora Felton arrived with her wedding dress over her shoulder and her entourage in tow.

Cora, of course, was sober as a judge, but the bridesmaids were clearly three sheets to the wind, having swilled brandy before, during, and after dessert.

"Well, hello, Studly!" Lois Greely brayed at the sight of the bare-chested keyboard player. "What is this, Chippendales?"

"Oh, like you've ever been to Chippendales!" Iris Cooper chided. "Hiya, Reverend. Where you want your bridesmaids?"

Cora Felton took in the scene at a glance, scowled, crossed to her niece. "Sherry, is that the band?"

"That's just what *I* want to know," Wendy Wallenstein declared.

Cora sized her up. "Mother of the bride?"

"That's right. I understand it's to be a double wedding."

"You got a problem with that?" Cora asked hopefully. "Because I'm not convinced myself."

"And yet you're doing it," Brenda's mother snorted, cutting Cora no slack.

Cora decided to ignore her, said to Sherry, "Raymond's not here yet?"

"No."

"Good, I gotta change."

"Cora, I have to talk to you."

"Not now. I gotta get dressed."

Cora hurried off, hopping nimbly over the booted feet of a sprawled-out, cable-running Tune Freak as she went. She skipped up the steps around the pulpit, and into the small anteroom where the Reverend Kimble had said she could change.

Cora hung her bridal gown on a hook, kicked off her shoes, began to undress.

Sherry Carter came in the door. "Aunt Cora, listen to me—"

"Yeah, yeah, I'm listening."

Cora hung her ruffly white blouse on a hanger, stepped out of her skirt.

The tattooed Tune Freak barged in the door, saw Cora, said, "Whoa, baby!" and barged out again.

"Well, I like that," Cora said. "You wanna shut that door?"

"Aunt Cora . . ."

"Fine, leave it open."

Cora took her wedding gown off the hanger, stepped into it, fed her arms through the sleeves, and shrugged it up over her shoulders.

It was a gorgeous gown of pure white silk, satin, and lace. A tribute to the designer's skill, the dress was at once virginal and seductive, naughty and discreet. Whatever the case, Cora Felton seemed to melt into it, became at once the most beautiful, blushing bride.

"Zip me up, my dear."

Reluctantly, Sherry stepped behind her aunt, pulled the zipper up her back.

Cora regarded herself in the mirror, beamed in satisfaction. "Love that seamstress. Impossible woman, great gown. So much better than the other way around."

Her face wreathed in smiles, Cora turned back to her niece. "Now then, dear, what is it?"

Sherry took a breath.

"Aunt Cora . . . it's about Raymond."

26

"I CAN'T BELIEVE WE'VE GOTTA GIVE THE OLD PHONY A RIDE," Dennis groused, as he and Brenda dressed for the rehearsal.

Dennis was wearing a suit and tie. Brenda was wearing a blouse and skirt and affecting a casual look. She was, however, taking more than twice as long as usual with her makeup.

"He's not a phony," she protested.

"Of course he is. Just look at him. It really burns me up."

"You care who Cora marries?"

"Well, why should she get taken for a sucker?"

Brenda laughed, a risky move when darkening one's lashes. "Do you think he's after her money? I don't recall Cora being rich."

"She has the fat residuals from her TV ads. Not to mention her alimony."

"Which she loses when she marries again." Brenda gestured with the eyelash brush. "Now, there's a conspiracy theory for you.

Raymond is a stooge hired by her last husband to marry her and get *him* off the hook."

"Go ahead and laugh. I tell you, there's something real wrong with that guy."

Dennis straightened his tie, checked himself out in the full-length mirror on the closet door. He nodded his approval at his own appearance, then glanced into the bathroom. "Ready yet?"

"Just about."

"You been in there forever."

"I want to look good."

"You look great. Sensational."

"I look like a raccoon. This eye shadow's way too dark."

"Then why are you putting more on?"

"I'm making it lighter."

"You're putting light shadow over dark shadow?"

"Yeah. Why?"

"No reason. So why do we have to take this geezer? Cora's at a hen party somewhere?"

"Some of her friends are taking her out to dinner to celebrate her engagement." Brenda stopped dabbing at her eyelids long enough to add, "Because it was announced in the paper."

"Hey, I told the guy. If he didn't use it, it's hardly my fault." Dennis glanced at his watch. "Come on. We don't wanna be late."

"We won't be late."

"We will if you don't stop layering your eyelids. Isn't that good enough?"

Brenda turned to him, smiled. "What do you think?"

One eyelid was dark, one light.

"Terrific. Gorgeous. Come on, let's go."

Brenda shook her head. "Men." And went back to working on her eyes.

"All right, fine," Dennis said. "I'll go get the geezer, you meet us downstairs."

"There's really no hurry," Brenda told him.

"Yeah, sure."

Dennis stomped out.

Brenda frowned. Dennis was certainly unduly agitated. As far as she was concerned, this whole wedding rehearsal was a bad idea. The four of them and Sherry? What was that all about? More like group therapy than rehearsal. It was a good thing she'd called her parents. They'd promised they'd make it. She hoped they would. Of course they would. When her mother said they were going to do something, they always did it. Her mother would come through again. But, boy, was she surprised to have the rehearsal tonight. Of course, it wasn't as big a shock as moving the wedding to Bakerhaven.

Brenda's musings brought her to the front window. She looked out, saw Dennis go in the front door of the house across the street. Oh, hell, she really did have to get ready. At least Raymond wasn't ready either, or he'd have come out instead of asking Dennis in. So she had a few minutes, but not many, not with Dennis getting so worked up. Not a good idea, she decided, to leave the two men alone for long.

She hurried back in the bathroom, attacked her eyes. The eyelid situation was out of control. The cover-up Dennis had scoffed at wasn't working.

Brenda grabbed cotton and cold cream, swiftly and expertly wiped the shadow off, then began applying the lighter shadow to the natural skin tone.

Much better. And it hadn't taken long. She was sure of it. A few quick touch-ups, and—

The bedroom door burst open.

Startled, Brenda smudged an eyelid. "Oh, hell."

She came out of the bathroom to find Dennis bent over his suitcase. "What are you doing?"

He wheeled around with a guilty start. "Oh. I was just looking for— What difference does it make? Harstein wasn't ready, so I came back."

"And you were rushing *me,*" Brenda teased. "How long's he gonna be?"

"A couple minutes, I guess. I'll go get him. You hurry up."

"Yes, but . . ."

Dennis dashed out the door.

Brenda shrugged, shook her head. Smiled indulgently.

She went back in the bathroom, fixed her eye shadow, and reapplied her mascara. She checked her face in the mirror, smiled a dazzling smile.

She waltzed out the door and came tripping down the steps to meet Dennis. Of course he wasn't there. Neither was Raymond. His next-door neighbors were both out on their porch, but aside from them the street was empty. That figured. After making her rush, the men were late.

Brenda considered going inside and shooing the two bridegrooms out, then rejected the notion. Raymond didn't need her around if he was trying to dress. She wished she had the key to the rental car. It wasn't cold, but it was dark, and the bugs were coming out. She slapped a mosquito on her arm, and decided to go back inside. Why not? Let Dennis come and get her.

Tires screeched around a corner, and headlights hurtled down the street. Brenda leaped for the sidewalk as a red Toyota fishtailed by and screeched to a stop in front of the house across the street.

The car door flew open, and Cora Felton came rocketing out like the top of an exploding wedding cake, her lacy white veil and train trailing out behind her. She descended on Brenda, demanded, "Why aren't you at the damn church?"

Brenda, considerably taken aback, replied, "Raymond isn't ready yet. Dennis went to get him."

"Oh, he did, did he?"

Cora turned, stalked across the street.

On their porch, the hippie couple were getting an eyeful. Cora glared at them as she pelted up the front steps and stomped inside.

Brenda caught up with her in the foyer. She had no idea what was going on, but she wasn't about to be left out. Cheek by jowl, the two brides-to-be turned the corner into the living room.

Cora stopped dead.

Brenda screamed.

Raymond Harstein III lay faceup on the living room rug. His head lolled at an unnatural angle. His tongue hung out of his mouth. His eyes were wide, accusing, staring.

He wore nothing but socks, boxer shorts, and a crisp white dress shirt. The front of the shirt was stained bright red from the blood that had pooled near the breast pocket.

Dennis was kneeling beside the body. In his right hand he held a butcher knife, poised just over the victim's heart.

27

Dr. Barney Nathan, dapper as ever in his scarlet bow tie, followed the EMS crew as they bumped the gurney down the front steps, ducked under the crime-scene ribbon, and loaded the gurney into the van.

Chief Harper caught up with the physician just as he was climbing into his Lincoln Town Car. "What you got for me, Barney?"

"Well, you got a dead guy, for one thing."

Harper snorted in exasperation. "I knew that."

"Actually, you didn't," Dr. Nathan retorted complacently. "There was blood flowing out of the wound. Could have been a sign of life. Could have been postmortem." The little doctor raised one finger, added pedantically, "Turns out it was postmortem."

"What does running blood do to your time of death?"

"What do you mean?"

"You're gonna give me a time of death. Is that gonna be when he was stabbed, or did he die later?"

"Hard to say."

"Great."

"But from the look of the wound, it was a very short time."

"That's more like it. How's Miss Felton?"

"Hysterical. I gave her a sedative."

"You calm her down?"

"I knocked her out. She was in bad shape."

"When can I talk to her?"

"Maybe tomorrow. I gave her a megadose."

The little doctor hopped into his big car, and sped off after the ambulance.

Chief Harper surveyed the street, which was filling up with curious neighbors. He scowled, ducked under the crime-scene ribbon, went back inside.

Dan Finley was processing the living room for prints. The eager young officer had already dusted all the obvious places, like the telephone, doorknobs, and light switches, and was now working on table surfaces.

Sam Brogan, the cranky, gum-chewing officer, watched in amusement. "Lookin' for fingerprints. Guy was *holdin'* the knife, but *he's* lookin' for prints."

"You get any prints off the knife?" Harper asked Finley, ignoring Sam.

"Got a whole bunch. At least three look clear enough to match."

Sam Brogan popped his gum. "Not real bright. Probably never killed anyone before."

"You read him his rights?"

"Oh, sure." Sam stroked his mustache, recited: " 'You got the right to go to court and hear a dozen people say you did it. You got the right to go to jail until some bleeding-heart parole board lets you out.' "

"Very funny. Did you read him Miranda?"

" 'Course I did. Ask him anything you like."

"Gee, thanks, Sam," Chief Harper said, sarcastically. "You got him in the lockup?"

"Yeah."

"Where's the girl?"

"There with him."

"You left them together?"

"Not at all. Pride's in the holding cell. Unless she's got a set of keys, she can't get back there."

"So where is she?"

"In your office. Figured you wouldn't mind. Her parents are there with her."

"Oh, hell."

Chief Harper hopped in his car, drove to the police station.

Brenda and her parents met him at the front door. The bride-to-be was trying to hold herself together, but she was clearly distraught. The artfully applied eye shadow and mascara ran down her cheeks, evidence of the fact she'd been weeping.

"He didn't do it!" she cried. "You've gotta believe me! Dennis didn't do it!"

"I'm sure he didn't, miss," Chief Harper soothed. He took her by the hands. "Now, if you'd come back inside . . ."

"If you know he didn't do it, why did you arrest him?" Wendy Wallenstein managed to sound as if Chief Harper had just given Dennis a C- on an American History paper.

"I didn't arrest him."

"Oh, no? He's back there in a *cell*."

"It's a holding cell. I'm holding him as a material witness."

"The cop read him his rights," Mrs. Wallenstein pointed out indignantly.

"We have to do that," Chief Harper told her. "To protect ourselves. In case anything should come out in our questioning. But that doesn't mean we expect it to."

Brenda put her hands to her temples and wailed: "Stop, stop. I can't take this anymore. First this horrible thing happens, then you arrest Dennis, then you act as if it's all just routine. It's *not* routine. He's back there in a *cell*."

"I know."

"So do something about it," Mrs. Wallenstein insisted.

"Okay. Come into my office, calm down, tell me what you want me to do."

"Want you to do?" Brenda cried. "I want you to let Dennis out."

Chief Harper guided them into his office, set Brenda in a chair. Her parents sat on either side. Her father put his arm around her and tried to console her, but her mother sat straight up glaring poisonously at the chief. He ignored her, said to Brenda, "Why don't you tell me what happened?"

"My daughter is far too upset to answer questions," Mrs. Wallenstein declared haughtily.

Chief Harper shook his head. "That's too bad. Then I guess Mr. Pride will have to remain locked up."

"Mo-*om*!" Brenda wailed, glaring at her mother. "I'm *fine*. Go ahead, Chief. I'm *fine*."

"So, what happened?"

"You know what happened! Dennis and I walked in and found him dead."

"How did you get in?"

"The front door was open."

"Standing open?"

"No, I mean it was unlocked."

"Who opened the front door?"

"Dennis."

"What happened then?"

"We went in the living room and there he was."

"What did you do?"

"I screamed."

"What did Dennis do?"

"Dennis ran to help him."

"Help him how?"

"There was a knife in his chest. Dennis pulled it out."

"You saw Dennis pull the knife out?"

"Yes. But it was too late. Raymond was dead."

"There," Wendy Wallenstein said impatiently. "There you have it. It's perfectly clear. The boy didn't do it. Now let him go."

"I'm afraid I have a few more questions."

"I fail to see why."

Chief Harper leaned back in his desk chair and waited.

There was an uncomfortable silence.

Brenda stared her mother down.

"You knew Raymond?" Chief Harper asked Brenda.

"Not well. We were supposed to give him a ride to the church."

"Had you ever been in his house before?"

"No."

"Did you call his name? Did you call 'Hey, Raymond'?"

"I don't remember."

"Did Dennis call his name?"

Brenda hesitated.

"Because the first time entering a strange house without being let in, that would be the normal thing to do. Call out, see if the occupant was home."

"I don't remember."

"Why not?"

At that, Wendy Wallenstein actually sprang out of her chair. "I think that's enough, Officer. My daughter's told you everything she knows and everything she remembers. When you start asking her *why* she doesn't remember, you've crossed the line."

"I wasn't aware there was a line, Mrs. Wallenstein," Chief Harper said gently. "Anyway, I think I'm done."

"You're going to let him go?" Brenda said.

"Not just yet."

Chief Harper left the Wallensteins in his office and hurried down the hall. He unlocked the door to the holding cells and slipped through, locking it behind him, in case the women took a notion to try to follow.

There were four tiny cells in the back of the police station. Only one was currently occupied. Dennis Pride stood with his hands gripping the bars. Pride looked like a caged animal. His eyes were haunted and frightened. But there was something else in his face too. A look of utter disbelief. How could this possibly have happened to him? Chief Harper had seen that look before, even on the most hardened of criminals. No matter how heinous their crime, they still could not believe they had been caught. Chief Harper wondered which one Dennis was: the trapped assassin, or the innocent man.

"Hey, let me out of here!" Dennis cried. "I didn't do anything."

"Glad to hear it," the chief said. "That will make my life a little harder, but I'm really glad, for your sake. You wanna talk this over?"

"I wanna get out of this cell."

Chief Harper nodded. "Seems reasonable." He jerked his thumb. "How about the two of us go in that room over there and have a little chat?"

Dennis scowled, took a raspy breath, blew it out. "Yeah, sure."

"Fine," Chief Harper said, as if Dennis had given in with complete good grace. He unlocked the cell, led the young man into the interrogation room. "This shouldn't take long," he said. He didn't mention that when he was done Dennis was going right back into the cell. He gestured to Dennis to sit at the interrogation table, then sat down opposite. "Tell me how you found the body."

"I already told you. We were supposed to give the guy a ride to the church. He was late, so we went in. We found him dead."

"You were going to your wedding rehearsal, and had agreed to give him a ride?"

"Yeah." Dennis looked Chief Harper right in the eye. "Not that I wanted to, mind. Frankly, I didn't care for the guy. But Cora asked me, and I couldn't get out of it."

"You didn't like the man?"

"No, I didn't. Geezer like that, always acting like he's God's gift to women. And like he's so smart just 'cause he's older than I am, big deal. Anyway, I didn't like him, but I'm stuck driving him to church, so I came to pick him up, and there he was."

"When you came to pick him up, there was no one out front?"

"That's right."

"You knocked on the door?"

Dennis hesitated a second before saying, "Yes."

"No one answered?"

"Obviously. I tried the doorknob. It was unlocked. So I pushed it open, stuck my head inside."

"Then what?"

"There was no one in the foyer. I went on into the living room, and there he was, lying on the floor in all that blood, with the knife in his rib cage. It was awful."

"Was he dead?"

"He looked dead to me, but do I look like Dr. Kildare? I ran to him, tried to help him. I bent down, pulled out the knife."

"Then what?"

"I guess it was the wrong thing to do. The blood started running again."

"Had it stopped running?"

"I don't know. There was blood all over his shirt." Dennis looked at his own cuffs, which were spattered with blood. "A real mess. But it might have stopped, I can't remember."

"This was the first time you'd been in his house?"

"Yeah, why?"

"The fact you walked in and found the body."

"It wasn't hard to find. Right there in the middle of the rug."

"That's what Miss Wallenstein said too."

"Well, there you are. Can I get out of here now?"

"We've got a few formalities to go through first," Chief Harper said.

Over Dennis's protests, Chief Harper locked him back up in the holding cell.

Harper tiptoed down the hall, peeked into his office. Brenda and her mother had their heads together and were whispering furiously. Her father was slumped in his chair watching them, expressionless, like a gray, slumbering bear.

Harper snuck on by to the outer office, sat at Dan Finley's desk, picked up the phone, and punched in a number.

A voice said, "Hello?"

"Hi, Judge Hobbs. Dale Harper."

"Aw, hell."

"Well, I like that," Harper said. "What happened to, Hi, hello, how are ya?"

"Calling me at home and using your first name instead of *Chief.* You want something."

"Now, don't be like that."

"What do you want?"

"Well, now that you mention it . . ."

28

CORA FELTON WAS STUCK IN A BOG. A DENSE, STICKY BOG SHE couldn't get out of. A pea-soup bog, so thick she couldn't see. No, that was fog. A pea-soup fog. She was slogging through the bog in the fog.

With a dog.

No. No dog. Alone. Alone and slogging.

To the altar.

No. Not the altar. The altar was altered. Like her ego. Her altar ego.

No, not ego. Raymond's not breathing. Raymond's bloody. Not British bloody, American bloody. Blood bloody.

Blood bloody. Blood buddy.

Bloody hell.

Cora reached out of the bog, but she couldn't escape. The more she moved, the worse it got. Covering every inch, pooling over her head, sucking her down.

"Nooo!" Cora moaned.

Her eyes snapped open. She glanced around groggily. She was in unfamiliar surroundings. The lamp. The bookcase. The window. Where was she?

And there was her niece, slipping through the doorway.

"Cora, lie down. You're not supposed to be awake."

Cora hadn't realized she'd sat up. Now she looked, saw what she was sitting on.

A bed.

Her bed.

Her room.

Strange.

With a rush, it all came back to her.

"Oh." Cora shivered, and her face twisted in pain.

Sherry ran to her, put her arms around her, held her. "There, there. There, there," she said. Perfectly meaningless words that couldn't help. Because no words could help.

"Sherry," Cora moaned. "Raymond's dead."

"Hush."

Cora rocked in Sherry's arms, whimpering softly.

"Shh," Sherry whispered. "There, there."

The moaning stopped. Cora relaxed. Sherry thought she was asleep.

"What about Dennis?" Cora asked.

Startled, Sherry said, "Huh?"

"Dennis. Where's Dennis?"

"Chief Harper took him in."

"Did he let him go?"

"I don't know. I suppose so."

Cora shook her head. "Not gonna happen. Police think he did it."

"I don't know about that."

"I do. Too much evidence. Gotta hold him."

"But he didn't do it."

" 'Course not."

"You really think so?"

Cora shook her head again. "Not Dennis's style. Type of guy likes to beat up women."

"Cora . . ."

"Fact is, he didn't do it."

Cora threw her legs over the side of the bed.

"Aunt Cora! You can't get up!"

"Says who?"

Cora struggled to her feet. Was surprised to find she was in her underclothes. "Where's my gown?"

"In the washing machine."

"The washing machine! Sherry, you don't put a silk wedding gown in the washing machine."

"Cora, remember what happened? You threw yourself on Raymond. You tried to revive him."

"Did I?" Understanding, Cora groaned, "Raymond . . ."

"So the gown's in the wash. I don't know if it can be saved."

"What difference does it make." Cora slumped back on the bed. "Sherry, I'm dizzy."

"Of course you are. The doctor gave you a shot."

"I'll sue the bastard for malpractice."

"You needed it, Cora."

"What time is it?"

"Ten thirty-five. You got barely an hour's sleep."

Cora lurched to her feet again. "What did Brenda say? To the police. What did she say to the cops?"

"I don't know."

"Didn't you hear?"

"I was looking after you."

"I gotta get over there."

"I can't let you."

"Why not?"

"You're in no shape to go anywhere."

"Says who?"

"The fact you're going out in your bra and panties is a pretty good indication."

Cora staggered to the closet, pulled down her Wicked Witch of the West dress. A loose, comfortable, tattered smock with cigarette burns and a liquor stain or two, it was Cora's favorite casual knock-around-home wear.

"Cora! You can't wear that outside."

"Why not?"

"It's a rag. You'll look like a beggar woman."

"What do I care?"

Cora spotted her drawstring purse on the night table. She snatched it up, fumbled in it, came out with her lighter and cigarettes. "I can smoke now," she declared. Tears streamed down her cheeks. "It doesn't matter anymore. Now I can smoke."

Cora tapped a cigarette out of the pack, stuck it between her lips, tried to light it. The flame wouldn't touch the cigarette. Her hand wasn't steady enough. "Help me, Sherry."

"Help you smoke?"

Cora's face hardened. "Do it myself."

She managed to get the cigarette lit. She sucked in a greedy drag, squeezed her eyes shut, shuddered.

"There, that's better. Come on, Sherry. Let's go see the cops."

"I'm not taking you anywhere in that condition."

"Fine. Do it myself."

"Aunt Cora, you can't drive."

"You are so negative today."

Her car keys were in the fruit bowl on the maple cabinet near the door, where she and Sherry always left them for each other. Cora snatched them from the bowl, careened out the door.

"Damn it, Cora!" Sherry said. "You can't drive!"

She sprinted after her, got there just as Cora slammed the car door in her face.

Sherry grabbed at the handle, but the doors automatically locked as Cora turned the key in the ignition. The engine roared to life.

"My God! Cora! Don't do this!"

But Cora was already backing the car into a U-turn. She did a one-eighty, wound up on the front lawn.

"Oops," Cora said.

She spun the wheel, swerved across the driveway and onto the lawn on the other side.

As Sherry watched in horror, Cora went speeding down the driveway in a series of S-turns, weaving from one side to the other. She reached the bottom, skidded the car into a turn.

"At least put your lights on!" Sherry yelled after her, as the automobile roared out of sight.

29

BECKY BALDWIN PUSHED HER WAY THROUGH THE THRONG OF curious spectators milling about outside the crime scene, and spotted Sam Brogan chatting with the neighbors in the dim light of the streetlamp. "Hey, Sam, where's the chief?"

Sam Brogan was one of the few men in Bakerhaven Becky Baldwin's wiles didn't work on. "If he's smart, he's home in bed. That's where I'd like to be."

"Not your shift, eh, Sam?"

"I'll say. This sort of stuff never happens on my shift."

"So where's the chief?"

"Most likely down at the station."

"Didn't see his car. Suppose he *did* go home to get some sleep?"

"Not likely. Called in ten minutes ago, told me to stick around."

"How come?"

" 'Cause it ain't my shift. This always happens when it ain't my shift."

"Why'd he want you to stick around?" Becky asked again, with commendable patience.

"Didn't say. First I'm going home after I talk to the neighbors, now I'm hangin' here."

Aaron Grant came pushing through the crowd. "Hi, Becky. Got any angle on this?"

"Don't look at me. I'm not involved."

"No client in the case?"

"No. And what client might that be?"

"I understand they took Dennis and Brenda in."

"On what charge?"

"No charge. They just took 'em in."

"They can't do that."

"Is that a fact?"

Becky grimaced. "Damn it, Aaron, you're just needling me for quotes."

"That's my job."

Razor, the Tune Freaks' lead guitarist, strode up. He was followed by two lesser Freaks. "You the lawyer lady?" Razor asked.

Becky raised her eyebrows at the grubby young man who'd accosted her. He appeared to dwell within the neverland of grunge rock, attractive if his group was successful, a filthy bum if it wasn't.

"Do I know you?" she asked.

"So you are her. I knew it. Just like Dennis said."

"You're friends of Dennis's?"

Razor looked at Becky as if she'd just revealed herself to be a half-wit. "Lady, we're the *band*."

"Oh, that's right. Dennis was in a band. And he described me to you?"

"He said the lawyer lady was the prettiest girl in town." Razor shrugged the hair out of his eyes, favored her with a dimpled grin he doubtless thought endearing. "I see he was right."

Becky cast a glance at Aaron, sharing her amusement at a guy who would flirt at a crime scene. "So, where is Dennis?" she asked mischievously.

"That's what we want to know," Razor replied. "I thought you'd know. You're a lawyer."

"I'm not his lawyer. Why don't you ask the cop?"

Razor made a face. "Don't get on with cops."

"I can't imagine why. Well, if I do see Dennis, I'll tell him you're looking. What's your name?"

"Razor."

Becky bit back a smile. "I'll tell him."

"I thought you were going to ask him if he was Gillette or Norelco," Aaron said as Becky walked off toward her car.

"Actually, I was toying with asking him if he was a *straight* razor," Becky confided.

"Oh, wicked," Aaron said. "So where you going?"

"To find Dennis. To tell him his band's looking for him. You want a ride?"

Aaron hesitated. "I might wanna leave before you."

"Suit yourself."

Becky climbed into her convertible, headed back toward town. Aaron, hopelessly conflicted, tagged along behind in his own car. He was leaving a crime scene, but Chief Harper and the murder suspect weren't there, so why stay?

Becky drove by the police station, but there was still no police car out front. She continued down Main Street and around the village green. The church was dark. So was the town hall. But there was a police car parked in front of the county courthouse. Becky pulled up behind it. Aaron pulled up behind her. They met on the pavement.

"Looks like you found the chief," Aaron said.

"Yeah. Wonder what he's doing here."

A car pulled out of the back lot, drove on down the street.

"Isn't that Judge Hobbs?" Becky said.

"Sure looked like it."

The front door of the courthouse opened, and Chief Harper came out, folding up his cell phone as he went. He slipped it casually into his coat pocket, nodded to Aaron and Becky.

"What's up, Chief?" Aaron asked him. "Is Dennis Pride under arrest for murder?"

Harper brushed the question away. "No one's under arrest. We're making inquiries."

"Those inquiries include an arraignment?"

"Not likely," Becky pointed out. "The suspect isn't here."

Chief Harper headed for his car.

Becky Baldwin blocked his way. "How about it, Chief. Where's Dennis at?"

"Sorry. Can't help you."

"He has the right to an attorney."

Chief Harper nodded. "*He* has the right to an attorney. *You* have no right to insist that the attorney be *you*."

"You read him Miranda?"

"Of course he was read Miranda."

"Then he *is* a suspect. I demand to see him at once."

"When did he hire you?"

"Don't be silly. He needs representation. You got a public defender hanging out at the police station?"

"Of course not."

"So he *is* at the police station?"

"I didn't say that."

"No, you didn't. Thanks, Chief."

Becky hopped in her car, drove on around the green, back down Main Street, and pulled up in front of the station. Aaron Grant and Chief Harper stuck right behind her.

Brenda and her parents burst out the door.

"You're back," Mrs. Wallenstein said to the chief. "It's about time."

"When are you going to let him go?" Brenda wailed. "He didn't do anything. I swear it."

Becky sized up the situation, said to Brenda, "You're the bride-to-be?"

Brenda frowned. "I know you. You're the lawyer. You're here to help Dennis?"

"If I can. What would you like me to do?"

"Get Dennis out of here. He shouldn't be in jail."

"I see." Becky raised her eyebrows. "I don't wish to seem crude, but do you have any money?"

Brenda turned to her father. "Da-ad," she implored.

Mr. Wallenstein spoke for the first time. "She has money."

The simple statement carried weight. Becky smiled. She said, "It seems the bride wants to hire me, Chief."

"To represent Dennis Pride?"

"That's right."

"Fine. He's in a holding cell in back."

"Gee, that wasn't like pulling teeth, now, was it?" She trotted up the steps, went inside.

Brenda and her parents started to follow. Chief Harper intervened. "One minute, young lady. You can help me out here."

"What do you mean?"

"You were with Dennis when he went in and found the body."

"Oh, for goodness' sakes," Mrs. Wallenstein snapped. "We've been over and over this. Yes, she was with Dennis when he went in and found the body. You don't have to take her word for it. That Felton woman was there too."

"If you don't mind," Chief Harper said, "I'd prefer to let your daughter tell me."

"She already has," Mrs. Wallenstein pointed out waspishly.

"Right," Chief Harper agreed. He managed to place himself between Brenda and her mother, so that he could face the one and turn his back on the other. "And was that the first time Dennis had been inside that house?"

Brenda frowned. "First time?"

"Yes. Had Dennis ever been in there before?"

"Not that I know of."

"Are you sure? Raymond was late, as I understand it. It would be only natural if Dennis ran over to see how he was coming along."

"It may have been natural, but it's not what he did."

"So Dennis wasn't over there shortly before you two found the body?"

"No, he wasn't."

"Interesting," Chief Harper said.

Becky Baldwin came out of the police station, mad as a wet hen. "Hey, the back room's locked."

"Of course it is," Chief Harper told her. "We can't have the prisoners escaping."

"They're in cells," Becky said.

"Exactly. Otherwise they'd run away."

"Damn it," Becky fumed. "You sent me in to talk to Dennis. I can't get near his cell because the back room is locked."

"I don't recall sending you in to talk to Dennis," Chief Harper said pleasantly. "But you're right about the back door. If you want to wait a moment, I'll open it for you."

A red Toyota screeched down the street with its headlights off. It fishtailed, clipped a stop sign, and hurtled toward the police station.

"Look out!" Harper yelled. He, Becky, Aaron, and Brenda and her parents scattered.

The car executed a breathtaking one-eighty and stopped on a dime.

Cora Felton erupted from the driver's seat and leveled a finger at Chief Harper. "Don't arrest that man!"

Harper stared at her. "Miss Felton, you're supposed to be in bed."

"Why does *everyone* keep telling me that?" Cora wobbled, glared at the chief. "And you're supposed to be solving this crime, but you're not. Instead, you're just making yourself look stupid."

Brenda's mother muttered, "Talk about the pot calling the kettle."

"I heard that," Cora said. She turned to Becky. "Are you his lawyer?"

"Yes, I am."

"How come he's still in jail?"

"I haven't even spoken to him yet."

"You're keeping him from his attorney?" Cora accused Chief Harper. She jerked her thumb at Aaron. "And in front of a reporter too. Very bad decision. You taking note of this, Aaron?"

"There's nothing to take note of," Harper interposed. "Miss Baldwin has just identified herself as Mr. Pride's attorney. And I was just taking her to her client. Right this way, Miss Baldwin."

"That's more like it," Cora said, starting up the steps.

"Not you. Or the rest of you, either. Just her."

"Harrumph," Cora snorted. Though still woozy from the medication, she managed to convey more meaning with that single grunt than your average Julius Caesar could with "*Et tu, Brute?*"

"Cora, you shouldn't be here," Aaron told her.

"Oh, my God, another one! Aaron, try to look at the big picture here."

"What big picture?"

Cora scowled. "How the hell should I know? I just got here, for chrissakes."

Aaron's cell phone rang. He jerked it out of his jacket, clicked it on. "Hello?"

"Aaron," Sherry said. "Cora woke up and took off. I'm afraid she'll wreck the car."

"She came close, but she's okay now. She's down at the police station, telling Chief Harper his business."

"Can you bring her home?"

"I doubt she'll take kindly to the suggestion."

"At least get her car keys before she kills someone."

"I'll do my best."

Chief Harper came out the door. "Okay, gang. Show's over. You can wait for Miss Baldwin if you want, but you can't go in."

"We're waiting," Brenda declared with stubborn resolution.

"Fine. You do that."

Harper started for his car.

"Where you going?" Cora demanded.

"Back to the crime scene."

"Cora, why don't you ride with the chief," Aaron suggested.

Chief Harper's mouth dropped open.

Cora frowned. "Oh?"

"Sherry needs the car back. If you wouldn't mind riding with the chief—"

"Aaron—" Chief Harper began.

"Unless you'd rather have her follow you, Chief. You could use your siren to clear the way."

"Why can't she go with *you*?" Harper asked.

"I gotta run her car keys out to Sherry. Got the keys, Cora?"

Cora jerked her thumb. "In the car."

"Great. Hope you didn't lock the doors."

Aaron retrieved the keys from the Toyota.

"Why don't you take Cora home while you're at it?"

"Good idea, Chief. Why don't you suggest it to her?"

Chief Harper looked at Cora.

It occurred to him he'd rather wrestle an alligator.

Two alligators.

30

"SO, WHAT'S YOUR THEORY OF THE CASE, CHIEF?" CORA DE-manded, as they drove back toward the crime scene.

"It's too early to have a theory of the case."

"Don't give me that. You made an arrest." Cora jerked her cigarettes out of her purse.

"You can't smoke in here."

Cora made a face. "In a *police* car?"

"In *my* police car. Put 'em away."

"I will if you tell me your theory."

Chief Harper sighed. "This is not exactly rocket science. The suspect was found kneeling over the victim with a knife in his hand."

"I know. I found him."

"And you're still not convinced?"

"Of course not. There's no way he did it."

"How do you know?"

"How do I know my fanny's round? Dennis couldn't have

killed Raymond. Raymond would have ground him up and spit him out like chewing tobacco."

"I understand it's personal—"

"You don't understand a thing." Cora snuffled. "Sure it's personal, but it's not just personal for me. It's personal for Sherry."

"She and her ex-husband were estranged."

"That's putting it mildly. A restraining order was in effect."

"Even so, you think it would upset her to have him charged with murder?"

Cora shook her head. "You don't understand. He didn't do it. You charge him with murder, he becomes the sympathetic hero, charged with a crime he didn't commit. Don't cast that jerk in that role."

"This is not a game, Cora."

"No kidding. This is deadly serious."

Chief Harper slowed his car near the crime scene. He frowned. It appeared half of Bakerhaven was there.

Harvey Beerbaum emerged from the crowd. "Cora, I just heard. I'm so sorry." He enfolded her in a clumsy embrace.

"I'm sure you are, Harvey. I'm sure you are."

Harvey was almost knocked off his feet by a stampede of Tune Freaks.

"Hey, man, where's our lead singer?" Razor demanded.

"If you mean Dennis Pride, he's talking to his lawyer."

"I'll *bet* he is," the portly drummer said, and rolled his eyes suggestively.

Harper and Cora tiptoed through the Tune Freaks to where Sam Brogan was standing with two witnesses. Cora had a momentary rush of dread as she recognized Raymond's long-haired hippie next-door neighbors, before the horrible realization dawned that she didn't have to be afraid of them anymore.

"These the ones?" Harper asked.

"Yeah." Sam rolled his eyes slightly as he introduced the hippie couple as Jack and Daffodil Dirkson. Their getup recalled the Beatles song in which John and Yoko looked like two gurus in drag. "They saw him go in."

"Is that right?" Chief Harper asked.

Jack Dirkson ran his hand through his long, thinning hair. His mind appeared blown by the question. "Wow, man. What a thing to say. When you say, like, 'Did we see him?' you mean, like, 'Did we *see* him?' "

"That's the gist of it," Harper said patiently. "Did you see him go in?"

"You gotta ask me that?" Jack whined. He pointed to Cora. "She was there. She went in. You don't need us."

"According to your wife, the young man came earlier," Sam Brogan prompted.

"Yes, he did," Daffodil Dirkson said. She seemed slightly more coherent than her spouse. Cora wondered if that had to do with their relative drug intake, or was just generally the case. "I was on the porch swing. He came out of the house over there, crossed the street, and went in."

"Did Raymond let him in?" Harper asked.

Daffodil frowned. "I'm not sure."

"Bummer!" Jack exclaimed. "You don't want a witness who isn't sure."

"No one's talking about being a witness right now," Chief Harper said. "I just need some guidelines to go on. So the young man came by himself, before everyone went in and found the body. Do you have any idea how much earlier that might have been?"

Daffodil shrugged. "I'm not that good with time."

"No kidding," Jack Dirkson put in. "Daffy, you're a space cadet. You don't know."

Chief Harper managed not to show amusement at Daffodil's nickname. "How long was he in there?" he asked her.

"Don't be a drag, man," Jack said. "She can't tell."

"Was it as much as five minutes?" Chief Harper persisted.

Daffy shrugged helplessly. "Could be."

"At least a couple?"

"Ah . . ."

"What I'm getting at," Chief Harper said, "is there's no way he just stuck his head in and came back out?"

Daffodil Dirkson tried to follow his logic, exhaled. "Wow."

"Did he do that, or did he go inside? Did the door close?"

"Ah . . ."

"Daffy, you can't make it up," Jack Dirkson said. "She's making it up."

"I'm not making it up. I'm trying to think."

"She's making it up."

"Your best recollection is he came alone, went inside for several minutes, then came back out again, prior to the time the others arrived?"

Daffy's eyes looked round as saucers. "Oh, wow," she murmured.

"Does she have to be a witness?" Jack demanded.

"I certainly hope not," Chief Harper said dryly.

The chief walked Sam Brogan out of earshot of the Dirksons. "Good work, Sam. Where's the owner of the B&B?"

"She was here a minute ago. Can't miss her, she's got red hair. Yeah, there she is. Right in front of her house."

"Fine, let's go serve the warrant."

"Warrant?" Cora Felton asked. "What warrant?"

Chief Harper wove his way through the crowd with Sam Brogan. Cora Felton stuck to his heels. He checked the name on the warrant, said, "Mrs. Trumble?"

The red-haired B&B owner tore herself away from her conversation with her neighbors, preening a little with her new-found celebrity status—after all, this *was* a murder, and she *was* talking to the chief of police. "Yes?" she all but simpered.

"I have a search warrant here for your address."

Her mouth fell open. The woman could not have been more astonished had the chief accused *her* of the crime. "What?" she stammered.

"Nothing to be alarmed about. But we have to check on one of your guests. This warrant empowers us to search any rooms occupied by him."

"This is most unusual."

"Actually, it's quite routine. Could you open up for us, please?"

"What are we looking for?" Cora demanded, as she followed them to the B&B.

"*You* are not looking for anything," Chief Harper reminded her. "This warrant empowers the police to search the premises. It does not empower private citizens."

"Oh, for goodness' sakes."

"And that's final," Chief Harper said firmly. "I am not having any evidence thrown out on the grounds the search was tainted. We're doing this strictly by the book. You stay here."

"Well, I like that," Cora Felton said, as Harper strode off.

With no siren but great honking of horn, the Channel 8 van drove right to the front of the crime scene and Rick Reed hopped out. Young, handsome, and as bright as your average fireplug, the on-camera reporter practically drooled when he caught sight of Cora Felton. In the past Rick Reed had always come out second best in his interviews with the Puzzle Lady. Now the sight of her dressed in rags seemed too good to be true. If she really was the grieving bride-to-be, she was a sitting duck.

"Get the camera! Get the camera!" he hissed desperately at the crew in the van. He buttoned his Channel 8 blazer, tugged on his tie. "Damn it, where's my mike?"

The video crew, struggling with their heavy equipment, came around the side of the van.

"Here you go, Rick," the soundman said.

"You wanna shoot a lead-in first, in front of the crime scene?" the cameraman asked.

"No, no, her," Rick Reed said. "I want her." He grabbed the mike, raced to Cora Felton. "Miss Felton, Rick Reed, Channel 8 News. I just heard of this terrible tragedy. You must be devastated. Is it true the victim was to be your bridegroom?"

Cora's first instinct was to punch him in the mouth, but some sense of self-preservation stopped her. "I have no information," she said primly. "But I understand the police have made an arrest."

Rick Reed had already framed his next question, but that stopped him dead. "An arrest? Who have they arrested?"

"Ask them," Cora said, and vanished into the crowd.

Rick Reed was left with egg on his face, and the suspicion he'd been gotten the better of again. Cora's terse statement was worse than "No comment." He'd be hard-pressed to justify using it.

Cora, escaping from the TV crew, barely sidestepped the solicitous Reverend Kimble, and fell right into the clutches of an overattentive Harvey Beerbaum.

"Cora," Harvey said. "I was attempting to convey to you how sorry I am."

"I know, Harvey."

"No, you don't. I've been awful. I resented the fact a stranger came into town and swept you off your feet. He was an outsider. I didn't want him here. I didn't like him. But I didn't want him dead."

"Of course you didn't, Harvey."

"It's just a coincidence, that's all."

"Of course it is," Cora said, but she had no idea what he was talking about.

"Anyway, I'm devastated. If there's anything I can do—"

"That's sweet of you, Harvey, but there's really nothing."

"Are you certain?"

Cora patted his arm. "Just don't tell me I should be home in bed."

"You must believe me, I never meant for this to happen."

"Of course I do, Harvey. Of course I do."

"Well, just so you know."

Harvey turned, trudged dejectedly back into the darkness.

Cora watched him go. Was he *too* upset about what had happened, or was she just woozy from the drug?

Cora shook her head to clear it. She certainly was woozy, or she'd be able to think straight. What did Chief Harper expect to find in Dennis and Brenda's bed-and-breakfast?

31

BECKY BALDWIN ARCHED ONE EXQUISITELY PERFECT BLOND eyebrow, and drummed her pencil on her yellow legal pad. She had pulled a folding chair up next to the cell, and was talking to Dennis through the bars. "*That's* your story?"

Dennis's smile was good-natured. "What's wrong with my story?"

"Well, in the first place, you call it a story."

"*You* called it a story."

"I'm a lawyer, and that's what it sounds like. But *you're* not supposed to think it's a story."

"All right, it's the naked truth." Dennis leaned forward on his bunk, his arms on his knees. "What's wrong with it?"

Becky consulted her legal pad. Not that she'd written anything important, just to gather her thoughts. "You were going to pick up Raymond to go to the rehearsal?"

"That's right."

"Cora and Brenda were with you?"

"They were right behind."

Becky doodled on the legal pad. "According to Brenda, you were all together."

"We were *practically* together. I went in, they came in after."

"That's not what Brenda says."

"Brenda's trying to protect me. Which is dumb. I didn't do anything."

"You had the knife in your hand."

"I pulled it out of the guy. I was just trying to help him."

"It didn't occur to you removing the knife might cause more damage, make him bleed out?"

"No, it didn't. You ever see someone stabbed by a knife?"

"No, I haven't."

"Well, neither had I." Dennis chuckled ironically, shook his head. "Trust me, you're not thinking all that. You're thinking, 'Jesus H. Christ, I hope he doesn't die!'"

"I thought you didn't like Raymond Harstein."

"I don't like a lot of people, but I don't want to stab 'em."

Dennis's good-natured grin was infectious, his boyish charm seductive. Becky avoided the sparkling blue eyes by concentrating on her doodling. She blushed as she realized she'd been drawing hearts.

"How'd you get in the door?" she asked.

"It was open."

"Open? Or just unlocked?"

"Oh. Unlocked."

"Did you knock?"

"I think I did."

"You *think*?"

Dennis shrugged. "It really wasn't important. If I'd known I was going to find a dead body, I'd have been sure to remember."

"Anyway, you turned the doorknob?"

"Yeah. It was open. *Unlocked*. I went in. I found the body."

"Right away? Could you see him from the open door?"

"No. He was in the living room."

"Why'd you go in the living room?"

"Are you kidding? Because I was looking for him."

"Did you call his name?"

"Yeah. He didn't answer. Now we know why."

"You came into the foyer ahead of Brenda and Cora. You stopped, called Harstein's name, got no answer. Entered the living room. At the time, Brenda and Cora had not yet caught up with you, is that right?"

"If you say so."

Becky frowned. She drummed her pencil on her hand. "Dennis, this is not a game. You're a murder suspect. I could use a little help here."

"I could use a little help too. I gotta get out of here."

"It's not as easy as you think."

For the first time, Dennis's cheery facade slipped. "Hey, what are you talking about? I'm in jail. I didn't do it. So get me out."

"Just how do you propose I do that?"

"You're the lawyer. Bail me out."

"You haven't even been charged yet. The police are holding you on suspicion."

"Can they do that?"

"Until a judge tells them not to."

"So get a judge."

"The courthouse is closed, Dennis."

"I can't stay here all night."

"You may not have much choice."

"Damn it to hell!"

"Hey, it's not the end of the world. You're in a private lockup. It's reasonably clean. You don't have a two-hundred-fifty-pound roommate who thinks you're cute. If I were you, I'd count my blessings."

"But I didn't *do* anything!"

"So you say. That will, of course, make everything much easier."

He glared at her in disbelief. "Are you telling me I'm not getting out of here tonight?"

"Finally, a meeting of the minds."

"Well, that's just great." Dennis rubbed his forehead. "Is Brenda still out there?"

"Last I looked."

"Could you bring her in?"

Becky shook her head. "Chief said no."

"Why the hell not?" Dennis said it with a cajoling grin. "It's not like she's gonna help me break out."

"You wanna talk to Brenda about the case?"

"I sure do."

"Why?"

"I wanna assure her I'm innocent."

"I thought she knew that."

"She does, but even so. It's only natural."

"So you're just gonna talk to her about what happened?"

"Yeah, so?"

"She's a material witness."

"Oh, for Christ's sake!"

"Dennis, there's nothing in your story you'd like to change, is there?"

"No, of course not."

"And there's nothing in her story you'd like to change?"

"No. I just don't need her to try so hard to give me an alibi. I don't want her getting in trouble."

"I'll convey that message."

"You won't bring her back here?"

"No."

"Damn!"

Becky leaned forward, stared into Dennis's smoldering blue

eyes. Tried to read his thoughts. "What is it, Dennis? What is it that you need to tell Brenda?"

"I just want to talk to her."

"About what?"

He shrugged. "Nothing special."

Becky wondered why she didn't believe that was true.

32

JUDGE HOBBS SAT AT THE BENCH AND FROWNED WITH DISPLEA-sure at his crowded courtroom. Chief Harper had warned him a rock group might be present. But he was unprepared for the grubby guerrilla warriors who sat just behind the press row. The band, hoping for TV exposure, had dressed in concert garb. All were, as usual, filthy, unshaven, with tangled hair. Today they sported accessories, such as the drummer's World War I German officer's helmet, Razor's aviator glasses, the bass player's ban-danna, and the keyboard player's eye patch. The skinny pianist had twenty-twenty vision; he just felt he needed something.

The band was not directly behind the defense table. That prime location was occupied by Brenda Wallenstein and her par-ents. Mrs. Wallenstein, who must have traveled with an extensive wardrobe, was decked out in an elaborate Versace dress that probably cost more than your average court proceeding. Mr. Wallenstein, steady as a rock, wore a business suit that could have been the one he'd worn the day before. The bride-to-be, perky in slacks and sweater, nonetheless sported a fashionably tear-stained face.

In the back of the courtroom, Sherry Carter whispered, "Now, remember, you behave."

"Well, I never," Cora Felton sputtered indignantly. Cora, who'd had a good night's sleep, showered, dressed in her tidiest Miss Marple gear of frilly white blouse and tweedy skirt, had all but shaken off the effects of the sedative.

"This is personal, you have no perspective, you back off."

"Just what I was about to tell you," Cora countered, sweetly.

"Huh?"

Judge Hobbs banged the courtroom to silence. "All right, what have we this morning?"

Henry Firth, the county prosecutor, shot to his feet. A little man with a thin mustache and a twitchy nose, he always re-minded Cora Felton of a rat. Today, pleased by the weight of a homicide charge to deliver, he seemed like a smug rat. "Your Honor, we have the case of Dennis Pride, arrested on a charge of murder."

"Ah, yes. Is the defendant in the courtroom?"

"I believe he's being brought in now."

A side door opened, and Dan Finley led Dennis into the courtroom. Dennis had spent the night in jail, and was somewhat the worse for wear. He was unshaven, and his hair was un-combed. His jacket and shirt were open, and his tie hung loosely about his neck.

And he wore handcuffs.

Dan Finley led him to the defense table, where Becky Baldwin was waiting.

Judge Hobbs said, "I see that Mr. Pride is represented by counsel. To the charge of murder, how do you plead?"

"We plead not guilty, Your Honor, and ask that the defendant be released on his own recognizance."

"On the contrary," Henry Firth said with a smirk, "we ask that the defendant be held without bail. He is not a resident of Bakerhaven, has no ties to this community, and poses a clear and present flight risk."

"Nonsense," Becky Baldwin bridled. "Mr. Pride is scheduled to be married next weekend in the Bakerhaven Congregational Church. If that's not a tie to the community, I don't know what is."

Henry Firth remained unshakably smug. "Ah, yes. That was scheduled as a double wedding, was it not? Might I ask how it is presently scheduled?"

"Is that relevant?" Judge Hobbs inquired.

"I should think so. Mr. Pride is charged with killing the other groom. I would think that would cause some sort of strain on the proceedings."

Judge Hobbs's gavel silenced Becky's angry retort. "That will do, Ms. Baldwin. I can handle this. Mr. Firth, I would hate to discipline a prosecutor for excessive zeal. Still, if I could ask you to keep your sarcasm within acceptable limits."

"Yes, Your Honor."

"That being said, I, too, raise the question. Ms. Baldwin, what is the status of this wedding?"

"We don't know, Your Honor," Becky said. She gestured to the front row, where Brenda Wallenstein sat behind Dennis. "My client has not been allowed any contact with his affianced bride."

"And why is that?"

"She's a witness, Your Honor," Henry Firth explained.

"Not if she marries him, she's not," Judge Hobbs said dryly. He nodded to Becky. "As I'm sure you've advised your client."

"We're getting far afield, Your Honor," Becky said. "I was requesting reasonable bail."

"I thought you were asking for recognizance."

"That was before Mr. Firth made such a splendid showing."

"Now who's being sarcastic?" Henry Firth whined.

"That will do," Judge Hobbs said. "Could we have some facts, instead of the usual histrionics? You say Mr. Pride is not a resident of Bakerhaven. Where does he live?"

"Here again we get into trouble," Henry Firth said ponderously. "Mr. Pride has no permanent address. He is a member of a 'rock band' . . ." Here Henry made a point of directing the court's attention to the scruffy men in the second row. ". . . and he's always on the road."

"Not so, Your Honor," Becky Baldwin said. "Mr. Pride is a *former* member of a rock band. And while the prosecutor took great delight in pointing them out, he merely makes my case. Even after a night in jail, my client looks nothing like his former group. That contention has no merit whatsoever."

Judge Hobbs frowned. "The contention was that the defendant has no permanent address. Do you contend that he does, Ms. Baldwin?"

"Absolutely, Your Honor."

"And where would that be?"

"New York City, Your Honor."

"At what address?"

"Seventy-four Spring Street."

Henry Firth shook his head. "Your Honor, there's no record of the defendant having any apartment at that address."

"The apartment is in the name of his fiancée, Brenda Wallenstein."

"Who he may or may not marry in the ceremony this weekend. You see, Your Honor, how tenuous this claim is."

"You say the defendant has left the rock band. Where is he currently employed?" the judge asked.

"At Wallenstein Textiles, in Manhattan."

"Oh, really?" Henry Firth said. "And when did he start work?"

"He starts work Monday."

Henry Firth smiled. "I submit, Your Honor, that Wallenstein

Textiles is no doubt owned and operated by the father of Mr. Pride's fiancée, Brenda Wallenstein, and this job that conveniently starts Monday is the result of a frantic discussion early this morning among the Wallenstein family members seated here in court, after the defense realized Mr. Pride would have no chance of making bail if he was unemployed."

"I object to the characterization *frantic discussion,* Your Honor."

"Your objection is noted, Ms. Baldwin. So is your failure to dispute any other part of the prosecutor's claim." Judge Hobbs drew himself up. "Very well. Is there anything else you would like me to consider before setting bail?"

"Yes, Your Honor," Henry Firth said. "In fact, at this time I would like to amend the complaint."

Judge Hobbs gawked at him. "Amend the complaint? Mr. Firth, the defendant is already charged with murder. Do you mean you are reducing the charges?"

"No, Your Honor. I'm increasing them."

There were stunned gasps in the courtroom.

"Increasing a murder charge. How is that possible?"

"In addition to murder, I am charging the defendant with possession of a controlled substance, possession with intent to sell, *and* grand larceny."

The courtroom was in an uproar. Becky Baldwin was practically apoplectic, trying to shout over the din. Judge Hobbs banged his gavel, but it was several minutes before he was able to restore order.

"Your Honor, this is disgraceful," Becky said hotly. "Amend the complaint, indeed! Out of the clear blue sky, the prosecutor is suddenly dumping in a bunch of brand-new charges."

"You maintain the prosecutor has no right to charge your client?"

"No, Your Honor, he has every right to charge him, but I wasn't informed."

"Please forgive me any breach of etiquette," Henry Firth said with an ironic bow, "but certain matters have come to light since the defendant's arrest."

"And just what might those be?"

Henry Firth unsnapped his briefcase, and raised the lid. "This, Your Honor." He pulled out a plastic evidence bag and held it high. "Approximately fifty-four grams of cocaine found concealed in the defendant's suitcase."

33

RICK REED COULDN'T HAVE BEEN HAPPIER, THOUGH HE SLAPPED on his most earnest face for the TV cameras. He positioned himself on the steps of the picturesque Bakerhaven courthouse, and delivered the breaking news. "In a stunning surprise today, police charged Dennis Pride, former lead singer of the Tune Freaks arrested last night on suspicion of the murder of Raymond Harstein III, with the felony possession of cocaine, which a search warrant revealed to have been concealed in his luggage."

Rick's eyes briefly lost focus, as he tried to assess whether that sentence had been coherent on the one hand, or grammatical on the other. He forged on. "Raymond Harstein III is a reputed drug dealer. Dennis Pride is accused of stabbing him to death for his drugs. That theory drew an indignant response from Rebecca Baldwin, Mr. Pride's attorney."

The camera cut to a shot of Becky Baldwin coming out of the courthouse. Becky, who looked furious enough to take a bite out of the camera lens, was holding herself back only with great restraint. "I can scarcely dignify this with a response. It's one thing to stand up and wave an exhibit, and quite another to establish a chain of evidence. We have only Henry Firth's assurance that cocaine was in my client's luggage. Did Mr. Firth see it there? I doubt it. There is no proof that it was there at all. If it was, I would like to point out there was every opportunity for it to be planted there last night, while my client was in jail."

Rick Reed looked duly impressed. "Strong words, from Mr. Pride's attorney." He brightened. "Razor, lead guitarist of Mr. Pride's rock group, Tune Freaks, had another take on the discovery of the cocaine."

Razor, looking rather stoned himself, shrugged at the camera. "Hey, man, we're a rock band."

"This is Rick Reed, Channel 8 News, live in Bakerhaven."

Cora Felton clicked the TV to MUTE, said, "Nice report."

Sherry, sitting next to her on the couch, looked at her aunt with concern. "Cora."

"What?"

"This has to be hard on you."

"It is."

"I wouldn't know it."

"What's the matter? I haven't filled the requisite grief quotient?" Cora chuckled. "Christ, Sherry. There's a sentence for the Puzzle Lady. Sounds like I actually know a few words."

"Cora, you're repressing your feelings. That isn't healthy."

"I'm not repressing squat. I'm dealing with the situation."

"How?"

"The only way I know. By making it make sense."

Cora got up from the couch, picked up her dinner plate. "Did I eat my dinner? Yes, I did. Was it tasty? Yes, it was. Did you cook it well? Yes, you did. And that's how you're dealing with things. Getting on with life. The daily routine. As if your ex-husband weren't charged with murder."

"It's not the same."

"I know. That's why I'm worried."

"Cora, you're not making any sense."

Cora scraped her plate in the garbage, dumped it in the sink.

"Hey, you actually scraped a plate. Now, if you could just manage to put it in the dishwasher."

"I never know if the dishes in there are dirty or clean."

"You have to look at them."

"Ah, well, you're an expert. You know all these inside tricks."

"Cora."

Cora turned on her niece angrily. "Sherry, I don't wanna talk about it. You hit me with this pack of lies about Raymond, and then before I can ask him, he's dead. Raymond wasn't like that. I know he wasn't. Now you want me to grieve for him, *and* you want me to think he was a bad man. You want me to be heartbroken on both counts. Well, it's too much, Sherry. It's too goddamned much. And I'm not gonna do it, even for you."

"Can't you do it for yourself?"

"Sherry, this is not the first time I've lost a man. It's the first time I've lost one this way, but, believe me, I've lost them before. And it isn't easy. Whether I married them or not, it isn't easy. And then you throw this at me with so many layers. So many layers." Cora took out her cigarettes, lit one up. "Just the fact I can smoke again makes me feel guilty. I'm relieved I can smoke again. I feel good I can smoke again. Does it mean I'm glad he's dead? No, it doesn't. But every time I take a drag I feel guilty."

Sherry said nothing. The elephant in the room was the fact Cora could also drink again, but she hadn't. Even in these trying circumstances.

A car roared up the driveway.

"Good," Sherry said, relieved. "That'll be Aaron. Maybe you can talk to him, if you can't talk to me." At Cora's raised eyebrows, she explained, "Not for publication. Just as a friend."

"Friend."

"Why do you say it like that?"

"Aaron was the one who dug up those lies about Raymond."

"Aunt Cora—"

"Yes, I think I would like to talk to Aaron."

With that polite pronouncement, Cora swept back through the living room and opened the front door.

Dennis strode up the path. When he saw Cora, he said, "I didn't do it. I swear to God, I didn't do it."

"Glad to hear it," Cora said, and slammed the door in his face.

Sherry came in from the kitchen. "Where's Aaron?"

"It wasn't Aaron."

The doorbell rang.

"Aunt Cora?"

"It's Dennis. Go back in the kitchen. I'll deal with him."

"You don't have to do that."

"It's my pleasure."

The doorbell rang again.

"Are you gonna answer it?"

"I already did. He doesn't seem to have gotten the message. Go back in the kitchen."

"Oh, for goodness' sakes." Sherry pushed by her aunt, flung open the door.

Dennis's face lit up when he saw her, made him look handsomer than ever.

"Sherry," he said. "It's so awful."

It was the perfect thing to say. He hadn't denied it, forced her support of his innocence. Instead he had stated a simple, universal truth about which there could be no dispute. Even Cora would have been hard-pressed to argue.

"How'd you get out of jail?" Sherry asked him.

"Brenda posted bail."

"You mean her father did?"

"Well, she doesn't have that kind of money."

"She must have pled a good case."

"It was touch-and-go. Her father's real antidrugs."

"No kidding."

Dennis closed the door, walked on into the living room.

Cora had a strong desire to grab him by the scruff of the neck and throw him out. She stifled it. She knew the more she attacked Dennis, the more Sherry would defend him.

He flopped down on the couch, sank back into the cushions, exhaled as if he'd been carrying the weight of the world on his shoulders.

Sherry sat at the other end of the couch.

Cora frowned. Sherry wasn't next to Dennis, but she was on the couch. Too close.

"Sherry, I'm scared." Dennis leaned in toward her, and edged her way a little. "Someone's out to get me."

Cora sucked in her breath. The he-man shows his sensitive side? Could Dennis really be pulling that?

"Who?" Sherry asked.

"I have no idea," Dennis said. "But I'm being framed."

"Now, there's a new one," Cora blurted. She swore she wasn't going to butt in, but she couldn't help herself.

Dennis shot her a dirty look.

So did Sherry.

Cora zipped her lip, sank into a chair across the room.

"Why would anyone want to frame you, Dennis?" Sherry asked.

"How should I know? I'm a stranger here in town. I have nothing to do with anyone. Except you guys. And what's that to anyone?" Dennis was all wide-eyed innocence.

"You didn't like him, did you, Dennis?"

"Of course I didn't like him. He was a big phony. Sorry, Cora, but that's a fact. But I didn't stab him to keep you from marrying him. That makes no sense."

"Of course not," Sherry said.

Dennis pressed his advantage. "You do believe me, that I'm not responsible for any of this?"

Before Sherry could answer, Cora jumped in. "No one seriously thinks you did it. It's no big deal."

"The cops think it is. Do you know how much it cost to bail me out? I feel like I have a price on my head."

"Oh, for goodness' sakes," Cora grumbled. "You're nothing of the kind. You wanna be a wanted man, you gotta *jump* bail. Leave the jurisdiction of the court."

Dennis frowned. Cora could practically see the wheels turning as he envisioned himself in that role.

"Of course, your prospective father-in-law won't be too thrilled, forfeiting the bail money. And you'll be living outside the law."

"Cora," Sherry said irritably. "What are you trying to do?"

"Put this in perspective. Right now the only law he's breaking is a restraining order against seeing you."

"These are extenuating circumstances, Cora."

"They certainly are," Dennis agreed. "This is a terrible thing, Cora. You've suffered a tremendous loss."

"I don't need your sympathy," Cora snapped, then realized she was playing right into his hands. She was sure he even smirked slightly, when Sherry wasn't looking.

A sound in the driveway interrupted the conversation.

Cora went to the window.

"Who is it?" Sherry said.

"I don't know," Cora said. "It's a car service."

The black car pulled to a stop behind Dennis's rental. Brenda Wallenstein stepped out. The car turned around and drove off.

"It's your fiancée," Cora told Dennis. Cora was quite proud of herself. She was sure there was no hint of malicious satisfaction in that pronouncement.

Dennis looked distinctly displeased. "In a car service?"

Brenda came up the path, looking concerned and stressed.

Cora met her at the door. "Come in, come in. We were just working things out."

Brenda pushed through the door, saw Dennis sitting on the couch next to Sherry. "Oh, there you are. You took off without a word."

"I told you I was going."

"Not a word. I came out of the bathroom and you were gone."

"So you hired a car service to come out here?"

"Well, you took the car."

"I was coming right back."

"You didn't say so. I've been waiting all night and all day for you. You finally get back, I turn around, and you're gone."

"I had to tell them I didn't do it."

"You think they don't know that?"

"No, I'm sure they do."

Brenda ran to him, flung her arms around him. "Oh, Dennis! I've been so worried!"

Dennis held her, but his embrace seemed rather perfunctory.

Cora Felton didn't like it.

34

DENNIS WASN'T PLEASED. HE GLANCED AT BRENDA IN THE PAS-senger seat, said, "You hired a car service?"

"I was worried."

"Why? I was in no danger. I was out of jail."

"You disappeared."

"Big deal. What if I just ran out to the store?"

"But you didn't."

Dennis scowled, whipped the car into an S-turn a little too fast. "Brenda, this isn't about you."

"That's the trouble."

He rolled his eyes. "Oh, boy. This is all I need. I'm hit with a murder charge, and you go screwy on me."

"I'm not going screwy on you. I'm just scared. I mean, I have no idea what happened here."

"That's the problem. Neither do I."

Dennis pulled up in front of the bed-and-breakfast. "Okay, here you are."

Brenda blinked. "Huh?"

"Go in, take it easy, read your book. Calm down, stop worrying so much."

"You're leaving again?"

"I'm not *leaving*. Boy, what drama. I just need to drive around, clear my head."

"You're not going back there?"

"Back where? To Cora's? Hell, no. That's taken care of. Cora knows I didn't do it."

"So where are you going?"

"I told you. I have to clear my head."

"You can't do that here?"

"No, I can't. Not with you *needing* me all the time." Dennis smiled. "I'm sorry. I'm just upset. There's a lot of crazy stuff happening I can't figure out."

"Like the cocaine?"

"Yeah, like the cocaine. Where the hell did *that* come from?"

"You didn't put it there?"

"No, I didn't put it there," Dennis snapped irritably. "My God, I'm in a lot of trouble if I can't make *you* believe me."

"Then where did it come from?"

"I told you someone went through my suitcase. That's why we moved."

"Yeah, but . . ."

"But what?"

"Before we moved, why would someone be framing you for killing Raymond? I mean, we weren't living near Raymond. No one knew we were going to give him a ride to the church."

"Exactly," Dennis said. "Which is why my head is coming off, and why I need to think." He smiled his most winning, most endearing smile. "Just give me a little time, a little time to think this out."

Brenda hesitated slightly. "You won't drink?"

His smile became frosty. "No, I won't drink. You ought to know that by now."

"Yeah, but all this pressure . . ."

"Doesn't make me wanna take a drink. Just makes me wanna take a drive. I just need a little space. A little space."

Brenda stared at his rock-hard, handsome profile. She heaved a sigh. "Of course."

Without another word, Brenda got out of the car and went into the bed-and-breakfast.

The minute she was inside, Dennis threw the car into gear and pulled out. He turned right at the corner, headed back toward town. Halfway there he took a side road that curved around through some farmland, and over a covered bridge. He turned right at the general store, and headed up into the hills.

The houses were fewer and farther between, then stopped altogether. The road was overhung by oak and maple trees. Soon he was in the deep woods. A stream sparkled alongside the road.

Dennis pulled the car off onto the shoulder. He cut the engine, got out, and walked around to the back. He popped the trunk and raised the lid.

The trunk was empty. Dennis reached in and lifted the bottom panel to get at the spare tire. He unscrewed the catch, lifted the tire out of the well.

Dennis leaned in, and grabbed the manila envelope that had been wedged into the well beneath the spare tire. He pulled the envelope out, undid the catch, and slid out the contents.

The top page read:

A=F	J=D	S=Z
B=C	K=A	T=E
C=K	L=O	U=M
D=X	M=G	V=H
E=P	N=W	W=L

F=R	O=V	X=Y
G=S	P=I	Y=Q
H=N	Q=T	Z=B
I=J	R=U	

XPFU IMBBOP OFXQ,
Dear Puzzle Lady,

QVM'UP GFAJWS F CJS GJZEFAP. ENJZ JZ F CFX GFEKN. JR
You're making a big mistake. This is a bad match. If

QVM'UP ZGFUE, QVM'OO CUPFA JE VRR, CPRVUP ZVGPENJWS
you're smart, you'll break it off, before something

NFIIPWZ. CPRVUP ZVGPVWP SPEZ NMUE. OPFHP NJG. LFOA
happens. Before someone gets hurt. Leave him. Walk

FLFQ, FWX XVW'E OVVA CFKA. JE'Z WVE EVV OFEP EV UPKEJRQ
away, and don't look back. It's not too late to rectify

ENP PUUVUZ ENFE QVM'HP GFXP. LFOA FLFQ LNJOP ENPUP'Z
the errors that you've made. Walk away while there's

ZEJOO EJGP. LFOA FLFQ.
still time. Walk away.

Dennis riffled through the pages. They were copies of the cryptograms, as well as master sheets of the substituted letters.

Dennis shoved the pages back in the envelope, fastened the catch. Then he stepped to the side of the road, and sailed the envelope down to the creek below.

It caught on a branch, hung there like a huge Christmas tree ornament, in plain sight from the road.

Cursing, Dennis plunged into the woods. He tromped down the hill until he was right underneath the branch. He leaped up, tried to bat the envelope free, but it was just out of reach. He glanced around, scanned the ground, came up with a stick. He hefted it up and batted the envelope out of the tree.

Dennis pounced on the envelope. He lined up a clear spot among the trees, and hurled it again.

This time it flew like a frisbee all the way to the brook. He watched with satisfaction as it drifted downstream.

Dennis climbed back up the hill to his car.

Officer Sam Brogan stood there waiting for him.

35

BECKY BALDWIN WAS INCREDULOUS. "WHAT ARE YOU, A MORON?"

"Hey, give me a break," Dennis said.

"A break? How much of a break do you need? You're charged with murder. I get you out on bail, and you get yourself arrested again."

"It's not my fault. Someone is trying to frame me. Can't you see that? Someone is setting me up!"

"Well, that's no reason to go ahead and help them," Becky said sarcastically. "Don't you see? The puzzles aren't that bad. It's getting *rid* of them that hangs you."

"Damn it."

"Are those your puzzles?"

"Of course not. Someone planted them in my car."

"Wasn't your car locked?"

"It's the country. You don't lock your car in the country."

"Even a city boy like you?"

He shrugged. "It's a rental car."

"So you left it unlocked?"

"*I* didn't."

"You mean Brenda did?"

"Hey, let's not attack Brenda. I was in jail. She was upset. Would she really be thinking about things like that?"

"Uh-huh," Becky said. "So you didn't find these puzzles until after you got out of jail."

"No, of course not."

"How did you come to find them?"

"I looked the car over."

"Why?"

"Someone was framing me. They planted cocaine. I wanted to see if they planted anything else."

"So you searched your car?"

"Yeah."

"When?"

Dennis scowled. "What?"

"When did you search your car? You got out of jail. Brenda picked you up in the car. Did you do it then? Did you search the car in front of her? Was she there when you found the puzzles? Can she back you up?"

Dennis shook his head. "No, that's the trouble. She didn't know I found them."

"Why not?"

"Because I didn't tell her. She was so upset, I just couldn't bear to."

"So when you searched the car, Brenda wasn't there?"

"That's right."

"When was that?"

"Later. When I went out."

"Where did you go?"

"To see Cora. To tell her how sorry I was, and tell her I had nothing to do with this mess."

"She buy that?"

Dennis looked at Becky sharply. He narrowed his eyes. "What do you mean, buy it? It's the truth."

"Of course it is. When you talked to Cora, assured her you had nothing to do with Raymond's death—did you know about the puzzles then?"

Dennis's eyes flicked. He considered.

"It's a yes or no question," Becky said dryly.

"Yes, I knew about them then. On my way to Cora's I stopped and searched the car."

"And found the puzzles?"

"That's right."

"In the trunk underneath the spare tire?"

"Uh-huh."

"You had to unscrew the spare tire to get them?"

"Yes, I did."

"When you found them, what did you do?"

"I didn't know what to do. I wanted to get out to Cora's."

"So you put them back in your trunk?"

"Yes."

"Under the spare tire?"

"That's right."

"And screwed it down?"

"Well, I didn't want anyone to find them."

"So you went to Cora's?"

"Yes."

"And you got rid of the puzzles on the way back?"

"No."

"Why not?"

"Brenda was with me."

"Oh? I thought you left her at the bed-and-breakfast."

"I did. She hired a car service and came out."

"Why?"

204 / PARNELL HALL

He shrugged. "Who knows why women do things."

"Who, indeed," Becky said. "So you drove Brenda home, got rid of her, and went out to ditch the evidence?"

"Sounds bad, doesn't it?"

"And earlier you got rid of her, and went out and *found* the evidence."

Dennis said nothing.

There came a knock on the interrogation room door, and Dan Finley stuck his head in. The young officer was apologetic. "I realize this is irregular, but Cora Felton is out front. She wants to talk to you. And the prisoner."

Becky frowned. "She wants to talk to my client?"

"I told you it was irregular."

Dennis looked concerned. "She can't do that, can she?"

Becky sized Dennis up. "She can if I say so. Send her in, Dan."

Dan Finley ushered Cora Felton into the room, and ducked out, closing the door behind him.

Dennis was the picture of consternation. "Now, look, it wasn't me. I'm being set up."

Cora sat down next to Becky. "Tell me about it."

Dennis looked shocked. "Tell? What's to tell? Someone's framing me, and they're doing a damn good job."

"Yeah. Like sneaking the puzzles into your car. How do you suppose they did that?"

"How the hell should I know? I was in jail. Anyone could have done it."

"You didn't send the puzzles to Raymond?"

"Of course I didn't send the puzzles. I didn't even *know* the guy. How many times do I have to say it?"

Cora studied his face impassively. "I'd like to believe you. The strike against you is, the puzzles are so easy to construct even a schnook like you could have done it."

"Hey!"

"Sorry, but that's a fact. If they were regular crossword puzzles I could eliminate you right now. But these cryptograms look bad. They were something you could have done. They were in your car. See what I mean?"

Dennis turned to Becky. "Do I have to talk to her? Get her out of here!"

"I'm afraid you're upsetting my client," Becky told Cora.

"I don't think *I'm* upsetting him," Cora said serenely, in her best Miss Marple mode. "I think the facts are. Look, kid. If someone is setting you up, the question is, who? Who would want to frame you for murder?"

"Nobody. Everybody likes me."

"Yeah, right," Cora said dryly. "Try again. Who has reasons *not* to like you?" She added with just a touch of malice, "I mean *specific* reasons."

"I don't know. I suppose Sherry bears a grudge."

"Sherry's not framing you for murder. Anyone else?"

"That newspaper reporter she's going out with."

"You think Aaron might be framing you?"

"Why not?"

"Fine," Cora said without enthusiasm. "Can you think of anyone else?"

"I don't know anyone else. Remember? I'm not from around here."

"What about Brenda?"

"Are you nuts? Brenda adores me."

"And you adore her. Till death do you part. And neither of you has any doubts. You don't have any doubts, do you, Dennis?"

"What are you trying to do?"

"Believe it or not, I'm trying to help you. All right, what about the band?"

"What?"

"The band members. They know you. Any of them want to do you in?"

"What, are you whack? They're the band. They're my guys."

"But you walked out on them, didn't you? And you were their lead singer. Don't you think that might have pissed them off?"

Dennis shook his head. "Boy, are you off base. The guys aren't mad at me. Hell, they want me back."

Chief Harper pushed his way through the door.

"Hey!" Becky said. "I'm in conference with my client."

"In the presence of a third party?" Chief Harper observed. "That's not a privileged communication."

Becky bristled. "You mean you listened in?"

"Why? You say anything interesting?" Harper shrugged. "Sorry to interrupt, but I got news, and it ain't good."

"What's that, Chief?" Cora asked.

"We got a lab report back on the cocaine. And it *is* cocaine. There's always the chance it's just a bag of milk sugar, but, no, this is the real deal."

"That's no surprise, Chief."

Harper scowled. "Maybe not. But we found the fingerprints of two people on the bag. One of them's Dennis here. The other's Raymond Harstein."

36

SHERRY CARTER WASN'T BUYING IT. "OF COURSE HIS FINGER-prints are on the bag. He's being framed. It was planted on him, so when he found it, he'd handle it."

"He didn't find it," Cora pointed out. "The police did."

"So? Dennis found it, left it there. The police found it later."

"And just when did he find it?"

"How the hell should I know?"

"Sherry, I'm not attacking you here."

"You're attacking Dennis."

"I'm not. I'm laying out the facts."

"No, you're interpreting the facts to implicate him."

"Raymond's fingerprints are also on that bag."

"So? The killer stole it from Raymond, planted it on Dennis."

"How?"

"What do you mean, how? The killer stuck it in his suitcase."

"Without being seen?"

"Dennis and Brenda weren't there at the time."

"I'm not sure that works. In terms of the autopsy report. We don't have the time of death yet. But what if it was when Dennis and Brenda were home?"

"It clearly wasn't."

"Even so, Sherry. It's a bed-and-breakfast. You can't just walk in and out. The owner would see."

"Oh, yeah? I bet I could walk in and out of any bed-and-breakfast in town you'd care to name."

"Sherry, don't do this!"

"Do what?"

"Don't get involved. Dennis is bad news. You know it. I know it. You don't want to get involved with him again."

"I'm not getting involved with him!"

"Don't get worked up."

"I'm not getting worked up!" Sherry took a breath, said more quietly, "I'm not getting worked up. But you're annoying me, Cora. Telling me things I already know. As well as ignoring facts."

"Oh? Just what facts am I ignoring?"

"Dennis complained about people going through his things way before this happened. It's the reason he changed B&Bs, if you'll recall."

"So?"

"So what if the killer planted it then?"

"That was way before the crime."

"It was way before the crime was *committed*. We don't know when the crime was *planned*."

Cora took her niece by the hands. "Sherry. I don't think Dennis bumped off Raymond. I think he's innocent. As far as him being framed goes, I can't tell if he's being framed, or if he's just so stupid he's framing himself."

"Dennis is not stupid."

"Well, he's not a candidate for Mensa. Throwing away those puzzles was a pretty dumb move."

"He was scared, for goodness' sakes. He'd just spent the night in jail. Then he finds the puzzles in his car."

"And how did he happen to find them?"

"What do you mean?"

"He gets out of jail and says, 'I think I'll look under my spare tire just in case somebody's trying to plant something on me'?"

"Now you're saying he *sent* the puzzles?"

"No. I'm just saying his story of how he found them needs to be given a little scrutiny."

"Scrutinize it, then. Cora, the puzzles are like the cocaine. It doesn't matter if someone planted them on Dennis before the murder or after."

"You mean he found them before the murder and just didn't bother to tell anybody?"

"I know that's bad, but it's a lot different than if he sent them. He wouldn't have sent them, Cora. You know he wouldn't."

Cora said nothing.

Sherry said irritably, "Don't you know he wouldn't?"

Cora grimaced. "Well, let me put it this way: I'm trying damn hard to prove he wouldn't."

37

The living room of Jack and Daffodil Dirkson's home was just as Cora Felton had envisioned it, with tie-dyed pillows on the couch, woven tapestries on the walls, and the faint aroma of marijuana in the air. The only anachronistic touch was the array of hearts and diamonds and clubs and spades on a green glowing monitor screen that Cora could see through the bead curtain to the study. She recognized the game as Free Cell, a variation of solitaire she sometimes played on Sherry's computer. Cora could imagine the Dirksons getting stoned out of their minds and staring at the screen for hours, trying to figure out which card to move.

Cora Felton wasn't happy with the Dirksons. And it wasn't just that they looked like an aging Sonny and Cher. Cora remembered the '60s quite fondly, had once worn flowers in her hair. No, what bothered her was the lack of harmony in the dynamic. An expert interrogator, Cora recognized it instantly. Daffodil Dirkson clearly had something to tell. Jack Dirkson clearly didn't want her to tell it.

Cora seemed to recall this from Chief Harper's interrogation of the Dirksons, but at the time she'd been woozy from Dr. Nathan's sedative, so it was only a vague recollection. Indeed, Cora was not even entirely sure their name was Dirkson.

"You're certain he went in twice?" Cora asked now. "Once alone, and once when he found the body?"

"That's right." Daffodil Dirkson's cornflower-blue eyes were wide. She had her hair in braids, and wore a "Fight AIDS" T-shirt, blue jeans, and purple Converse sneakers. She looked like a schoolgirl being brave and answering difficult questions.

"No, it's not," her husband said irritably. "What's with the found-the-body bit? I thought he offed the guy."

"He's innocent until proven guilty," Cora said. "I'm not going to go around saying he killed Raymond and leave myself wide open to a slander suit."

"See, Daffy," Jack Dirkson told his wife. "*She's* protecting *herself. She's* not going to say anything."

Cora hadn't remembered Mrs. Dirkson's nickname was Daffy. It made her momentarily lose her train of thought. When she recovered, she said, "There's a difference between making unfounded accusations and telling what you know."

Jack looked like processing the phrase *unfounded accusations* might short-circuit his memory banks. "Whoa! Heavy!"

"We told the police what we know," Daffy said. "Why are you asking again?"

"New evidence keeps popping up."

"Against him?"

"I'm afraid so."

"Like what?"

"It will be on the evening news. The puzzles were found in his car."

Daffodil Dirkson's mouth fell open. "Puzzles? What puzzles?"

"Cryptograms, warning me not to marry Raymond."

"And the boy had them? These cryptograms?"

"It would appear so," Cora said. She felt no need to mention Dennis had actually been apprehended in the attempt at getting rid of them.

"Whew. Bummer." Jack Dirkson shook his head. "So what more do you want?"

"Frankly," Cora said, "I'm not entirely convinced the young man did it. If he didn't, I wanna nail the guy who did."

"But he must have done it," Daffy said. "I'd feel awful if I told on him and he didn't do it."

"That's why you keep your mouth shut," Jack said.

Cora ignored him, said, "So, if there was any evidence that pointed to anyone else . . ."

"Well, there isn't," Jack Dirkson said. "Look, lady, we don't know diddly-squat. After dinner we came out on the porch, and we saw you guys go in, that's all we know."

"And before dinner?"

"We were inside," Jack said forcefully.

Cora looked at his wife. Daffy Dirkson was playing with one of her straw-colored braids, and would not meet Cora's eyes. Nor would she meet her husband's. She snuffled her nose like a rabbit, or perhaps a sulky girl. She didn't speak, but she did not look happy.

Cora left, having learned nothing. But it occurred to her that if Jack Dirkson didn't want his wife to talk, he was playing it all wrong.

Next time, Cora decided, she would make a point of talking to Daffy alone.

38

CORA COULD HEAR THE RACKET A BLOCK AWAY. SHE SUPPOSED IT must be music, though it certainly seemed more like noise, made her feel like an old fogy as she drove up to the house.

There seemed an inordinate amount of cars out front, even for a bed-and-breakfast. Cora pulled up behind a white Land Rover, and got out. She realized the din was coming from the two-car garage. She walked up to the door, cocked her head, and listened.

Buried in the electric buzz of the guitar, a gravelly voice was croaking, "I'm an angry man. If I can't have you, no one can." Then came a note that sounded bad, even within the context of the discordant music. The drumming and loud electric strumming dissolved into a torrent of vile, varied curses. Cora cocked an ear, hoping to hear something new. Alas, Tune Freaks seemed no more versatile with their sexual and scatological references than they were with their lyrics.

Cora grabbed the handle and pulled. The garage door slid upward, revealing a jungle of amps and music stands. The latter were clearly for show. No sheet music of any kind was in evidence. Cora doubted if a Tune Freak could read music.

Razor stood at the front mike, wearing a guitar. To his right a scrawny Freak sat at an electric keyboard. To his left stood a tattooed Freak with an electric bass. A plump Freak sat behind him at a drum set. From the dynamic, Cora gathered that Razor, distracted by his singing chores, had played a wrong note on the guitar, and was somehow blaming the keyboardist.

Cora took all this in with a glance, beamed at the band. The four Freaks gawked at her. Cora realized they were young men, but couldn't help thinking of them as boys. Again she felt a twinge of age.

Razor stuck out his chin. "What are you doing here?" he demanded.

"I need to ask you some questions."

Clearly he would have liked to tell her to go to hell, but after all, her fiancé had just been killed. Instead, he fell back on the simple but actually insightful, "How come?"

"Your lead singer's in a lot of trouble."

"He's not our lead singer anymore," Razor pointed out reasonably.

"You resent him for that?"

Razor shrugged. "Man's gotta do what a man's gotta do."

Cora suppressed a smile. She had encountered that phrase before in the course of mystery fiction, but this was the first time she had ever heard it applied to taking a job in the textile industry. "If Dennis changed his mind, would you guys take him back?"

"And how!" the keyboardist exclaimed. Razor shot him a dirty look. "Nothing against you, man, but we need you on guitar."

"I *am* on guitar."

"Yeah, but your attention's, like, divided. And your notes, man, they are too beautiful to divide."

To Cora, the fact Razor took that declaration at face value indicated he was either too stoned to notice, or so utterly self-absorbed that the sycophantic praise seemed perfectly natural. In any event, he calmed down enough to inquire, "What's with Denny? We hear he was picked up again."

"News travels fast."

"For drunk driving."

"Though not very accurately. Dennis wasn't drunk. According to the police, Dennis was attempting to dispose of something that was hidden in his car."

The keyboardist's eyes widened. "The murder weapon?"

"No, doofus," Razor said. "He was *holding* the murder weapon."

"Then, what could it be?"

"More drugs," the drummer suggested. He cackled happily at his own wit.

"Nah, that can't be it," the bassist scoffed. "They already busted him for drugs. That would be like double jeopardy."

Cora managed not to roll her eyes. It took a huge effort.

"Well, if it's not drugs, what is it?" the keyboardist asked.

"The puzzles," Razor said. "They must have caught him with the puzzles."

Cora's flesh tingled. "You know about the puzzles?"

"Sure," Razor said.

A copy of the *Bakerhaven Gazette,* folded open to the sports page, was lying on one of the amps. Razor scooped it up, folded it back to the front page.

THE VICTIM WAS WARNED ! ! !

screamed the headline.

"'In a bizarre twist,'" Razor read aloud for Cora's benefit, "'Raymond Harstein, the murdered intended bridegroom of Cora Felton of Bakerhaven, Connecticut, was warned against the upcoming marriage in a series of anonymous cryptic letters. The coded messages, when deciphered by the bride-to-be, threatened Mr. Harstein in the event that he did not break off the match.' "

Cora frowned. With everything else that was going on, she hadn't taken the time that morning to look at the paper.

"The cops catch Denny with the puzzles?" Razor asked her.

"Would that surprise you?"

"Are you jazzin' me? Why the hell would Dennis care if some geezer got married?" Razor flushed slightly. "No offense meant," he mumbled.

"Right. Listen, Razor, could I talk to you outside a minute?"

Razor frowned, said, "Take five, guys," and followed her out into the driveway.

Cora lowered her voice. "Look, I can tell you're in charge of this band. The others do what you say. So I want your opinion, because that's the only one that matters. This thing that's happened to Dennis. Any way you slice it, it's gonna be messy. He'll have a rap sheet. Assuming he doesn't go to prison, can the band get by that? Would you stand behind him and welcome him back?"

Razor grinned. "Are you jazzin' me? Lady, I don't know what kind of music you dig, but, boy, are you out-of-date. You think we'd dump him for that? Up till now, our big claim to fame was trashing a hotel room two years ago in Schenectady. But this. This is a natural."

"So you're standing by him. Good. Glad to hear it."

Cora watched Razor walk back into the garage and pull down the sliding door. She felt somewhat smug. She wasn't nearly as out-of-date as Razor imagined. The idea that Dennis being accused of murder raised him to celebrity status and was thus an asset for the band was exactly how she expected the members of Tune Freaks would see it. It was nice to have one's theories confirmed so thoroughly.

Inside, the tune cranked up again. At least, Cora assumed it was a tune. She certainly couldn't discern any melody, but it sure was loud.

As Cora went down the driveway, the front door of the B&B opened and the owner came out. Cora recognized her as one of her fellow maids a-milking from last year's Christmas pageant. Cora had occasionally chatted with the woman but didn't know her name.

"Oh, Cora," the woman cried, throwing her hands in the air. A birdlike woman several years Cora's senior, the B&B owner seemed particularly distraught. "I'm so sorry. So sorry to hear. The young man squiring you around town, and all of us hoping, and then the wedding just announced. This is such a blow."

Cora accepted the sympathy graciously, though she couldn't help a tinge of amusement that the woman was old enough to refer to Raymond as young.

A particularly deafening burst of noise made the two of them wince.

"Oh, my goodness," the B&B owner said. "When he rented the room, I had no idea he had an orchestra."

"A band," Cora corrected. "Didn't they all come together?"

"No, he came first. Not that it mattered. I was happy to rent the extra rooms. But he didn't say they were for an orches—a band. And when he wanted the garage, I thought it was for a car. You know, one of those fancy new ones they didn't want to leave on the street. Then they show up with the amps and the preamps and the reverb and what have you. And I'm telling you, it's a wonder someone hasn't called the cops."

The woman flushed, perhaps realizing the cops were otherwise occupied at the moment.

"You say one of them came first?"

"Yes. He calls himself Razor." She leaned close and winked. "But the name on his credit card's Ralph Millsap. What do you think of that?"

"I think if my name were Ralph Millsap, I might change my name to Razor," Cora replied.

The two women giggled conspiratorially.

Another blast from the garage practically shook the framework of the Victorian house.

"Do you hear that?" It was clearly a rhetorical question. The B&B owner winced. "And they play till all hours of the morning."

"After midnight?"

"Oh, sure. I asked them to turn it down. I should have just said no music."

"Then you'd have lost the rental."

"Oh, I doubt it. I should have just been firm."

"You think he'd have still booked the rooms?"

"Razor had already booked the rooms. Over the phone. When he got here, he wanted the garage. I could have just said no."

"Well, that's different. Of course you could. He's lucky you even had a garage."

"Oh, Razor knew that."

Cora blinked. "He knew that? How?"

"Oh." The B&B owner smiled. "Because he stayed here just last month."

39

SHERRY CARTER WAS VERY UPSET. "AUNT CORA. YOU LEFT ME here."

"I didn't leave you here."

"You drove off while I was in the bathroom."

"Did I? I had no idea."

"Really? I didn't hear the car start."

"Oh?"

"And I always hear the car start. But you didn't start it, did you? You simply took the brake off and coasted down the driveway."

"Why would you think that?"

"Because I know your devious ways. And don't light a cigarette," she added, as Cora reached into her purse. "You weren't going to smoke in the house anymore."

"That was for Raymond. It doesn't matter now."

"Don't change the subject."

"You're the one who changed the subject." Cora whipped out

her lighter, fired up a cigarette, looked around. "Oh, right, you got rid of them."

"Got rid of what?"

Cora pulled open a cabinet, grabbed a saucer, flopped down at the kitchen table. "Ashtrays," she answered. She took a drag, blew a perfect smoke ring. "You know how long it's been since I've been able to do that?"

"You sound like you're glad he's dead."

Cora's face hardened. "Bite your tongue."

"Sorry," Sherry said. "That was awful. I didn't mean it. My nerves are raw."

"And mine aren't?"

"I said I was sorry."

"Yeah, I know. So guess what?"

"What?"

"Razor was here last month."

Sherry blinked. "What?"

"Isn't that something. The band got here yesterday. Or the day before. Or whenever it was." Cora shook her head. "Anyway, the landlady where the band's staying says Razor was here a month ago, all by himself, scoping things out."

"Scoping what out?"

Cora put up her hands. "Sorry. That's not what she said. That's a conclusion on my part."

"And what does it mean?"

"I don't know yet. But it's fascinating, isn't it?"

"It's more than fascinating. It's completely off the wall. It's before Dennis ever thought of coming here. Probably before he even thought of getting married."

"Exactly."

"What do you mean, 'exactly'? You mean *Razor* is the killer? *Razor* is the one masterminding all this?"

"Someone is," Cora said, ominously.

"But why? What would he have to gain?"

"He stops the marriage. He gets his lead singer back. And the publicity helps the band."

"Oh, come on."

"What's wrong with that?"

"You said he stops the marriage. I thought we agreed Razor was up here before the marriage was even an issue."

"I admit I haven't thought it all out yet."

"I'll say." Sherry shook her head. "And how does that stop the marriage? What if Dennis still goes through with the marriage?"

"You think he will?" Cora asked.

"There's no reason to think he won't."

"Except for Brenda's parents. They ain't too pleased with this turn of events."

"So? Dennis and Brenda are adults. They don't need her parents' consent."

"No, but they need her parents' dough."

"Cora!"

"You think Dennis would marry her if her parents cut her off without a dime?"

"That's not going to happen."

"Which?"

"Now *you're* playing word games? Wonders never cease."

The phone rang.

"That's probably Aaron," Sherry said.

"Or *one* of your gentlemen callers," Cora said archly.

Sherry flashed Cora a look, scooped up the kitchen phone. "Hello?"

An anxious female voice said, "Cora Felton? You're not Cora Felton. Is Cora Felton there? May I talk to her?"

Sherry cradled the phone against her side, said, "It's for you."

"Who is it?"

"I don't know. It's a woman. She seems upset."

Cora lunged from the table, grabbed the phone. "Hello."

"It's you? Oh, thank God, it's you! I was afraid I wouldn't get you! I need to see you right away."

"That's very interesting," Cora said, "but who the hell are you?"

"Oh, oh, I'm sorry. It's Daffodil. Daffodil Dirkson. I really need to talk to you. But Jack doesn't want me to get involved."

"What do you want to tell me?"

"No. Not over the phone. I gotta get off the phone. I don't have time. Jack would kill me if he caught me."

"Yes, but—"

"Meet me at the Congregational church. Out front. If no one's watching. If someone is, I'll duck inside."

"What's this all about?"

"The murder, of course. I— Oh!"

The phone went dead.

40

CORA FELTON SLAMMED THE CAR INTO AN S-CURVE. THE TIRES spun wildly, searching for pavement.

"Good God, slow down!" Sherry cried. "It's not a race!"

The Toyota shot out of the curve, rocketed down the road.

"You didn't hear that woman's voice!" Cora hissed.

"Yes, I did. Remember, I took the call."

"How'd she sound to you?"

"Frightened!"

"No kidding."

"But not as frightened as I am! Slow down, will you!"

"Relax! Almost there!"

The Toyota hurtled toward the village green. Cora spun the wheel, swerved in the direction of the Congregational church.

The psychedelic VW microbus was parked right outside.

Cora snorted in disgust. "That's inconspicuous as all hell. Like no one knows she's here."

Cora pulled in and she and Sherry got out.

"So where is she?" Cora demanded. "She said she'd be out front unless someone was around. There's no one around, including her."

"Maybe someone scared her off, she went inside, and they went away."

"Yeah. Maybe."

Cora yanked the doors open and they entered the church.

The anteroom was empty. To the right was the door to the Reverend's office. To the left, the stairs to the organ loft and the bell tower. Ahead were the double doors leading into the church. Cora pushed them open, strode through.

The light pouring through the multicolored panels of the stained-glass windows revealed the pews were empty, as was the pulpit.

"She's not here," Sherry said.

"She must be."

Cora strode down the aisle, looking left and right among the pews. She reached the front row and stopped so abruptly, Sherry bumped into her.

A foot protruded from behind the pulpit.

It wore a purple Converse sneaker.

Cora grabbed Sherry by the arm.

"Oh, my God!" Sherry said.

Cora sucked in her breath. She scooted up the three steps to the raised pulpit, peered around.

Daffodil Dirkson lay facedown behind the pulpit. Her head was twisted to the side. Her left eye was glassy, bulging. A carving knife protruded from her back. Blood stained the back of her white T-shirt, presumably the "Fight AIDS" one she'd been wearing earlier that day.

"Is she dead?" Sherry whispered.

"I'd bet my poker stake on it."

"We gotta call the cops."

"Good. Go call 'em. I'm gonna look around."

"Aunt Cora—"

"Go, go. Take the car if you need it."

There came a sound from the shadows off to the right.

Cora wheeled around. Her hand was in her drawstring purse.

A shadow loomed up in the darkness, a menacing figure silhouetted in the unearthly light pouring through the stained-glass windows, a rainbow halo around his head.

Cora whipped a gun from her purse. "All right!" she cried. "Hold it right there!"

The shadow raised his hands. They were empty.

"Cora? Sherry?" he said.

It was Aaron Grant.

41

CHIEF HARPER WAS TRYING TO BE CALM. IT WAS DIFFICULT UNder the circumstances, what with a murder in the church, and so many witnesses on hand. As a result, the chief was cutting corners on proper police procedure, and interviewing them all at once, instead of taking individual statements. Since it was Sherry, Aaron, and Cora, Chief Harper didn't see how that could hurt. After all, it wasn't the first of his crime scenes these three had showed up at. Also, he was eager to get back to the church, where he had left Sam Brogan in charge. It would not be great for public relations to have cranky Sam making statements when the TV crews arrived.

To keep the witnesses out of the way of the media, Chief Harper was conducting his interviews across the village green in the county courthouse. As court was not in session, they had pulled up chairs around the defense table while Chief Harper listened to their stories.

"It's very simple," Cora said impatiently. "Daffy called, claimed she had something urgent to tell me, and asked me to meet her at the church. She said if she wasn't out front, to look inside. She wasn't, so we did, and found her lying there behind the pulpit right where you saw her."

"You and Sherry came together?" Chief Harper asked.

"That's right."

"What about Aaron?"

"He came by himself."

"You came in response to the phone call from the woman?"

"Yes."

Chief Harper turned to Aaron. "Why did you come?"

"Same thing. I got a phone call from the woman."

"Where?"

"My desk at the paper. She called up, said she had something important to tell me, and to meet her at the church."

"She give you any idea what it was she wanted to tell you?"

"No. Just that it was important and it was about the murder."

"She tell you anything else?"

"She told me not to drive."

"What?"

"She said she didn't want my car parked outside the church so people might think we were in there together."

"Why did she want to meet in the church?"

"I have no idea."

"How about you?" Chief Harper asked Cora.

"She was going to meet us *outside* the church. Unless there were people around."

"She tell you that?" the chief asked Aaron.

"She said she'd be behind the pulpit."

"Uh-huh. So you walked in the church expecting to meet Daffodil Dirkson behind the pulpit, and found Miss Carter and Miss Felton there?"

"No, I didn't."

Chief Harper frowned. "Huh?"

"When I got to the church, no one was there. I looked behind the pulpit. Daffodil was lying there dead. The next thing I remember, Sherry and Cora were standing there."

"Next thing you remember?"

"Right."

"Your mind's a blank?"

Aaron grimaced. "That sounds bad, doesn't it?"

The door to the back of the courtroom banged open, and Becky Baldwin barged in. "All right, what's going on?" she demanded fiercely.

Chief Harper frowned. "Nothing that concerns you."

"Well, I'm certainly glad to hear it." Becky strode toward them, hands on her hips. "You can give me your assurance my client Dennis Pride has nothing to do with the second murder?"

"I thought he was in jail," Harper said.

"No. Mr. Wallenstein bailed him out again. So I'd just like to be sure you're not trying to connect him to this second crime."

"You're the first one to suggest such a thing," Sherry said icily.

"Sweet," Becky said. "But this is not such a novel idea the police could not have come to it on their own. They've accused him of one crime. It would seriously undermine their case to admit he had nothing to do with the second."

"So he's out, eh?" Harper said. "Since when?"

"I wasn't there at the time. Mr. Wallenstein charged in on his white horse, waved some money at the judge."

"May I quote you on that?" Aaron Grant said.

"Heavens, no. We're off the record here, aren't we? I mean, no one's taking anything down. No one's advised anyone of their rights. None of these three are suspects, are they, Chief?"

"Why do you care?" Harper asked. "You're not their lawyer, too, are you?"

"Of course not. That would be a conflict of interest." She smiled. "Unless you'd like to drop the charges against Dennis. In light of the fact he had nothing to do with this. Then I'd be free to accept other employment."

"Oh, for Christ's sake," Sherry said irritably. "Could you all stop sparring? A woman is dead. Dennis didn't kill her. Aaron didn't kill her. Let's stop playing games, pool our information, and find out who did."

"Good idea," Chief Harper said. "I haven't heard your story, Sherry. Is everything Cora told me true and accurate?"

"Absolutely."

"She leave anything out?"

Sherry hesitated.

"I knew it," Chief Harper said. "Instead of answering the question, you're evaluating the effect of your answer. Do I understand in your terminology this does not fall under the definition of playing games?"

"I wasn't evaluating the effect of my answer," Sherry said. "I was trying to remember if there was anything at all."

"And was there?"

"I can't think of a thing. Except . . ."

"Except what?"

"Aaron did seem somewhat stunned. In light of his statement that he can't remember what happened, you should look into the possibility he was hit on the head."

"Aaron can't remember?" Becky said it incredulously.

Chief Harper leveled his finger at her. "If you blow that up for your own use . . ."

"The fact one of the other suspects' mind's a blank for the time a homicide took place? Chief, any attorney who *failed* to mention such a thing could probably be sued for malpractice. If not disbarred." Becky smiled. "But, seeing as how Dennis was with Brenda

230 / PARNELL HALL

and her father the *entire time* this second murder might have occurred, I see no reason to raise the inference."

The door flew open again. This time, Brenda Wallenstein
burst in.

"Where's Dennis?" she cried. "He went out and never came
back. He's been gone for hours!"

42

THE CRIME-SCENE RIBBON STRETCHED FROM ONE SIDE OF THE church to the other, right across the front steps. A noisy crowd had gathered, although there was nothing to see. The townspeople stood in the street and on the village green, talking amongst themselves. None of them really knew what had happened, so a lot of the details were wrong. The victim, for instance, was speculated to be anyone from a passing stranger to the Reverend Kimble. The cause of death ranged from gunshots to drowning. The latter seemed somewhat unlikely in a church, yet there was a rather complicated theory circulating involving holy water.

The Reverend Kimble, who showed up very much alive, was shocked at the proceedings. "What the devil is going on?" he demanded, immediately ascribing any such turmoil to the Prince of Darkness.

Sam Brogan shrugged and popped his gum. "It appears someone's been using your church as a crime scene, Reverend. You happen to know anything about that?"

The Reverend could not have looked more nonplussed had Sam smacked him with his nightstick. "I *beg* your pardon?"

Luckily, Chief Harper arrived just then, and was able to put a more tactful spin on the inquiry. Cora, Sherry, Aaron, Becky, and Brenda, who had followed the chief across the green, all listened while he filled the Reverend in.

"Oh, how awful," Reverend Kimble lamented. "And in the church. I find that hard to believe."

"I do too," Chief Harper said. "I'm amazed such a thing could be done. The killer getting in and out of the church, I mean. Without you seeing him."

"I wasn't there," the Reverend said.

"But how could the killer know that?" Cora pointed out.

"Maybe the killer got lucky," Chief Harper hypothesized.

Cora shook her head. "You have to go on the assumption the killer intended to get away with the crime. You don't walk into a church, murder somebody, and walk out again, and not expect to be seen."

"I don't want to debate it right now," Chief Harper said. "I want to get the Reverend Kimble's statement."

"Right," Cora agreed. "Look, Rev—"

"If you don't mind," Chief Harper interrupted, "*I'd* like to ask the questions here."

"Yes, of course," Cora said, sweetly. "Ask him who knew he'd be out."

Chief Harper shot her a dirty look, then turned to the Reverend.

"No one knew I'd be out," the Reverend Kimble protested unhappily. Once again, the wretched man seemed to take the remark as an accusation of complicity in the crime. "Someone might have seen me leave, but I didn't tell anyone where I was going."

"Where exactly were you?"

The Reverend's eyes widened. "Where was I? I was at the old

folks' home. I'm sorry, you have me flustered. I mean the retirement community. I help out there twice a week, bringing comfort to those who aren't able to make it to church."

Cora, who hadn't been able to make it to church for decades, said, "Is that a regularly scheduled thing?"

"Oh, yes. Every Tuesday and Thursday from two to three."

"Who knew that?"

"Heavens, I have no idea. The retirement community, of course. And anyone who wanted to schedule an appointment with me would see those times were taken."

"See where?"

"On the bulletin board outside my office. It has my schedule on it. Everyone knows it's there. That is, everyone in the parish."

Chief Harper did little to hide his disgust.

"And anyone at the wedding rehearsal," Cora appended.

"Or anyone who *wasn't*," Becky Baldwin amended dryly. "The church is open. Anyone could walk in and look at that bulletin board at any time."

Dr. Barney Nathan came walking up. The little coroner looked smug as usual. "Chief. Could I have a word with you?"

Chief Harper shot a glance at the jostling throng around them. "Yeah. Over here." He led the doctor off to one side. "What you got, Doc?"

"Cause of death's a single knife wound to the back. There appear to be no contributing factors."

"You came all the way over here to tell me that?"

"No. I just thought you'd like to know I pinned down the time of death."

"Oh?"

"I wanted to let you know, because you always make such a big deal over the wide latitude we doctors leave in our estimates. As if we didn't *want* to be more exact, when the medical facts simply don't support it. And a two-hour window is actually a pretty good estimate."

"Are you saying you can do better this time?"

"Yes, I am."

"You can give me the time of death within an hour?"

"I can give you the time of death within a minute."

Chief Harper's jaw dropped. "What?"

"In the ambulance the decedent exhibited a faint but unmistakable pulse. This was maintained by the EMS workers until the patient was presented to me in the hospital. Despite heroic measures to save her life, the patient succumbed to her wound at three forty-seven, in the operating room."

Chief Harper digested that information. "Well, that doesn't tell me when she was stabbed."

Barney Nathan smiled. "I never said it would."

On the far side of the crowd a car pulled up. Dennis climbed out.

Cora Felton, inching closer to try to eavesdrop on the doctor and the police chief, spotted Dennis, glanced around, saw that no one else had noticed him.

Cora moved to intercept Dennis. Unfortunately, Chief Harper and Barney Nathan were right in her way. Instead of trying to avoid them, she barged right up. "Chief, while you've got the doc here, we should check out Aaron for a head wound, see if he's been coshed, like Sherry thinks."

Harper frowned. "Not now. I'm talking to the doctor. Go on, get out of here."

"Yes, sir," Cora said meekly.

She twisted away from the two men, disappeared into the crowd, and made a beeline for Dennis. She grabbed him by the arm, dragged him back behind his car.

"What's going on?" he demanded.

"You don't know?"

"I just got here."

"Where have you been?"

"None of your business."

"Actually, it is."

"Is Sherry over there?"

"Yes, she is. And Brenda. And your attorney."

"Oh." Dennis didn't sound entirely pleased.

Cora smiled. "Lotta women all at once, isn't it? Even for a charmer like you."

Dennis scowled. "You got something to say to me, say it."

"Sure. The dead woman in the church. Did you know her?"

"Dead woman in the church?"

"What did you think this was, a potluck supper? There's been another murder. Someone else has croaked. Which would have been real convenient for you if you'd been behind bars doing time. Too bad Daddy Warbucks bailed you out."

"Who's the dead woman?"

"Good question. It's not only relevant, but asking it implies you don't know the answer."

"So who is it?"

"You have no idea?"

"Someone said the neighbor."

"Oh? Who might that someone be?"

"Lady in the crowd. Just now. Was she right?"

"Yes, she was."

"So who's the neighbor?"

"You know the hippie couple next door?"

Dennis snorted. "Those stoned geezers? It's one of them?"

"Yeah," Cora said. "It's one of the stoned geezers."

"Which one?"

Cora grimaced. "No. Bad move. Pretending you didn't know who the victim was was a good touch. Pretending you didn't know which stoned geezer—what a delicate characterization—is just dumb. We've already discussed the dead *woman*. Which stoned geezer do you think that might be?"

Dennis thought it over.

"You're gonna need to talk to the police, Dennis. When you do, you better have your story straight. A little rehearsal wouldn't hurt."

"What do you mean, *story*? I don't have a story."

"Then your ass is grass," Cora said with relish. "Refusing to talk and demanding to see your lawyer may be your constitutional right, but it's not gonna make you real popular with the cops. Or get you on the tube. If you're not gettin' 'em publicity, even your bandmates may begin to think this is a pretty bad habit."

Dennis frowned, irritably. "Cool it. I'm trying to think."

"Better think fast. Here comes the fuzz."

Chief Harper pushed his way through the crowd. He did not look happy. "Damn it, Miss Felton. I thought I told you to stay put."

"Actually, you told me to leave. I ran into Dennis here, figured you might wanna chat with him."

"I sure do. Where'd you go when you got out of jail, Pride?"

"Don't answer that," Becky Baldwin advised. She thrust herself between Chief Harper and Dennis.

Brenda rushed to her fiancé's side, threw her arms around him.

Sherry, watching her, frowned.

Watching Sherry, so did Aaron.

So did Chief Harper. "Miss Baldwin, that's not a particularly wise tack to take. If your client has an alibi for the present crime, it will go a long way toward clearing him of the first."

"Nice try, Chief. But my client's not saying one word until he talks to me. Unless the charges against him are dismissed, in light of this second crime."

Chief Harper didn't dignify that suggestion with a response.

"Well," Aaron said, "if no one's talking, I'm gonna go write this one up."

"You're not charging him?" Becky asked the chief.

Dennis frowned. "Charging who?"

"Aaron Grant here," Becky said. "He was found under almost the same circumstances as you were. And by the same person. Cora Felton came to meet the woman, found her dead and Aaron right there on the spot. You know, Chief, it really seems like favoritism, you charging Dennis and not Aaron."

"Was Aaron holding the knife?" Chief Harper asked.

"Not at the time. But then again, only someone trying to help would be holding the knife."

"You don't have to try your theories out on me, Miss Baldwin. But I feel it only fair to point out the dead woman happens to be one of the witnesses who saw your client enter the first murder scene."

Becky looked at Chief Harper as if he had just revealed himself to be an utter moron. "Gee, Chief, as my client was *found* at the first murder scene, a witness who saw him go *in* hardly seems particularly damning. I can't see what he gains by shutting her up."

"We don't know what she intended to say. Did she give you any hint, Miss Felton?"

Cora shook her head ruefully. "Not one damn thing."

43

CORA FELTON TRACKED JACK DIRKSON TO THE WAITING ROOM of Bakerhaven Memorial Hospital. The man was distraught. His eyes were red, his face was wet with tears. He was dressed in a tie-dyed shirt, a buckskin vest, bell-bottom jeans, and a string of love beads. He looked totally lost.

Cora slid into a chair next to him and said, "How are you doing?"

It was as if there was a time lag before he realized she was talking to him. His head swiveled, and his right hand snaked up to push the stringy hair off his forehead. Cora could see white roots, realized the man must dye his hair. That seemed out of keeping with the hippie garb.

A bleary eye fixed on her. Dull. Bewildered. Uncomprehending.

"Sorry," Cora said.

The man said nothing, stared back down at his sandaled feet.

"You should go home," Cora told him. "I stopped by your house, but you weren't there. I figured you might be here. Actually,

I couldn't think of anywhere else to look. Even so, this is no place to be. Why don't you go home?"

After a moment, Jack heaved a ragged sigh. "Got no wheels."

Of course he didn't. Too late, Cora remembered his VW bus was parked in front of the church. He didn't have a car because his car was now part of a crime scene. No one had thought to drive him home.

"I'll give you a ride," Cora told him. "Would you like that?"

He shrugged, uncaring.

"Come on. My car's outside."

Cora took him by the arm, led him through the automatic sliding doors, down the marble steps, into the parking lot. The large, modern Bakerhaven Memorial Hospital seemed too big for such a small town, which indeed it was. It served the entire county. Cora guided Jack to her Toyota, installed him in the front seat. She buckled his seat belt to make sure he'd stay there.

Cora resolved to get out of the parking lot before she made another attempt at conversation, but Jack beat her to it, even if his contribution was only a whine. "I told her," he moaned. "I told Daffy to keep out of it. She wouldn't listen. Not that she knew anything. That's the irony. Daffy didn't know anything. But somebody thought she did."

"What could she have known?" Cora asked. "I mean, what could someone have thought she knew?"

"They thought she saw something. But she didn't."

"How do you know?"

"Daffy would have told me."

"Hmmm."

Jack looked at her numbly. "What do you mean by that?"

"You were very negative."

"I didn't want her to get hurt."

Cora made no comment, drove several blocks. "What did you see?"

"Nothing."

"You were out on the porch, though, when we all went in the house."

"So?"

"So you saw us go in. Dennis and me and Brenda."

"Big deal. Everyone *knows* you went in. You all saw each other go in. Why involve us?"

"Witnesses lie," Cora said.

Jack's ravaged face hardened instantly. "Are you saying Daffy lied?"

"No, I'm not. I'm just saying people aren't always accurate. Dennis, Brenda, and I saw each other go into Raymond's house. We don't seem to remember it the same way. Maybe your wife saw something we didn't."

"That got her killed?" he said incredulously. "You mean she *saw* something that got her killed?"

"I don't know, but I'm going to find out. Was that the *only* time you saw Dennis that day?"

Jack hesitated. "I saw him with you. And what's-his-name. With Raymond. Gettin' the dude a ride."

"Yes. In front of the bed-and-breakfast. But aside from that. Did you see Dennis enter Raymond's *house* at any other time?"

"No way."

"Did you see anyone else?"

"I told you. No."

"Too bad."

Cora turned off the highway just past the Mobil station. It was a route she'd traveled many times to Raymond's house. In minutes Jack would be out of the car. "How about the reporter? Aaron Grant? Do you happen to know him?"

"Why?"

"Just wondered. You're relatively new in town. I don't know who you know."

"No, I don't know him. I think Daffy mentioned him, though."

Cora almost drove off the road. "Really," she said, casually. "And what did she say?"

"I don't remember. It wasn't important."

Cora heroically restrained herself from saying, *I'll be the judge of that.* "It must have been a while ago."

"Dunno."

"And you have no idea what it was?"

"No, I don't," Jack said, irritably. "Who *cares* what it was?"

It appeared the police had not been forthcoming with the details of his wife's demise. Cora wasn't about to enlighten him.

"You didn't see Aaron Grant around your house the day of Raymond's murder, did you?"

"I don't even know what this Aaron Grant dude looks like."

"Then you can't be sure."

"Yes, I'm *sure*!" Jack exploded.

Cora gave him a moment, then asked gently, "How are you so sure?"

"Because I didn't see *anyone*!" Jack Dirkson's bloodshot eyes were wild. His cheeks were red and caked with tears. "Just what I *told* you, lady. No more, no less. I can't *help* you." A sob racked his body. "And you can't help me."

Cora said nothing as she pulled into his driveway.

She was pretty sure she couldn't help him, either.

44

NORMAN WALLENSTEIN LOOKED TIRED. HE'D SENT WORD DOWN with Mrs. Trumble, the red-haired landlady, that he wasn't up to seeing anybody. Cora Felton had sent word back that if Mr. Wallenstein valued his only child's health and happiness he damned well better dance himself down to see her. Now Norman stood on the front steps of the bed-and-breakfast, leaning against the rail. He wore no jacket or tie. His Brooks Brothers shirt was open at the neck. His sleeves were rolled up.

As Cora had expected, the businessman was not one to mince words.

"All right, what the hell's so damn important?" he demanded. It was the longest sentence Cora had ever heard him say.

"The wedding arrangements," Cora told him.

Wallenstein blinked. "Huh?"

"Your daughter and I were having a double wedding, remember? My wedding's off. Is hers still on?"

"Are you serious?"

"No, I came over here after my fiancé was murdered just to yank your chain."

"You want to know if the wedding's on?"

"Yeah. Have you decided yet?"

"It's not my decision."

"No, but you've got clout. I doubt if Brenda would marry if you forbid it. On the other hand, I wonder if Dennis would marry into the family if he figured you were cutting Brenda off."

Wallenstein frowned. "Where did you get that notion?"

"If *my* daughter were marrying Dennis, *I'd* cut her off. But that's not the way you wanna play it, is it? You, with the show of solidarity, bailing the kid out. Though, I suppose you felt you had to."

Wallenstein took a breath. "I'm sorry for your recent loss, Miss Felton. But that doesn't give you the right to insult me."

"I don't mean to. I'm actually sorry for you. You're in a bit of a bind. You have to back your daughter's choice, which you don't wanna do, or dump him in his time of need, which will turn your kid against you. Definitely a lose-lose situation."

Wallenstein pondered that. He eyed Cora with new interest. "What do you know about it?"

"I know Dennis. I know what he's like. Sherry hates him. I suppose you know he beat her?"

"Dennis swears it wasn't like that."

"I'm sure he does. The point is, Sherry thinks he's dirt. But even she doesn't think he's a killer. She gets protective of him when he's threatened. And he knows it, and he plays off it. He knows all the angles."

"You don't paint a very pretty picture."

Cora shrugged. "At least I'm not accusing him of murder. Frankly, I don't think he did it."

"Then what's your point?"

"Just what I said: Do you intend to go through with the wedding?"

"Do you think I should stop it?"

"No, I think you should encourage it. I think the wedding should take place exactly as planned."

Impassively, Norman Wallenstein studied Cora's face. "Why?"

"Because," Cora told him, "someone's gone to an awful lot of trouble to see that it doesn't."

45

SHERRY WAS IN THE KITCHEN, MAKING HERB-CRUSTED PORK tenderloin, spinach, and new potatoes. The meal was one of Cora's favorites, and Sherry hoped to tempt her with it. Cora had shown no signs of letting the tragic demise of her intended ruin her appetite, but Sherry was taking no chances. She had the pork roast in the oven and was concocting a red pepper and hazelnut sauce to go with it when the doorbell rang. She rinsed her hands off and went to answer the door.

Dennis had cleaned himself up since she had last seen him. His slacks were creased. His sherbet-colored polo shirt was tucked in. He was shaved and his hair was combed. Only his eyes betrayed him. They were glassy and bloodshot.

"Oh," Sherry said.

She stood there with her hand on the doorknob. She didn't invite him in, but she made no move to close the door, either.

"Sherry—" Dennis said.

She put up her hand. "You don't have to tell me. I know you didn't murder Daffodil."

"That isn't it."

"Oh? What is it, then?"

"May I come in?"

"That's not a good idea."

"Why?"

"Dennis, there's a restraining order."

"As if that matters now."

"Dennis—"

"I want to discuss the wedding."

"Wedding? You're going ahead with the wedding?"

"Saturday, as planned. May I come in?"

Sherry stepped back. That was all the invitation Dennis needed. He pushed by her into the house.

Sherry stood there for a moment, then closed the door.

Dennis stepped aside to let her precede him into the living room. Everything in his manner was polite, restrained.

Except for barging in the door.

But he hadn't really done that.

She'd invited him in.

Dennis sat on the couch, gestured for her to do the same.

Sherry hesitated. She couldn't stand there talking to him while he sat, but she didn't want to sit on the couch with him, either. Instead, she sat in the chair opposite. Dennis did not protest. In fact, he acted as if that was exactly what he'd intended.

"So," Sherry said. "You say your wedding's going forward?"

"That's right."

"Whose idea is that?"

"That's what I want to talk to you about. It seems to be your aunt's."

"I beg your pardon?"

"Apparently she spoke to Brenda's father, convinced him it would be a good idea. He's called the wedding back on, and what Norman Wallenstein wants, Norman Wallenstein always gets."

"You don't *want* to marry Brenda?"

"I didn't say that."

"I know you didn't say that. That's why I asked."

"It's not that I don't want to marry Brenda. It's just that under the circumstances . . ."

"What circumstances?"

"Well, with everything up in the air."

"What's up in the air? There's been a murder. Two murders. But they have nothing to do with you. If you want to get married, nothing's stopping you."

He shook his head. "It was to be a double wedding, Sherry. The other groom is on a slab in the morgue. Don't you think that might cast a certain pall over the festivities?"

"So you *don't* want to get married?" Sherry said.

Dennis frowned. "I think I made my feelings clear. What isn't clear is your aunt's motivation. Why is she pushing the wedding?"

"You're asking me? This is the first I've heard of it."

Dennis sniffed the air. "What's that?"

"Oh, the pork loin!" Sherry wailed.

She jumped up, raced into the kitchen. She grabbed pot holders, jerked the oven open. She took the roast out, stuck in a meat thermometer.

Dennis had followed her into the room. "That smells good," he said. "You always were a fantastic cook."

Sherry didn't answer, instead inspected the thermometer.

"I don't think you ever made that, though. Is it a new recipe?"

"Something Cora likes."

"It's hot in here. You got anything to drink?" Dennis swung the refrigerator open. "Hmm. Diet Coke. You on a diet?"

"No. I just don't need the sugar rotting my teeth."

"Come on. You always had great teeth."

Sherry flushed, embarrassed that the conversation had turned personal.

The doorbell rang.

Sherry left Dennis in the kitchen, went to answer the door.

"Hi," Aaron Grant said. "I see you've got company. Whose car is that?"

Dennis stepped into view behind Sherry. He was smiling and casually holding his glass of soda, right at home. "Oh, hi there, Grant. Don't mind us. We're just having drinks while the pork tenderloin is cooking."

Aaron scowled and his face turned red.

Sherry had never seen him like that before. It threw her, made her hesitate a moment before she could think of what to say.

"I guess I'm intruding," Aaron said stiffly.

He turned, stomped back toward his car.

"Aaron, wait!" Sherry cried.

She followed him a few steps down the drive, then stopped, hopelessly torn between wanting to run after Aaron, and not wanting to leave Dennis alone in her home.

While she vacillated, Aaron's Honda sprang to life. It backed up, and tore down the drive, sending up an angry cloud of dirt.

Sherry heaved an exasperated sigh, then turned back to Dennis. "You have to leave. Now."

"Because some reporter throws a jealous snit?" Dennis smiled, condescendingly.

"No. Because I say so. Come on. Get out. Get out."

"I haven't finished my Coke."

"Yes, you have. Chug it down, or give me the glass."

"Sherry, look what you're doing here. I haven't done any-thing. That reporter's flippin' out, so you're taking it out on me. We were having a drink together, calm, social, and suddenly you're throwing me out of the house. Does that seem right?"

"Dennis, I don't have time for this."

"You don't have time for *me?*" Dennis said incredulously. "I'm charged with murder, but you don't have time for *me?*"

"No, you're right. *You* don't have time for this."

"I'll always have time for my maid of honor."

Sherry shuddered. Calmly, she said, "You better go look after the bride-to-be."

"Brenda's not here. Her mother took her to pick up the wed-ding dress."

"She doesn't have a dress yet? What's the matter? Didn't she think you'd go through with it?"

"Sherry—"

"No. I don't want to talk about it. You have to go."

"Can I give you a ride somewhere?"

"No."

"Because you don't have a car. You're kind of stranded here, aren't you?" Dennis looked around. "No near neighbors."

Sherry felt a chill. She suppressed another shudder, kept up a bold front. "I gotta get back to work, Dennis. With all this I'm behind on the column."

"I thought you were cooking dinner."

"I am. I can do both."

"Yeah," Dennis said. "And nobody knows it." He pointed down the driveway. "That reporter. Does he know? That you're the Puzzle Lady? He does, doesn't he? You really ought to be more careful who you tell."

A car pulled up the driveway. A red Toyota.

Sherry had never been so happy to see Cora in her life.

Dennis didn't look thrilled. He hopped in his rental, backed around, and roared down the driveway, before Cora was even out of her car.

"Well," Cora said. "What the hell was *that* all about?"

The dam finally broke. Sherry flung herself into her aunt's arms, weeping uncontrollably.

46

Cora gobbled up the last slice of pork loin, then greedily sopped up the gravy with a biscuit. "This is fantastic. Simply fantastic."

"Glad you like it."

"Like it? I love it. You should open a restaurant. Or teach cooking classes."

"Then we'd each have a career," Sherry said.

"Oh, low blow," Cora said. "You must be in a particularly rotten mood."

"What gave you your first clue?"

"I haven't heard that expression in years. Are you sure you're younger than me?"

"Younger than I. Stop trying to humor me, Cora."

"I'm not trying to humor you. I'm just trying to find out if you're calm enough to talk about what happened."

"Nothing happened."

"I thought Aaron caught you making out with Dennis."

"I wasn't making out with Dennis."

"Don't tell me. Tell Aaron."

"His cell phone isn't on."

"What about his office phone?"

"No answer."

"Gee. Maybe he isn't there."

"A brilliant deduction."

"He probably went looking for a story. Of course, Dennis wasn't available. He was making out with you. So Aaron's probably talking to his lawyer. That's the first thing men do when they get jealous. Run to another woman."

"Are you enjoying this?"

"Not at all."

"You seem to be."

"Do I? I can't imagine why. Could it be the years of listening to you needle me about one man or another? And now the shoe's on the other foot. . . ."

"Dennis says you're the one pushing the wedding."

"Pushing? I wasn't aware that I was pushing. Of course, he's not the best bridegroom in the world if he feels he's being pushed."

"He says you went to Brenda's father. Advised him to go ahead with the wedding."

"You mean as if the whole thing was Dad's idea and the kids had no say?"

"Nice evasion, Cora. Did you do it, yes or no?"

Cora shook her head. "I must have gotten to you with that lawyer crack. Now you're cross-examining me."

"The only thing keeping me from *strangling* you is the fact you've had a personal loss. Come on, Cora. I need help now. Maybe not as much as you, but I do. Would you please help me figure out what Dennis is up to?"

Cora took her niece by the hands. "That's the whole point,

Sherry. You don't *need* to figure out what Dennis is up to. You just need to decide that whatever Dennis is up to doesn't concern you."

"Oh, really?" Sherry's eyes blazed. "What am I supposed to do, call the police, say he's harassing me? The guy's on the hook for a murder he didn't commit. Every bit of bad publicity only sinks him deeper. I should call the cops on him, get him more bad press? I did it before, it didn't matter. I do it now, it gets on TV."

"Is that all you're feeling?"

"You'd like more?"

"I certainly wouldn't. Did you ask Dennis where he was at the time of Daffy's murder?"

"No."

"No? It would seem a pertinent question. If he had a good alibi for the second crime, it would go a long way toward proving he didn't commit the first."

"That's the difference between us," Sherry said bitterly. "I don't *need* any evidence to prove he didn't commit the first."

"I'm sure you don't." Cora cocked her head. "What about the cryptograms? You believe he didn't send them? The ones that were in his car? The ones he tried to get rid of?"

"It could have happened just the way he said."

"Sure it could."

"There is nothing in those cryptograms to prove he sent them."

"Is there anything to prove he didn't?"

"How could there be?"

"I don't know. You seem so sure. Did you look for something?"

Sherry's gaze faltered.

Cora pounced. "You did, didn't you?" she said. "You've been over those cryptograms with a fine-tooth comb trying to prove Dennis didn't send them. And you can't do it, can you?"

"So?" Sherry said. "Never mind *proving* anything. You can't find anything to even *suggest* he did."

Cora's eyes narrowed. "Oh, yeah? Where are they?"

"On the computer."

"Lead me to 'em."

Cora followed Sherry into the office. Sherry sat at the desk, clicked on a notebook icon similar to the one on Raymond's laptop.

The cryptograms opened up.

```
1. Dear Puzzle Lady,
   XPFU IMBBOP OFXQ,
```

```
You're making a big mistake. This is a bad match. If
QVM'UP GFAJWS F CJS GJZEFAP. ENJZ JZ F CFX GFEKN. JR
```

```
you're smart, you'll break it off, before something
QVM'UP ZGFUE, QVM'OO CUPFA JE VRR, CPRVUP ZVGPENJWS
```

```
happens. Before someone gets hurt. Leave him. Walk
NFIIPWZ. CPRVUP ZVGPVWP SPEZ NMUE. OPFHP NJG. LFOA
```

```
away, and don't look back. It's not too late to rectify
FLFQ, FWX XVW'E OVVA CFKA. JE'Z WVE EVV OFEP EV UPKEJRQ
```

```
the errors that you've made. Walk away while there's
ENP PUUVUZ ENFE QVM'HP GFXP. LFOA FLFQ LNJOP ENPUP'Z
```

```
still time. Walk away.
ZEJOO EJGP. LFOA FLFQ.
```

```
2. Dear Bridegroom,
   LQXS KSTLQZSUUD,
```

```
You think you're so smart but you're not. Butt out of my
RUJ FGTPO RUJ'SQ VU VDXSF KJF RUJ'SQ PUF. KJFF UJF UB DR
```

business, or this wedding isn't going to happen. This is
KJVTPQVV, US FGTV AQLLTPZ TVP'F ZUTPZ FU GXHHQP. FGTV TV

a warning. I'm getting angry.
X AXSPTPZ. T'D ZQFFTPZ XPZSR.

3. Dear Puzzle Lady,
   AWIE QPVVGW GIAU,

Shut him up, if you know what's good for you. I don't
XLPC LZY PQ, ZO UKP BDKR RLIC'X JKKA OKE UKP. Z AKD'C

have to take this from anyone.
LIHW CK CIBW CLZX OEKY IDUKDW.

"Okay," Sherry said. "There you go. What can you tell from that?"

Cora skimmed swiftly through the translations. Which told her absolutely nothing. Cora considered the prospect of bluffing her niece. It seemed a losing proposition.

"Well?" Sherry prompted.

"Give me a break. I've read over the messages. Now I'm examining the possibility the writer revealed himself in his choice of substitute letters."

"Talk about desperate," Sherry scoffed.

Cora continued to scan the letters. Then she frowned. "Hey, wait a minute. What are you trying to pull? This isn't the second cryptogram."

"Sure it is."

"Like hell. The second one is the one Raymond and I solved. And that's not it."

"Don't be silly."

"Hey. I saw it on his laptop. Not the solution, the code. I mean, the cryptogram. The substituted letters. And it wasn't them."

"Like you really remember the letters."

"Hey, goosey. I know what I saw. And it sure didn't start out *RUJ FGTPO RUJ'SQ*. Nothing repeated and there wasn't an apostrophe. I don't even think the first word was three letters."

Sherry, who'd been preparing a sarcastic reply, instead blinked at her aunt. "You saw *this* on Raymond's laptop?"

47

A BLOCK FROM RAYMOND'S HOUSE, CORA PULLED THE TOYOTA to the curb and killed the lights.

Sherry, peering out the window, said, "The crime-scene ribbon's still up."

"Of course it is. There's no one living there to take it down."

"Don't the police usually do that?"

"The cops are busy. They got this new case to crack."

"That's why they didn't take the ribbon down?"

"Stands to reason."

"If we're not breaking into a crime scene, why park here? Why don't you pull right up to the house?"

"Sherry. Sweetie. Dennis and Brenda are staying across the street. So are Brenda's parents. There's no reason to involve them in this."

"*This?*" Sherry raised her eyebrows. "Seldom has a demonstrative pronoun been used with such reckless abandon."

"I beg your pardon?"

"The *this* you don't want to involve them in is probably broad enough to include everything in the penal code."

"You're starting to sound like Becky Baldwin."

"Bite your tongue."

Cora and Sherry got out of the car and crept down the street, keeping in the shadows. There were two cars parked in front of the B&B, Dennis's rental and the Wallensteins' Mercedes. And the lights in the house were on.

Cora detoured across the street, found herself in front of the Dirksons' house. The porch swing was empty. The house was dark, except for a dim light from one of the rooms in the back. Cora could imagine Jack Dirkson sitting in the dark with the TV on, smoking dope, and having the worst trip of his life.

"Okay," Sherry said, joining her. "Do we take the crime-scene ribbon down?"

"Not our job."

"I thought you said the owner of the house would."

"We don't own the house."

Cora went up the steps, ducked under the ribbon, tried the door. It was locked.

"Gonna open it?" Sherry said.

"There's a problem."

"What's that?"

"I don't have the key."

"Is that right? I don't recall you mentioning that."

"It didn't come up."

"You said we weren't breaking in because it was your house. You didn't mention you didn't have a key to your house."

"You set such store on details."

"This is not a detail."

"It will be."

Cora reached into her floppy, drawstring purse, came out with a gun.

"Aunt Cora!"

"Shhh."

Cora stepped up to the front window, gripped the gun by the barrel, smashed a pane of glass with the butt. She reached in, undid the lock, and raised the window.

"Well, that's a relief," Sherry said. "I thought you were going to shoot your way in."

"Are we attracting any interest?"

"Not that I can see."

"Good. Let's go."

Cora brushed the glass off the sill and climbed through the window. Sherry was right behind.

"Can we risk a light?" Sherry asked.

"Not here. We can in the study. The window's in the back."

Cora led Sherry through the foyer, past the door to the living room, and into the study.

"Okay. Close the door and I'll hit the light."

Cora groped on the desk, switched on the lamp.

The little laptop sat closed in the middle of the desk.

"Oh," Sherry said. "It's a Dell."

"What's the matter? Can't you use it?"

Sherry gave Cora a look, elbowed her away, and sat at the desk. Sherry raised the top, switched the computer on. "Hmmm. Simple dial-up modem. You can't use the phone while you're on-line."

"Yeah, yeah," Cora said impatiently. "What about the code?"

"The machine's gotta boot up."

"And that takes time?"

"Didn't you ever turn a computer on?"

"Why would I?"

"You're an anachronism," Sherry told her.

"Whatever," Cora grumbled. "All the technology in the world, and they can't design a machine that just turns on."

"Is there another computer in the house?"

"Why? This is the one we want."

"Yeah, but is there another?"

"No. Why?"

"This one is networked."

"It's what?"

"It has a wireless network adapter. So it could be part of a system, if you had more than one machine."

"Well, we don't. Maybe he did in San Diego."

"I suppose."

Icons filled the screen.

"That's it!" Cora said. "That little notebook!"

"Got it."

Sherry clicked on the icon.

The notebook page filled the screen.

DADTT DIHNA NERMR OUFSH UCEGE DEORY OPOAA NBNEP IANSU RNNNW HATED NIDOO EFVLE ISARO SASOE ATUPA RPEHZ RNETM LIOWB WTEWN OFMNO LTOEA KTAAR

"That's it," Cora said. "See? It's not at all the same."

"It sure isn't," Sherry said. "Wow, that's amazing."

"What?"

"It's a cipher."

"Right, and we gotta crack it. Come on, come on. Print a copy."

"That's a problem."

"Why?"

"There's no printer."

"No printer?" Cora was indignant. "How can there be no printer?"

"It's a laptop. It would have to be connected to a printer. You would have to have a printer, and connect it to the printer. Otherwise there's no printer."

"Don't talk down to me."

"Well, how do you want me to say it? There is no printer. Unless there's one someplace in the house. Did Raymond take the laptop into another room to print things out?"

"If he had, don't you think I'd have mentioned it?" Cora said sarcastically. "So, how do we print this?"

"The traditional method. A pad and a pen."

"With my handwriting? Fat chance. Can you do it?"

"I'd rather not."

"Sherry—"

"But I don't have to. I can simply go on-line and e-mail it to myself."

"You're not on-line?"

"Of course not. I gotta dial up."

Sherry opened the screen, clicked on CONNECT. Lights flashed and the numbers beeped as the modem dialed.

Cora watched with increasing impatience.

"It's a slow modem," Sherry explained.

There came the sound of a busy signal.

Sherry reached to click CONNECT again.

Cora grabbed her arm. "Aw, the hell with it."

Sherry looked at her in surprise. "You don't want the code?"

"Of course I do."

Cora switched the computer off, closed the lid, unplugged the modem and the power cord, and stuck the laptop under her arm. "Let's vamoose," she said.

48

CORA RIPPED THE PAGE OUT OF SHERRY'S PRINTER. "ALL RIGHT, let me at it!"

Sherry's lips twitched. "You're going to crack the code?"

"Why not? I solved the other ones. So maybe I had a little help. But I know how to do it. Cracking a code is not like solving a damn crossword puzzle. It's just substituting letters. I can do that all day."

"It's a little harder than that."

"Oh, don't be a killjoy. Hang on, and let me plug in the salutation."

Cora squinted at the page:

```
DADTT DIHNA NERMR OUFSH UCEGE DEORY OPOAA NBNEP IANSU
RNNNW HATED NIDOO EFVLE ISARO SASOE ATUPA RPEHZ RNETM
LIOWB WTEWN OFMNO LTOEA KTAAR
```

"Hey! Wait a minute! *DADTT* can't be *Dear*. It's five letters, and there's two *D*'s and two *T*'s!"

"Yes, there are," Sherry said. "You notice anything else, Cora?"

"I sure as hell do! It doesn't say *Puzzle Lady,* either!"

"I was speaking more generally."

"Yeah, well, speak more general English, then. How the hell do you solve this? There're no apostrophes, and no single-letter words! What a rip-off!"

"Do you know *why* there're no single-letter words?"

"Do you want a fat lip?"

"Look at the words, Cora. How many letters are they?"

Cora's eyes widened. "They're *all* five letters!"

"That's right."

"Well, what the hell does that mean?"

"I don't know. It might mean they're not words."

Cora refrained from strangling her niece, but it was a close call. "Could you be more explicit?" she said through clenched teeth.

"Sorry," Sherry said. "What I'm trying to say is, this is a code. I don't know what kind of code. But each grouping of five letters might stand for something. A single letter, perhaps. Or the letters might be real, but rearranged. You see what I mean?"

"Not at all. Can you solve it?"

"I hope so. But it's going to take time. I may have to do some research. This is out of my field of expertise."

"Oddly enough, it's also out of mine. What's the story?"

"In the other cryptograms we had a one-to-one correspondence of substituted letters."

"Say that in Croatian. Maybe I'll understand it then."

"Cora, you're brilliant at solving crimes. Why are you an utter moron when it comes to language?"

"Why are you such a moron when it comes to *tact?* Just spit out what you mean. And never mind this one-on-one corespondent bit. To a woman who's been married as often as I, the word *co-respondent* has a rather nasty aftertaste."

"You know, you're much more adept verbally when you get angry."

"I'm much more adept physically too. You want me to tan your bottom? What's the deal?"

Sherry sighed. "I told you, this is not like the other cryptograms, where one letter equals another, like *A* equals *D*. Instead, it would appear to be a transpositional cipher."

"You got a Code-Breaking for Dummies definition for that?"

"Actually, Code-Breaking for Dummies is exactly right."

"Thanks a heap."

"I mean the code-breaking part. That's exactly what this is. Not a cryptogram, but a *code*. The letters are not substituted. They're merely transposed into a different order."

"How?"

"I don't know. I've never done codes before. But I think it has something to do with columns, and there may be a clue in the fact there's five letters in each word."

"A *clue*? Jesus Christ, can you solve this or not?"

"I don't know. I gotta look some stuff up on the Internet."

"What stuff?"

"Transpositional ciphers. The Enigma code."

"The *Enigma* code? That's World War Two, isn't it?"

"Right. It's the code the Germans used. It took the Allies nearly a year to break it."

Cora groaned, and fumbled in her purse. "You sure know how to build up a person's confidence." She pulled out a crumpled pack of cigarettes. It was empty. "Damn!" She crumpled it tighter, hurled it in the vague direction of the wastebasket. "Well, come on. Get crackin'."

"I could do a lot better if I were able to concentrate. Committing grand larceny at the scene of a homicide makes me anxious. I don't do my best work."

"Okay," Cora said. "Division of labor. You solve the code, I'll get the smokes."

49

"CORA! CORA!"

Cora Felton was ripping the cellophane off the pack of cigarettes she'd just purchased at the Route 9 convenience store. She glanced up to discover the plump form of Harvey Beerbaum trotting past the gas pumps toward her car. Cora had to stop herself from making a face. Harvey might mean well, but he was truly annoying. Cora didn't need to hear him apologize one more time for not having cared for her defunct intended. She hoped to God that wasn't what Harvey wanted.

It was.

"I've been trying to talk to you," he said, "but you're always so busy, so busy. I understand, of course, but it's so frustrating to carry the burden around and not be able to set it down."

Cora sucked in her breath. She had half a mind to tell Harvey that it was *her* burden that was being toted here, and he could jolly well not add to it, thank you very much. Instead, she tore open the pack of cigarettes and fired one up. She took a drag, leaned against her car door, and prepared herself to supply the appropriate nods and "uh-huh"s.

"I . . . just didn't want you to hear it from somebody else," Harvey was saying. "You know how things get distorted. It's like the telephone game. A word gets changed here or there, and before you know it the whole meaning is lost."

Cora, on whom the whole meaning of Harvey's explanation was *already* lost, nodded sagely, took a deep drag on her cigarette, and made a conscious effort not to look at her watch.

"I can't understand why no one's spoken to me," Harvey continued. "I keep waiting for someone to speak to me, but no one does. So when I see you avoiding me—"

"I'm not avoiding you, Harvey."

"Well, you're not talking to me, either. I would have thought you'd have come to talk to me."

"And why would I do that, Harvey? So you and Raymond didn't get along. Big deal. It's not like you *did* anything."

Harvey's eyes shifted.

The blood drained out of Cora's face. Suddenly she felt lightheaded. It couldn't be. It simply couldn't be. *Please,* Cora thought. *Don't let it be.*

But it was.

Cora knew instantly. There was no mistaking what she'd just seen. She was too good an interrogator. It was what she'd trained herself to look for. The guilty reaction.

But Harvey?

Not Harvey.

Never Harvey.

Cora hung on to her cigarette as if it were a lifeline. Hoped she didn't look as overwhelmed as she felt. But why shouldn't she? First Dennis, then Aaron, then Harvey. Time was out of joint. Nothing was as it seemed.

Could Harvey really be a killer?

Cora said evenly, "Get in my car, Harvey."

He gaped at her.

"You want to talk to me, get in the car."

He gawked a moment, then moved to comply. He made his way around the back of her Toyota.

Cora took one last drag, and tossed her cigarette away. She eased the door open, slid into the front seat.

There. At least she could sit down, keep her balance. She hefted her drawstring purse into her lap, felt the weight of her gun in it. The incongruity of it overwhelmed her. Even without being a linguist, Cora knew the words *gun* and *Harvey* didn't belong in the same sentence.

There came a knock on the window. Harvey's door was locked. Cora reached for the master lock, clicked all buttons open. Harvey slid into the passenger seat, closed the door.

"All right," he said. "What did you want to talk to me about?"

It was all Cora could do to keep from laughing. "Harvey, you've been trying to talk to me for days. Here's your chance."

"Oh." Harvey began to fidget.

"Okay," Cora said. "I'll supply the topic of conversation. You're trying to apologize to me. You wonder why no one's wanted to talk to you. At the suggestion you didn't do anything to Raymond, you nearly plotz. You wanna tell me what you *did* do?"

"Oh, my."

"That's a start."

"You mean no one's come forward at all?"

"Not to me. I can't speak for Chief Harper."

"Oh."

"So what is it someone might tell Chief Harper about you?"

Harvey took a breath, then blurted, "I was there."

"You were where, Harvey?"

"You mean no one's told you?"

Cora gritted her teeth. "Harvey, I have a very low patience threshold right now. If you stall one more time, I'll have to mutilate you. Now, assume no one's told me squat. So you tell me. You were where?"

"At Raymond's."

"When?"

"Oh, God!"

"That bad, huh? Better tell me about it."

"It's embarrassing. . . ."

Cora snorted. "If embarrassing is your only problem, you've got it made."

Harvey still couldn't meet her eyes. "Well, you were all at the Country Kitchen. . . . Having some sort of celebration. Because of the nuptials. I guess it was an engagement celebration. Anyway, you were all laughing a lot and talking rather loud. And then this one woman said something about how she was glad you weren't marrying me. Do you remember that?"

Cora did indeed. As she recalled, the *something about* included the phrase *nerdy little puzzle guy*. "Go on."

"I was shocked. Humiliated. There was no call for such an insult, but she'd said it, and I'd heard it. And some of the women at the table could see that I'd heard. Which was even worse. I turned around and walked out."

"Harvey, what did you do?"

"I drove out there. Where he was staying. Just as I was about to get out of my car, a kid came out the front door of Raymond's house and hurried across the street."

"When you say *a kid*—?"

"I don't mean a kid. I mean the young man. The bridegroom. The one they arrested."

"You saw Dennis Pride come out of Raymond's house?"

"That's right."

"How did he look?"

"Furtive. Guilty. As if he'd done something egregiously wrong. He ran directly in front of my car."

"Did he see you?"

"I don't believe so. His mind was clearly elsewhere. He ran right into his B&B."

"What did you do then, Harvey?"

"I exited my car, crossed the street, and rang the bell. There was no answer. Then I noticed the door was open. In his hurry to get out, the boy hadn't closed it all the way. I pushed it open and went in."

"What then?"

"I called out Raymond's name and got no answer. I called again, louder. The foyer was small and there was a door leading to the adjoining room. I ventured in and there he was."

Ventured, Cora thought. She said, "What do you mean, there he was?"

"Lying on the floor. Dead. With a knife in his heart."

"What did you do?" Cora said it quietly, knowing he needed a prompt, but not wanting to frighten him.

"I was terrified. I don't know why. Maybe because of the emotions I'd experienced just before I went there. Or perhaps because of the women mocking me in the restaurant. Or because I'd never seen anything like that before. Such a horrible thing. And I didn't know what to do. I knew I shouldn't touch anything. And I don't have a cell phone. So I ran out, got in my car, and drove off. To find a phone. To call."

Cora frowned. "But you didn't call."

"No."

"Why not?"

"As I drove away, I glimpsed that bizarre woman. There on the veranda. Sitting on the swing. Regarding me."

"Daffodil Dirkson saw you go into Raymond's house?" Cora translated.

"That's correct."

"It was just her? Her husband wasn't there?"

"No, just her. Alone on the porch swing. Smoking a cigarette."

"You're sure she saw you?"

"How could she not? Consequently, I'll confess, I panicked. I was convinced she'd identify me and the police would apprehend me. And the women in the restaurant would all say I had a motive. The bottom line is, I didn't call."

"So what did you do?"

"I drove back to Raymond's house. To see if anyone had found the corpse and reported it. If they had, I could keep quiet. If they hadn't, I didn't know what I was going to do. My mind was awhirl. But I had to know. So I drove back. Before I got there a vehicle raced by me, going quite recklessly. I drove along behind, saw it come to a stop. You emerged from it, followed the boy and his young bride into the house. I figured the boy must have honored his civic responsibilities and summoned the police and that somehow you'd beaten them there. Anyway, there was clearly no longer any necessity for me to call the authorities.

"I was going to get out of the car, but Daffodil and her husband were on the porch next door, and I didn't want her to see me. I don't know why. She'd *already* seen me. I knew she'd tell the police. Or tell you. I don't know why she didn't."

It occurred to Cora the woman might have tried.

Harvey wrung his hands. He looked absolutely miserable. "It's been driving me mad. I don't know what to do." He peered at her with anxious eyes. "Should I tell the authorities?"

Cora patted him on the cheek.

"Not just yet."

50

Cora got home to find Sherry cutting out strips of paper on the dining room table.

"What are you doing?" Cora asked.

"Breaking the code. What's with you? You look like you've seen a ghost."

"Nah, just Harvey Beerbaum."

"Oh?"

Cora filled Sherry in on her talk with the amorous cruciverbalist.

Sherry was amazed. "Harvey found Raymond? And didn't say anything?"

"He was going to. He was just too late."

"And he was going to confront Raymond? I wouldn't have thought the little guy had it in him."

"Me neither."

"Cora. You're not getting gooey-eyed over Harvey now, are you?"

"Don't be *absurd*. But it's flattering to have a man fight for you. So what's with the paper strips?"

"I wanna try something. There's a hundred and fifteen letters in the cipher."

"Go on!"

"Not different letters. I mean total. A hundred fifteen in all. Now, if there were five columns, then there would be twenty-three letters in each. See what I mean?"

"Sure. And Albert Einstein and I dreamed up E = Mc² together."

"Okay, look. This is lined notebook paper. I cut it so there's exactly twenty-three lines. Now I'm cutting it into five strips with twenty-three spaces in each. Now, if I lay them out next to each other, they would form a diagramless crossword puzzle with five spaces across by twenty-three spaces down."

Cora groaned. "Does it *have* to be a crossword puzzle?"

"It *isn't* a crossword puzzle. It just *looks* like one. Now what we do is we take the strips and we copy the letters onto them."

"Why? Oh, never mind. Just do it."

"Okay," Sherry said. "So we copy the cipher down the strips, like so."

D
A
D
T
T
D
I
H
N
A
N
E
R
M

R
O
U
F
S
H
U
C
E

"Up and down?" Cora said. "Why are you writing it up and down?"

"If I'm right, doing it vertically is the way to solve this. Now, the next line."

Sherry continued onto a second strip of paper.

G
E
D
E
O
R
Y
O
P
O
A
A
N
B
N
E
P
I
A
N
S
U
R

"And so on," Sherry said.

She continued to write out the rest of the message on the other three strips. When she was finished, she had five strips laid out on the table in front of her.

D	G	N	O	O
A	E	N	S	W
D	D	N	A	B
T	E	W	S	W
T	O	H	O	T
D	R	A	E	E
I	Y	T	A	W
H	O	E	T	N
N	P	D	U	O
A	O	N	P	F
N	A	I	A	M
E	A	D	R	N
R	N	O	P	O
M	B	O	E	L
R	N	E	H	T
O	E	F	Z	O
U	P	V	R	E
F	I	L	N	A
S	A	E	E	K
H	N	I	T	T
U	S	S	M	A
C	U	A	L	A
E	R	R	I	R

"Still gibberish," Cora said.

"Yeah. Now we play with it."

"How?"

"Easy," Sherry said.

She began swapping the positions of the strips. Soon she had this configuration:

G	O	O	D	N
E	W	S	A	N
D	B	A	D	N
E	W	S	T	W
O	T	O	T	H
R	E	E	D	A
Y	W	A	I	T
O	N	T	H	E
P	O	U	N	D
O	F	P	A	N
A	M	A	N	I
A	N	R	E	D
N	O	P	R	O
B	L	E	M	O
N	T	H	R	E
E	O	Z	O	F
P	E	R	U	V
I	A	N	F	L
A	K	E	S	E
N	T	T	H	I
S	A	M	U	S
U	A	L	C	A
R	R	I	E	R

Cora's mouth fell open. "It's words!"

"Sure it is," Sherry said. "See how it was done, Cora? The message was written in five columns, the columns were mixed, and the letters were written down in groups of five."

"Never mind that. What does it say?"

"Let's see: 'Good news and bad news. Two to three day wait on the pound of Panamanian red. No problem on three oz of Peruvian flake. Sent this A.M. usual carrier.' "

Cora's face was hard. "I know what you're thinking."

Sherry couldn't meet her eyes. "Aunt Cora—"

"No. Raymond may have had the message, but Dennis had the drugs."

"Dennis *found* the drugs. Raymond's fingerprints were all over the bag they were in."

"Dennis had the cryptograms, Sherry."

"Not this one."

"We don't know that."

"Oh? Was it in the packet the cops found? Funny no one mentioned it. Funny no one brought it to you to solve."

"They may not have noticed. *I* didn't notice."

"It's a completely different kind of code. Dennis couldn't have done this."

"He could if someone taught him. How hard is this, if you know the secret?"

"Oh, come on. Why would he use *two* codes?"

"Don't be silly. He *wants* the other cryptograms solved. They're warnings. But he doesn't want anyone cracking his code about drugs."

"It's not his code. He didn't have it on his laptop, Raymond did."

"And wound up dead."

"Oh, come on!"

"I'm sorry, Sherry. But if Dennis made up the other cryptograms, it's a good bet he made up this one."

"But there's no proof that he made up the other ones. Aside from the fact he had them. And they could have been planted. You went over them yourself. You couldn't find anything. Could you?"

"No."

"Cora, I know you don't want to think badly of Raymond. But Dennis didn't send the cryptograms. And Dennis didn't kill Raymond. I know it."

"Oh, yeah?" Cora said. "Then who did?"

51

THE BAND WAS PLAYING WHEN CORA PULLED UP TO THE CURB. She could imagine the bed-and-breakfast owner tearing out her hair. Actually, the Tune Freaks weren't playing that loud, perhaps having the good sense to tone it down after dark. The sound seeping from the garage was relatively restrained. It was also relatively melodic. Compared to the noise she'd heard the other day, this music seemed to have a tune. In addition, the singer was not noticeably off pitch.

It was also intelligible. As Cora neared the garage, she found she could make out the words.

> "He's taking your heart
> And he's tearing it apart
> If you stay with this man
> You must pay

"While there's still time
Turn around on a dime
Walk away, don't look back
Walk away."

Not the most original lyrics in the world, and the tune was rather familiar, too, but at least it *had* a tune, a rather upbeat, bouncy tune, in contrast to the heartbreak theme of the lyrics. All in all, it was a vast improvement over what Cora had heard the other day. She wondered if just turning the amplifiers down could make that much difference.

Instead of knocking on the door, Cora walked around the garage. A window on the side wall led to a tool closet, but through the open closet door she could see the boys rehearsing. Actually, from that angle she could see the drums but not the drummer, the edge of the keyboard, the bass player, and the lead singer and lead guitar.

The lead guitar was Razor.

The lead singer was Dennis Pride.

Dennis stood at the microphone in short hair, white shirt, and tan slacks, a preppy in the midst of punk rockers, a Tune Freak who was not a freak and who could actually carry a tune.

Dennis, back with the band. After all his protestations. After all his good intentions. After all his promises.

Did Brenda know?

Of course not.

There he was, the lying, scheming weasel, showing his true colors again.

Cora couldn't wait to hear what he'd say about this.

And then it all fell into place. Dennis sneaking off all the time. Running out on Brenda. Ditching her parents. Disappearing for hours at a time. Not being able to tell where he'd been.

Of course he couldn't. The son of a bitch was going back to his band. Just as soon as he married Brenda on the promise of working for her dad. How long would that last? A week? A month? Before he quit the job. Before Brenda's loft became a rehearsal space. Before his wife became just one of the groupies he saw when he happened through town. Nothing more than a place to crash, a wealthy dad—and a tie to Sherry.

With a shock, Cora knew how long it would all last. Till the wedding. *At* the wedding. As soon as they were legally married.

Dennis was going to perform at his wedding.

The slime.

The incredible slime.

Cora couldn't wait to tell him off.

As she reached for the handle of the garage door, Cora could hear Dennis singing inside to another girl of his dreams.

"Walk away, don't look back
Walk away."

Cora felt like she'd been punched in the stomach. She could barely catch her breath.

She heard the words again.

"Walk away, don't look back
Walk away."

Cora did.

52

"You gotta be there for Sherry."

Aaron looked exasperated. "I am there for Sherry. I don't know what more you want me to do."

"I'm here to tell you."

"Well, you picked a bad time. We go to press in half an hour, and I'm not done with my story."

"What's your lead? *Ace Reporter Conked on Head, Can't Recall Crime?*"

"That's not funny."

"No, it's not. I assume someone else is writing that story."

"The lead story, yes. I've been asked for a personal account."

"Are you doing it?"

"I'm trying."

"I wouldn't. Not without a lawyer's advice. Too bad Becky Baldwin's got a big-time conflict of interest."

"Yeah," Aaron said curtly. He turned back to his computer.

"Look," Cora persisted. "I don't know what you think you

saw, but if you wanna blame Sherry for the fact Dennis is harassing her, that's probably the dumbest thing you ever did in your life."

"Harassing?" Aaron spun his chair around. "They were having *drinks*. She was cooking him *dinner*."

"Cooking *me* dinner, moron. The jerk barged in and helped himself to a drink. What do you expect her to do? Throw him out physically? A guy who beat her up? There all alone. Playing with dynamite. Praying it won't go off. Then you barge in, make things worse, storm out in a jealous snit, and leave her alone with him, and *you're* mad at *her*? You're lucky she didn't wind up in the emergency room. You'd never be able to forgive yourself."

His gaze faltered. "Damn it."

"But that's over now. We've moved on. The point is, Sherry's gonna need a lot of help, sympathy, and understanding. And it can't come from me. Not the way things are shaping up. That doesn't leave many options. So you better wise up and be there for her."

"Why? Why won't you be there for her?"

"Because I'll be busy catching Raymond's killer."

"Oh." Aaron couldn't keep the lack of enthusiasm from his voice.

"I know what you think of him," Cora said. "And you're wrong. You didn't know Raymond like I did. I know what you heard about him. Just because a reporter tells you something doesn't mean it's true."

"Yeah."

"What does that mean?"

Aaron grimaced. "There's more coming in all the time, and it just gets worse and worse. Raymond Harstein was busted three years ago for selling heroin. Never did time. Pled guilty, suspended sentence."

Cora set her jaw. "So?"

"Only one way that happens. He rats. He rolls over on his friends. Names names. They go down, he walks. Goes right back to dealing."

"You know that for a fact?"

"Come on, Cora. Dennis stole Raymond's cocaine. The bag had Raymond's fingerprints all over it. Believe me, if Raymond hadn't been killed and you'd married him, he'd have been busted before too long. You'd have been visiting him in a maximum security prison."

"Is that right?"

"Yes, it is. According to my source in San Diego. The narcs don't like it when a pusher gets busted, gets off by turning in his friends, then starts dealing again. You do that, they go out of their way to hunt you down."

"Oh." Cora sighed. It was a deep, heavy sigh that shook her from head to toe.

"Are you all right?" Aaron asked.

Cora looked at him, smiled sadly. "No, Aaron, I'm not. Actually, it'll probably be some time before I'm all right again."

"You want some water or something? Anything I can do for you?"

"Be a friend to Sherry."

"Besides that."

"That's a lot. But I think you'll find it easy to do."

Cora put her head in her hands, closed her eyes.

Aaron stopped himself from asking her again if she was all right. Instead, he sat there helplessly, wondering what to do.

Cora raised her head, opened her eyes. "Your source in San Diego. Can I talk to him?"

"Probably not a good idea—"

"Hey, I'm not going to hurt him. He's in San Diego. I just wanna talk. On the phone."

"It's not gonna help you any. It will just make you feel worse."

"How could I feel worse? Please."

Aaron sighed. "Aw, hell." He looked up the number, wrote it down. "Here you go. Anything else I can do?"

"No," Cora said. She folded the paper, stuck it in her purse. "As a matter of fact, yes, there is something you could do. You got the whole town on your Rolodex?"

"Just about. Why?"

"Can you do me a big favor and look up the listings for the local real-estate agents?"

53

Knauer Realty was a one-woman operation, so when Judy Douglas Knauer was out showing a property, there was no one there. Cora arrived at the office to find the plastic hands of the clock on Judy's back at sign set for one-thirty. At least Cora didn't have to wait outside. The back at sign was not on the front door, but propped up on Judy's desk. The door was unlocked. There were chairs and magazines. Visitors were clearly welcome to hang out and read.

As a New Yorker, Cora found this hard to relate to. When Judy came in the door, Cora had to resist the impulse to act casual, like she hadn't jimmied the door open and broken in.

Judy wasn't sure how to play it, either. Her sales pitch was generally chipper, as befitted a rental agent. In light of the terrible tragedy in Cora's life, she knew that wouldn't really do. Cora could practically see the poor woman's mind whirling, trying to formulate an I'm-sorry-your-man's-dead-would-you-like-to-rent-a-smaller-house-instead spiel.

Cora forestalled this with an allusion to the Daffodil Dirkson incident, and the two women were soon off happily discussing the second murder.

It was some time before Judy got around to asking, "Why are you here?"

"I was hoping you could help me," wily Cora said.

Judy's eyes gleamed with excitement. "How?"

"The B&B Dennis rented. Mrs. Trumble's place. I wonder if that was through you."

"Yes, as a matter of fact it was. Why?"

"Can you tell me about it?"

Judy grimaced. "I really hate to talk about a client. . . ."

"Of course," Cora said. "But real-estate agents don't have the same privileges as doctors and lawyers, do they? I mean, you can't get on the witness stand and say 'I'm sorry, I won't answer that, I'm a real-estate agent.' "

"No, of course not," Judy said. "Still . . ."

"If you don't want to discuss it, I quite understand," Cora said.

That did it. Judy fell all over herself trying to backtrack.

"I didn't say I wouldn't discuss it, of course, I'll discuss it, I mean, it's just you and me, and we're not in court or anything. If we were in court, I guess it would be different, but that's not what we're talking about here, we're just talking."

"Yeah, we're just talking," Cora agreed, with astounding patience. "So tell me about Dennis."

"Well, he said he was staying in town at a bed-and-breakfast, but he didn't like it. He'd rented it through another agency." Judy snorted. "Hillside Agency. I'm not at all surprised. Gave him a room that didn't work out. Typical." She flushed. "But don't quote me on that."

"What did he want from you?" Cora prompted.

"A room, of course. But not just any room. Once bitten, twice shy. The guy's fussy beyond belief. Rejected offhand the first dozen places I showed him."

"You took him to a dozen places?"

"No, no. In the catalogue. I'm showing him houses, and he finds something wrong with all of 'em. I show him one on Piper Street."

"The one he rented?"

Judy shook her head. "No. He looked at the one I showed him, he said he liked the street but not the house, did I have any other houses on the street. I sure did. I mean, some of them are rented, some of them don't rent rooms, some of them are for sale, some of them rent the entire house, which he didn't want. I showed him on a Bakerhaven street map—this is rented, this is rented, this is a B&B. Then we looked 'em up, and came up with the one he's staying in."

"You took him to the B&B?"

"For a room rental? Not on your life. Not unless it's a very slow day. I just book the room and take my commission."

"This wasn't a slow day?"

"It was, but I didn't have to go. I called Mrs. Trumble and sent him over."

"Dennis picked the B&B out of a catalogue?"

"No, like I say, he picked it off the map. I was pointing out houses, I said this one's a B&B, he said do they have any rooms, so I called Mrs. Trumble."

"Could I see the map?"

Judy frowned. "What for?"

Cora sighed, smiled. "Really, just to feel like I'm doing something. You know, life goes on, and all that. A lot of what I'm doing is just busywork, but it's better than sitting on my duff."

"Ain't that the truth."

Judy went to the bookcase, selected a huge album from the

bottom shelf. She flopped it down on a table, began leafing through pages of street maps.

Cora, looking over her shoulder, saw each two-foot-square map covered about three blocks of a street. The houses were designated by perimeter line drawings containing the street numbers.

Judy hit a map for Piper Street, looked, turned another page, and referred to a master list. "There," she said, pointing. "That's the Trumble place. Right across the street from Raymond's house. Of course, you know that."

There was a pause. Judy cleared her throat. "I'm sorry. I really don't know who to ask. If the police are finished with Raymond's house now, what's going to happen to it? I mean, you're not actually staying there, are you?"

By the end of her spiel, Judy was blushing bright red.

It didn't help when Cora peered at her sideways and asked, "You want to rent the house?"

"I don't mean to be insensitive. I just have a business to run. And if the house is vacant . . . I know the owner will want to rent it out again."

"That's one of your houses?"

"Well, it's not *my* house. I'm the broker for it."

"Raymond rented it through you?"

"Of course he did."

"You rented the house to Raymond *and* the room to Dennis?"

Judy seemed taken aback by the tone of the question. "I assure you, there's nothing sinister about that. I rented both places. I also rented the Dirkson house. I broker most of the property on that street."

"Oh, really?" Cora said. For the first time in a long while, her eyes were shining. "Tell me about it."

54

CORA DROVE PAST THE CONGREGATIONAL CHURCH. THE YELLOW crime-scene ribbon was down, but the VW microbus was still parked in front. Apparently Jack Dirkson had no way to get it, and no one had thought to bring it to him.

Cora wondered if he cared.

There was a black circle drawn on the back of the microbus. As Cora drew near, she saw the circle had an upside-down Y inside, or rather a perpendicular diameter with two extra radii in an upside-down V. It was a peace sign, the black-and-white symbol college kids in the '60s had worn on buttons. Someone, Cora recalled, had come out with a gag button that looked like a peace sign, but had been subtly altered with little blips for engines to resemble a B-29 bomber, with the motto DROP IT. The emblem had enraged many of the hard-core peaceniks. At the time, Cora had merely found it funny.

It seemed strange to see a peace sign after all these years. Cora

290 / PARNELL HALL

couldn't recall the last time she had. But there it was, adorning the back of the Dirksons' microbus as Cora drove by.

DROP IT.

Cora slammed on the brakes, fishtailed to a stop. The front of the microbus was in her rearview mirror. There was no peace sign there, just two huge sunflowers with headlights for centers. The VW emblem looked remarkably like a peace sign, but was merely the nucleus for a series of psychedelic sun effects.

Cora threw the Toyota into reverse, backed up past the microbus.

And there it was. The rear of the bus with the huge peace sign. It wasn't a bomber. It didn't say DROP IT. But if it had, Cora could have seen it.

Cora frowned.

She sat and stared, transfixed by the symbol from her distant youth.

55

Jack Dirkson's eyes were as red as roses. Cora wondered if it was from grief or drugs. Jack had taken a long time to answer his door. He clung to it now as if for support, and made no move to invite Cora in.

"Yeah?" he demanded. His smoker's rasp was more pronounced than usual. When he spoke, the odor of marijuana was overpowering.

"Sorry to bother you," Cora said, "but I have your van."

That seemed more than his brain could process. "My what?"

"Your microbus. I had the police bring it back."

Cora stepped aside, gestured to the driveway where Dan Finley stood next to the VW microbus.

Jack Dirkson's bloodshot eyes widened in alarm at the sight of the uniformed officer standing next to the psychedelic vehicle. "The cops!" he exclaimed.

"It's all right," Cora said. "Dan Finley just drove it over. I wanted to, but they wouldn't release it to me. I followed Dan in my car. I'm driving him back. Anyway, here's your keys." Cora dangled them in front of his face. "I thought you'd rather I gave them to you than have a police officer knock on your door."

Jack reached up, took the keys.

"And while you're at it, take a look at this." Cora shoved a metal clipboard into his hands.

Jack gawked at the clipboard. "What's this?"

Cora pointed. "Look."

There was an 8-x-10 color photograph attached to the clipboard. The picture was of five long-haired young men looking at the camera. All seemed self-conscious, in the manner of amateurs attempting a professional pose.

Jack frowned. "Who's that?"

"Do you recognize any of those men?"

"No."

Jack thrust the clipboard back at Cora. She made no move to take it.

"Look again. You know at least one of them. There. The one in the middle. Take a look at him."

Jack shrugged helplessly. "Don't know him."

"Yes, you do. He just has shorter hair. That's Dennis Pride. Our young murder suspect. That's his band. You've seen them too. They were hanging around here the night Raymond was killed. The question is, have you ever seen any of them before? Not necessarily on the day of the murder, but anytime at all. Have you seen any of these guys prowling around?"

"Oh, wow."

"Have you?"

"No."

Jack shoved the clipboard back in Cora's hands and slammed the door.

Cora stuck her foot in. Luckily, the door was not that solid, and her shoe was hard. The pain was tolerable.

"Hold on," Cora said. "Look, I know how you feel. I'm probably the only one in town who does. We've both lost someone dear to us. I don't know about you, but I intend to do something about it. I would think you'd want to do something about it too."

Jack took a deep breath. He looked totally overwhelmed. "Aw, lady—"

"You say you never saw anyone in the photo. Maybe you didn't. But maybe you did. Dennis was in the photo, and you didn't know him."

"He had long hair."

"Right. And maybe you saw one of these other guys with his hair tucked up under a hat. The point is, it's a lot different seeing someone in person and seeing him in a photo."

"So?"

"Dennis is getting married this Saturday at the Congregational church. I need you to do me a favor."

"What's that?"

"Go to his wedding."

56

IT WAS A GORGEOUS DAY. THE SUN WAS OUT, THE SKY WAS BLUE, with no threat of rain. The white fluffy clouds looked ornamental, like the frosting on a wedding cake.

The actual wedding cake was a sight to behold. It was not from Cushman's Bake Shop, of course, but had been supplied by a specialty wedding shop in New York City. It was truly awesome. Ten tiers high on a three-foot stand, it dwarfed the bride and groom, and would have to be lowered before the bride cut the first slice.

The wedding cake was in the church, but would be served on the village green, where the caterers had set up a huge tent to house the wedding reception. The tables were set to feed five hundred, but there were more tables and settings on hand if needed.

Inside the church, only those with invitations were guaranteed a seat. Otherwise, it was catch-as-catch-can. Uninvited wedding guests spilled out the front doors and crowded together on the steps. Those who wanted to sit had come early. With the spectacular tragedies surrounding the proceeding, the wedding was the hottest ticket in town. As a result, it took only two ditzy women queuing up on the church steps the night before to trigger a stampede. At least a dozen townsfolk sat in line overnight, just as if they were teenagers and the church was showing a preview of the latest Star Wars movie. In return for their vigil, those zealots were seated in the third, fourth, and fifth rows, on the aisle, so as not to miss a thing.

The Reverend Kimble stood at the altar, checking the bookmarks in his Bible. Not that he hadn't performed hundreds of wedding ceremonies—still, it would never do to lose his place.

To the left of the altar, Dennis Pride stood with his best man. Dennis looked quite handsome in his tux. Razor looked quite uncomfortable in his. Razor's hair was tied back in a ponytail.

To the right of the altar, maid of honor Sherry Carter stood with the other bridesmaids, none of whom were Bakerhaven residents, and all of whom had been squeezed into sugar-pink gowns Brenda's mother had supplied. The out-of-town bridesmaids were young, passably attractive, and having a great time.

Sherry Carter was gorgeous and very worried.

The bridegroom was paying far more attention to her than was appropriate. Nor could she imagine him letting a little thing like a wedding ring dissuade him. The idea he might be marrying her friend to get at her didn't seem farfetched at all.

Sherry looked out over the pews.

Wendy Wallenstein sat in the first row. Her husband, of course, stood in the back of the church, waiting to escort the bride. Mrs. Wallenstein was dressed in a golden gown and more jewelry than you'd find in your average pawnshop. Sherry got the impression the woman lived to flash her wealth, and would have let her daughter marry almost anyone, just for the opportunity to show off her money.

Becky Baldwin, attorney for the groom, sat next to jilted puzzle constructor Harvey Beerbaum, whom Cora had unknowingly slighted. That seemed an unlikely pairing, particularly since Becky was unaware of just how valuable a witness Harvey might actually be.

Chief Harper, who no longer had the responsibility of giving Cora away, sat with his wife and daughter. The chief wore his best suit. His hair was slicked down, and his tie was crooked. He looked like he'd rather be practically anywhere else.

Officers Sam Brogan and Dan Finley, also out of uniform, sat on the aisle near the back. Sam looked cranky, but that was the way Sam always looked. Dan looked bright-eyed and eager.

Judy Douglas Knauer, rental agent of the crime scene, sat with her fellow former bridesmaids, Selectman Iris Cooper, general-store owner Lois Greely, and young housewife Amy Cox. The women, who had not been bridesmaids long enough to rate gowns, wore dresses of various pastel hues.

Jack Dirkson had come at Cora's request. The aging hippie sat halfway back in the middle of a row between Mrs. Cushman of Cushman's Bake Shop, and Mrs. Trumble of Trumble's Bed-and-Breakfast. Jack's wife's violent demise was no protection from the two women, who jabbered back and forth across him as if he wasn't even there.

Cora Felton, bride-not-to-be, sat on the aisle in the last pew in the very back of the church, next to best-man-not-to-be Aaron Grant.

Aaron was still rather testy. "You don't have to sit with me," he complained. "I'm quite all right."

"I'm sure you are," Cora told him. "That's not why I had you sit here. I need your help."

"What for?"

"To save my seat."

Cora got up and slipped out the door. The anteroom was

crowded with people, including the father of the bride. Mr. Wallenstein looked smart in his tux. He also looked rather nervous. Cora wondered if that was normal prewedding jitters, or due to the fact his daughter was marrying a murder suspect.

There was no sign of the bride-to-be. Brenda was holed up in the Reverend's office, which had been designated as a changing room, and was either making last-minute preparations or having last-minute doubts. Whatever the case, Brenda wasn't ready. Cora still had time. She pushed her way through the crowd out onto the front steps.

Rick Reed and his camera crew had been barred admission, and were set up on the lawn in order to record the departure of the bride and groom and shoot interviews of all concerned. Rick's spirits brightened at the sight of Cora, then dampened again as she dredged a pack of cigarettes from her purse and proceeded to light up. Cora could practically see his mind racing, weighing his chances of fighting his way through the crowd to get an interview. It was clearly not to be.

Cora looked for cars. All three parking lots were full, not just the church lot, but the county courthouse and the town hall lots as well. And there were cars all around the edge of the village green. But they were all parked. There were no more cars arriving. All the wedding guests were already here.

Cora frowned. She stamped out her cigarette, and ducked back inside the church.

"You went out to smoke?" Aaron said as she sat down.

"Among other things."

"What other things?"

"Praying for a miracle," Cora muttered.

"Huh?"

"Oh, my God, it's starting!"

It was. The church organ had just struck up the unmistakable strains of "Here Comes the Bride."

Down the aisle came Mr. Wallenstein, with his daughter on his arm. Brenda looked lovely. Her white dress rivaled the one Cora had worn for rehearsal. Custom-made, exquisitely tailored, it made Brenda look anything but plump. The silk and lace train of the gorgeous gown streamed out behind her. Her hair was up, her wedding veil in place. Her makeup today was perfect, discreet, understated. Her face was lit up with a radiant smile.

She looked beautiful.

Cora's shoulders heaved in a sigh of compassion.

She felt terrible about what she was about to do.

Brenda reached the altar. Her father handed her off to Dennis, and stepped aside.

Brenda smiled at Sherry Carter, then turned to face the altar.

Dennis smiled at Sherry too. The smile was quick, and Brenda didn't see it. Dennis made sure of that. Then he, too, turned to face the altar.

The Reverend Kimble opened his book.

"Dearly beloved," he intoned. "We are gathered here today to join together Dennis Pride and Brenda Wallenstein in holy matrimony. If there is anyone here who has any reason why these two should not be joined together, let him speak now, or forever hold his peace."

Sherry Carter fought down the urge to cry out, to stop the wedding, to save her friend. With all her heart she wished that someone would.

Cora Felton stood.

Sherry Carter's mouth fell open. The shock of having her wish granted overwhelmed her. Was her aunt really going to speak up?

She was.

"I have a reason," Cora said.

57

THERE WAS A STUNNED REACTION IN THE CHURCH.

The Reverend Kimble, who in his own mind had moved on to the next order of business, froze with his mouth open and his hand raised, as if Cora had just pressed the HOLD button on the VCR.

Dennis and Brenda both glared, Brenda in anger and bewilderment, Dennis in shock and apprehension.

There was a brief time lag, merely an instant, then every head in the church swiveled to look at Cora. With all eyes on her, Cora made her way down the aisle, talking a mile a minute as she went.

"I know, I know," she said. "It's merely a formality. The minister has to ask if anyone has any objections, and no one ever does. But I happen to have some, and, as people who know me know, I'm not the type to forever hold my peace. So I guess I gotta have my say now."

Cora stepped up between the bride and groom and next to the Reverend Kimble. "Okay, Reverend. Where am I supposed to do this? Of course, you don't know, do you, because no one ever does. So why don't I just take your place for the time being. Right here between the happy couple. Dennis. Brenda. Is that okay with you? It probably isn't, but this is the one part of the ceremony where you don't get to choose. Reverend, if you'd like to stand over there on the other side of the bride, I'll let you know when I'm done."

The Reverend Kimble, utterly overwhelmed, gawked openmouthed from bride to groom to Cora, then did as instructed.

"Fine," Cora said, nodding. "Just for the uninitiated, in case there are any, let me bring you up to speed. I'm Cora Felton. This was supposed to be a double wedding, and I was supposed to be Bride Number Two. The reason I'm not is because the other bridegroom was murdered. And this bridegroom, Dennis Pride, has been arrested and charged with the crime." She grimaced. "Now, I know it's not kosher to bring up a bridegroom's police record, but I don't see how I can avoid it. Because this wedding is largely a vote of confidence on the part of the bride's parents that Mr. Pride was in no way responsible for the murder."

Cora frowned, shook her head. "That strikes me as a rather poor basis for a wedding. I would think this marriage was premature, at best."

"Damn it," Brenda fumed. "You're the one who told us to go ahead."

"I know," Cora agreed sweetly, "and it's not the first time I've screwed up. Though usually my mistakes result in *me* getting married. But that's neither here nor there. The point is, your husband-to-be is accused of some rather dastardly deeds. Sending anonymous threats and murdering a couple of people. Neither of which are exactly what one would look for in a prospective bride-groom."

Brenda's father pushed forward. "Have you lost your mind? I know you're distraught. This would have been your wedding too. But there's no excuse for such outlandish behavior. Unless you have proof. Do you have proof? Do you have anything to back up what you just said?"

"That's the problem. I really don't. I don't have anything at all." Cora shook her head. "It's embarrassing, really. Me standing up in front of you, prattling on like a fool, when I just don't have the goods."

"So will you get out of the way and let us get on with it?"

Dennis's tone was most unpleasant. And the phrase he chose to refer to his marriage ceremony, *get on with it,* was unfortunate, at best. Brenda shot him a look. So did her father. Dennis was flustered, which only added to his irritation.

Cora loved it.

It was almost worth looking like such a fool.

"I'm sorry. You do want to 'get on with it,' don't you?" she said, rubbing it in. "I'm sorry to be prolonging things. I'm sure you'd like to rush this through before anyone finds any proof. So I will try to be brief." She frowned. "Let me see, now. Where was I? . . ."

"Den . . . nis! Den . . . nis!"

The shrill sound cut through the hushed air of the church. It was a wonder none of the stained-glass windows shattered. The woman's braying voice made Wendy Wallenstein's sound like a whisper.

To Cora Felton, it was the answer to a prayer.

Not to Sherry.

A chill ran down Sherry's spine. A chill she had not experi-enced in some time. Except last week when Dennis had walked into the Country Kitchen.

In the doorway of the church stood the two last people in the world Sherry Carter wished to see.

The in-laws from hell.

Randy and Gretchen Pride.

Dennis's parents.

58

THE REVEREND KIMBLE, LIKE EVERYONE ELSE IN CHURCH, gawked at the Prides.

Tall and thin, with a nose like the beak of a woodpecker, Gretchen Pride looked like a walking warning against cosmetic surgery. The skin on her face, tight as a drum, raised her eyebrows, lips, and pointed nose to such an extent as to give the impression she was actually a rather short woman, one who had been stretched on a rack into the monstrosity she had become.

Her husband was the exact opposite. A short, pudgy man, on whom every ounce of fat seemed to be doing its best to reach his feet. His stomach spilled over his belt. His jowls hung down like a bulldog's. A very old, very lazy bulldog. Who probably couldn't be bothered to even scratch himself.

The chance of these two incredibly unattractive people producing an offspring as handsome as Dennis had to have been about as likely as winning the Connecticut state lottery.

Gretchen Pride strode down the aisle like a drill sergeant. Her husband waddled behind like a raw recruit. One destined for KP duty.

Gretchen Pride hopped up next to the altar, practically elbowed Cora and the Reverend Kimble aside to get to her son. "Dennis. Whatever is the meaning of this? We could hardly get in the door. It's standing room only, and there're TV crews outside. Apparently you killed someone and you're getting married. Now, what is that all about?"

Dennis was totally taken aback. "Mom! Dad! I didn't kill anyone!"

"Well, I should hope not," Mrs. Pride declared. "That is not the way I brought you up."

Everyone gawked at her, rendered speechless by that monumental understatement.

She glowered at her husband. "Aren't you going to say something?"

"Son—" Randy Pride began dutifully.

"And look who's here," Gretchen Pride sliced in, wheeling on Sherry Carter. "I should have known. I suppose this is all your idea. Can't you leave my son alone? He divorced you, for goodness' sakes. Can't you take a hint?"

Sherry Carter was in no mood for this. "I *beg* your pardon."

Gretchen snorted. "Did you hear that, Randy? Do you hear the way the woman talks to me? No respect, and she never had any. Young lady, I thought we'd seen the last of you. And yet, here you are, horning in on your ex-husband's wedding, just because you happen to know his new bride."

"It's not my idea," Sherry said evenly.

"Of course not. It's that aunt of yours. Miss Puzzle Person." Mrs. Pride wheeled on Cora. "That's right, isn't it? You're the one who set this up." Gretchen nudged her husband, indicated Cora. "She was going to marry the dead man!"

"He was alive at the time," Cora pointed out.

"Is that funny? I suppose you think that's funny. My son is charged with murder, and you're to blame! And all you can do is make jokes!"

"Leave her alone!" Sherry raged.

"Oh, you again?" Gretchen stuck out her chin at Sherry. "Why don't you leave *my son* alone? Here he is, marrying a nice, respectable girl from a nice, respectable family, and you have to horn in."

Sherry's eyes blazed. "You think I want to do this? You think this is my idea? They *asked* me, for God's sake!"

Randy Pride opened his mouth. The layers of baby fat he spoke through suggested his message would be a conciliatory one of childlike innocence. Instead, in pedantic, petulant tones he whined, "Of course. You left them no choice. Threw yourself at them. What else could they do?"

Gretchen couldn't bother to listen to him. As usual when her husband spoke, she was already on to another subject. "Dennis!" she cried. "How could you do this to us? Are we such bad parents? So we disapproved of your first wife, is that a crime? You don't even tell us you're marrying again. What kind of a son is that?"

Dennis could not have been more mortified. "Mom—"

"And what's this?" Gretchen had spotted the best man. "I thought you'd quit the band. Clearly you haven't. At least I *hope* you haven't. God forbid you know someone like this who's *not* in a band."

"No, it's me, Mrs. Pride," Razor said with a sheepish grin.

Gretchen, appalled at being addressed by the young man, hastily turned her attention to the bride. "And you, young lady. Do I understand you wish to marry my son?"

"I don't know," Brenda replied gamely. She had grown *very* pale. "I hadn't realized the ceremony would be quite so—complicated."

Gretchen smiled approvingly. "Well said. And you would be the father of the bride? I don't believe I've had the pleasure."

"I'm sure you haven't," Norman Wallenstein answered. "It was my understanding that Dennis was estranged from his parents."

"Oh, you know how children are." Gretchen said it airily.

"I'm not sure I do. Anyway, I'm Norman Wallenstein, Brenda's father."

Randy Pride pushed forward. "Norman Wallenstein? Of Wallenstein Textiles?"

"That's right."

"And you've offered my son a job?"

Norman Wallenstein coughed. "Perhaps we could discuss this in private?" he said icily.

The Reverend Kimble ventured tentatively, "I take it this wedding is to be postponed?"

"No!" Brenda all but stamped her foot. She turned to her father, her face twisting into the wheedling look she always used to get her own way when she was a little girl. "Da-ad-dy!"

In all the confusion, Cora snuck off. She slipped down the aisle and fought her way to the door of the church. It was hard to do, as the crowd was pushing forward to hear what the bizarre newcomers had to say. Cora had to grab the doorknob just to keep from being shoved back in. She clung to the knob, dug her right foot into the molding six inches from the bottom of the door. With an effort, she managed to claw herself up, peer out over the crowd.

At the far end of the village green, Jimmy Potter, the librarian's son, was riding a bicycle. A tall, gawky boy of college age, Jimmy had always been a little bit slow. At the moment, he had his head down and was pedaling toward the church in dogged determination.

Cora let out a sigh of relief. Her foot slipped from the molding. She slid down and was lost in the crowd. She didn't care. She began elbowing people, battling her way out of the church.

At the altar, the Reverend Kimble had nearly restored order. Dennis's parents had run out of steam, and, aside from not liking Sherry, the pair seemed to have no serious objections to the match. Cora might have had some, but she was now nowhere to be seen. There was no reason not to proceed.

The Reverend turned to a shaken-looking bride and groom. "Are you ready?"

"Yes."

"Yes."

Brenda said it first. Dennis a half a beat later. Brenda looked at him. His smile seemed somewhat forced. But under the circumstances, it would be.

"Are you sure?" Brenda asked Dennis.

"Yes!"

He said it almost irritably. Turned resolutely toward the Reverend.

After a moment, Brenda followed suit.

The Reverend cleared his throat. "If I may have quiet, please. Let us continue." He consulted his Bible. "Do you, Dennis, take Brenda to be your lawfully wedded wife, to have and to hold, to love and to cherish, from this day forward, for richer and for poorer, in sickness and in health, as long as you both shall live?"

Dennis shot a look at Sherry Carter, seemed to implore her one last time, before his eyes returned to his new bride. "I do."

"And do you, Brenda, take Dennis to be your lawfully wedded husband, to have and to hold, to love and to cherish, from this day forward, for richer and for poorer, in sickness and—"

RING! RING! RING!

All heads swiveled at the sound of the bell.

It came from the back of the church.

Down the aisle came Cora Felton, pedaling a bicycle.

It was years since Cora had been on a bike, and she'd sort of lost the knack. She was wobbling back and forth, just trying to

308 / PARNELL HALL

stay upright. Had the aisle been any narrower, she'd have bumped into the pews. As it was, she barely squeaked by. She was steering with one hand, and ringing the bike bell with the other.

Cora pedaled up to the altar, stopped, and dismounted, like a Wild West hero riding up to save the day.

"Hold it there, Rev," Cora said. She stamped her foot on the kickstand, knocked it down, leaned the bike on it. Looked rather proud of the accomplishment. "Well, I finally got my proof. I know who set this whole thing up, and why. Would you like to know?" She turned to the wedding guests seated in the pews. "How about it, gang? Would you like to know what happened?"

A rumbling swept through the mesmerized crowd.

"I'll take that as a yes," Cora declared. "Okay, here's the scoop. To begin with, you wanna know why Dennis had all those puzzles he got caught with?"

Cora smiled and spread her arms. "It's a no-brainer. He had 'em because he *sent* 'em."

Cora had to raise her voice over the din that greeted that announcement. She pointed at the bridegroom. "Dennis Pride sent the messages, and caused all the trouble. I have proof."

Brenda looked up at Dennis in disbelief, waiting for him to dispute it, to deny it, to make it right.

Dennis didn't.

Dennis stood there, egg on his face, stunned.

"Just as I have proof who committed the murders," Cora went on doggedly. "With this bike, I can prove who killed Daffodil Dirkson." She looked out over the congregation. "Mr. Dirkson, will you come up here, please? This is your big moment. I'm going to prove who killed your wife."

Jack Dirkson was already out of his seat and climbing over people to reach the aisle. And when he did, he bolted for the back of the church.

He might as well have flung himself at a brick wall. Before he could even attempt to get out the door, Dan Finley and Sam Brogan grabbed him from either side. Dan snapped the cuffs on, while Sam began the drone. "You are charged with the murder of Daffodil Alice Dirkson. You have the right to remain silent. Should you give up the right to remain silent . . ."

59

"Damn it, Cora," Chief Harper demanded, "what the hell do I tell them?"

"Oh," Cora said, innocently. "Didn't I make that clear?"

"No," the chief said, with heavy irony. "All you told me was to post Sam and Dan near the door to stop anyone who tried to flee."

"Worked like a charm," Cora said. "I don't know what more you could need."

"There are a few gaps," Chief Harper pointed out dryly. "Would you mind filling them in?"

"Not at all, Chief. What would you like to know?"

"Practically everything. I have Jack Dirkson back there in a holding cell. His lawyer's driving up from New York. Before he gets here, you wanna tell me why I arrested his client?"

Cora groped in her drawstring bag, came out with a pack of cigarettes.

"There's no smoking in my office," Harper snapped irritably.

WITH THIS PUZZLE, I THEE KILL

"Sorry to hear it." Cora got up and headed for the door.

"Where are you going?"

"Where I can smoke."

"Get back here."

"Sorry, Chief. I need a cigarette."

"I need an explanation."

"We seem to be at an impasse."

"Damn it!" Harper heaved himself out of his desk chair, stomped out in the hall, and came back with a coffee cup. "Here's an ashtray. Burn your damn lungs out, see if I care."

"Thanks, Chief." Cora accepted the cup, fired up her cigarette.

"Now, would you mind filling me in?"

Cora took a drag on her cigarette, blew out smoke. "Just one thing, Chief. While you're in such an agreeable mood, would you mind getting Sherry and Aaron? They should hear this too."

Cora would not have thought Chief Harper's face could have gotten any redder, but it did. "You want our meeting written up in the newspaper?"

"Not at all, Chief. And of course I'll make that clear to Aaron. This is personal, and not for publication."

"Oh, great," Harper growled. "You're only going to humiliate me in front of two other people."

Chief Harper trudged gloomily out the door, returned minutes later with Sherry and Aaron.

"Sit down, kids," Cora told them. "We're having a post-mortem." She grimaced. "Bad choice of words. But that happens to be the case. Anyway, there's some things about this that you ought to know. And they're not for publication, Aaron."

"Oh, for Christ's sake!"

"You'll get your story. There's just some things you can't print."

"And you'll tell me what?" Aaron said irritably.

"No, I leave it to your discretion. That won't be hard. But I expect you to make the chief look good. That may be harder."

"Hey!"

"Sorry, Chief. Couldn't resist."

"Yeah, yeah, fine," Harper grumbled. "We're all here. You wanna tell me what you meant by your Wicked Witch of the West impression?"

That took Cora aback. She wasn't wearing her Wicked Witch of the West dress, but she had a moment of panic where she looked to check. No, of course she wasn't. She was wearing basic black, out of respect for Raymond.

Her eyes widened. "Oh. You mean on the bicycle. I'll get to that. There're more important things here." She turned back to Sherry and Aaron. "The most important thing is that you two don't split up. Because that's what this was really all about. Aside from the murders, I mean. The murders were incidental."

"I beg your pardon," Chief Harper put in. "They are not incidental to me."

"Yes, yes, I'll get to them. The point is, this is all about Sherry. Dennis just can't give her up. Understandable, but unfortunate." Seeing that the chief was about to explode, she added hastily, "So here's the score:

"Dennis, still obsessed with his ex-wife and drinking himself to death, takes the kill-or-cure step of quitting his band, sobering up, and falling in love. Unfortunately, it's not a clean break. If he can't have Sherry, he fixates on her friend. That friend just happens to come from money, and he plans to marry into the family business."

"That's hardly fair," Sherry protested.

"Sure, defend him," Aaron snorted.

"Kids, kids, let's get on with it. Chief Harper is gonna bust a gut. Anyway, that might have been the end of it except for one thing.

"The band.

"The band is lost without Dennis. Not that he's so good, but he can at least carry a tune. The lead guitarist never met a note he couldn't mangle. He can't sing and play guitar. Chaos results. The Tune Freaks are on the verge of breaking up.

"When something happens.

"Razor, the lead guitarist, spots Sherry in a bridal shop. He assumes she's getting married. She's not, she's just there with me. But Razor misunderstands. He follows Sherry to Bakerhaven, tags around for a couple of days to see who she's planning to marry." Cora smiled, gestured to Aaron. "Decides it's you."

"Are you kidding me?" Aaron said.

"Absolutely not. What does Razor do? He rushes back to New York, hunts up Dennis, says he just ran into his ex-wife and that she's getting married, too, isn't that a coincidence, why don't they have a double wedding? Like it's a big joke.

"Only Razor knows Dennis won't think it's a big joke. Just as Razor intended, Dennis and Brenda rush up to Bakerhaven to find out if it's true. Because if Sherry's really getting married, Dennis plans to stop her. He prepares cryptic messages, intended to drive her suitor off."

"Wait a minute," Chief Harper protested. "Those letters weren't to her, they were to you."

"Yes," Cora said. She flashed a glance at Aaron and Sherry before beginning her prevarication. "Dennis wrote the first message to Sherry, knowing I'd translate it for her. Before he sent it, however, he found out that Aaron wasn't engaged to Sherry at all, it was Raymond who was engaged to *me*. Lucky for Dennis, his message didn't mention Sherry by name, and could apply to me as well. So he just added the salutation 'Dear Puzzle Lady,' and left the cryptogram at the police station, figuring you'd bring it to me, Chief. He couldn't leave it at my house because Brenda was there talking to Sherry. Besides, he didn't know where I lived."

"Why does he send it at all?" Chief Harper said.

"He's just agreed to a double wedding, but he doesn't want it to come off. He's obsessed with Sherry, and he doesn't really want to marry Brenda. Anything that interferes with his marriage to Brenda is fine with him."

"So Pride sent *all* the letters?"

"Sure he did. He became obsessed with Raymond because he was obsessed with me because he was obsessed with Sherry. This was aggravated by the fact Raymond walked in on him while he was manhandling her."

"While he was *what*?!" Aaron exclaimed.

"That was right before he moved out of his bed-and-breakfast. He hunted up the real-estate agent who had rented Raymond's house, and sweet-talked her into getting him a room at the B&B across the street."

"I got all of that," Chief Harper said. "So how does that trigger a murder?"

"It sets the stage." Cora took a drag, stubbed out her cigarette. "Jack Dirkson's been looking to do Raymond in. He and his wife are out on the porch when Raymond and I arrange for Dennis to give him a ride to the wedding rehearsal. So they know Dennis is going to pick Raymond up, and they know what time. All they have to do is frame Dennis.

"Which isn't hard. Dennis is a refugee from a rock band. He'll be susceptible to drugs.

"Just before Dennis is due to pick Raymond up, Jack Dirkson slips next door. Stabs Raymond in the living room, and plants a plastic bag of cocaine on the floor in the foyer. He leaves the front door unlocked, and lets nature take its course.

"Things couldn't have worked out better. Dennis comes

alone, goes inside, finds the drugs, and can't resist the opportunity to rip them off. He sneaks out, runs back across the street, and stashes 'em in his suitcase.

"Then he goes back to get Raymond. This time poor Brenda is right behind him. And I drive up and join the party, just in time to see him pull out the knife.

"Which is too bad, because Sherry, *who is not interested in him in the least,* knew, just like I knew, that he never could have done it. And that," Cora said, looking directly at Aaron, "was her *only* interest in the matter. Dennis played it for all he was worth in the hope of driving you two apart, but I can't imagine you being so stupid as to fall for it."

"Fine, fine," Chief Harper interposed. "Not that this story of young love isn't fascinating, but I got a perp in the back on a murder charge, and I got half the town out there who'd like to know why. I'd sure like to know what to tell 'em."

"Tell 'em Jack's a drug dealer and Raymond was a narc."

"What? You're saying Harstein was a cop?"

"That surprises you? I should think it was fairly obvious."

"Raymond was not a narc. He was a dope peddler with a record."

"Whereas a narc would list himself as a narc," Cora said sarcastically. "Perhaps have an office with a sign NARC on the door, so pushers could drop in."

"Okay, okay, I get your point. But give me a break. The feds send a narc all the way from San Diego to track down the Dirksons? I mean, maybe they smoked a little dope, but they didn't exactly look like drug czars."

"They weren't," Cora said. "They were just low-level dealers, hardly worth notice."

"Then why'd the feds send Raymond?"

"They didn't. He came on his own."

"Why? What was so important about the Dirksons?"

"They got busted."

Chief Harper frowned. "What?"

"Jack and Daffy got caught selling drugs. But they didn't go to jail. They made a deal. They rolled over on their friends. By the time they were done, a lot of people went down. And Jack and Daffy walked."

"So?"

"The Dirksons didn't know Raymond, or they would have turned him in too. But some of the people they ratted out were Raymond's friends."

"You mean—"

"There's nothing sticks in a narc's craw so much as a dealer who gets busted, rats everybody out, gets off, and goes right on dealing. Raymond followed the Dirksons here, found out where they were living, managed to rent the house next door. You can verify that with Judy Knauer of Judy Douglas Knauer Realty."

"You knew this all along?"

Cora shook her head. "Raymond never told me. I found out through Aaron's source. On the San Diego paper."

"What!" Aaron exclaimed. "He never told *me*!"

"He didn't know." Cora smiled. "I said *through* your source. I had him refer me to the proper authorities. They were willing to cooperate, now that Raymond's dead."

"Well, I'll be damned," Chief Harper said.

Cora took out her cigarettes.

"Are you gonna light up again?"

"Sorry, Chief. I'll go outside."

"Sit down, sit down. Smoke the damn thing. How do you know Dirkson killed Raymond?"

"Actually, what tipped me off was Harvey Beerbaum. Hypothetically, suppose Harvey overheard some things at my engagement party which upset him and he went to call on Raymond? Harvey walked in, found Raymond dead, panicked, and split."

"What?!"

"Hypothetically."

"And you'd like me to cover this up?" Chief Harper said incredulously.

"It doesn't do you any good, and there's no reason to embarrass the poor man. The point is, when Harvey went in there, Daffodil Dirkson was on the porch."

"So?"

"Daffy didn't say anything. The reason *why* Daffy didn't say anything was, she and Jack were framing Dennis, and they didn't want to muddy the waters. But Harvey saw Daffy and Daffy saw Harvey. The fact Jack hasn't mentioned it is a strike against him."

"If I confronted Jack on it, he'd claim Daffodil never told him."

"Don't bother. Nail him on his wife."

"How?"

"After your Wicked Witch of the West crack, you have to ask?"

"All right, all right, so what's the bit with the bike?"

"That's Jack's alibi. When his wife was killed, she left the microbus in front of the church. Dan Finley had to pick Jack up at his house, take him to the hospital. I found him there, drove him home. And that's where Jack Dirkson overplayed his hand. His wife has been dead for hours. He's sitting alone and forgotten in the waiting room. Why? Because he doesn't have a ride home? No. Because he's waiting for someone to *notice* he doesn't have a ride home. The same reason he never picks up his microbus. To build up the image of the poor husband stranded at home. Who couldn't possibly have killed her because he didn't have a ride to the murder scene. He might have gotten away with it if it hadn't been for the peace sign."

"What peace sign?"

"On the back of the microbus. A great big peace sign's painted there. I saw it when I drove by the church. I realized I hadn't seen it before. You know why? Because it was covered up by a bicycle. There was a bicycle on the back of the bus. That's how he got home from the church. He drove there with his wife, killed her, left the microbus in front of the church for everyone to see, climbed on the bike, and pedaled home. Just in time for Dan Finley to pick him up and take him to the hospital. The bike was his alibi. That's why he freaked out when he saw it at the wedding."

"That was his bike?"

"Sure it was. I had Jimmy Potter get it for me. Jimmy hid out until Jack left for church, then got on the bike and rode over. It took him a while. It's a long ride. Jimmy got there just in time."

"You're lucky Dennis's parents showed up to slow things down."

"Lucky, hell. I called 'em."

"You *called* them?" Sherry exclaimed.

"I needed a diversion. Until Jimmy showed up."

"You might have told me."

"You had enough on your plate. I figured you didn't need to know."

"But really," Chief Harper said, "when you talk about giving Jimmy Potter time to get there, you mean in time to stop the wedding."

"What's your point?"

"Were you trying to stop the wedding, or nail a killer?"

"Both. Brenda's a good kid. She ought to go into marriage with her eyes open. I thought she should meet the in-laws. And see how Dennis reacted around them. That and the fact he wrote the letters ought to give a girl pause."

"Can you prove he wrote them?"

"I could make a good case. Dennis isn't very creative. For part of his first letter, he used some of the band's song lyrics."

"Oh, come on, he couldn't be that stupid," Aaron said.

"Trust me, he's that stupid," Sherry assured him.

"You drop the charges against him yet, Chief?" Cora asked.

"That's the prosecutor's decision, not mine."

"Well, you might point out that even though he isn't a murderer, he did possess a controlled substance. Not to mention stealing it. He's also violating a restraining order just being here."

"Never fear," Chief Harper said. "I'm not even sure getting the murder charge dropped will be that easy. When you come right down to it, there isn't much hard evidence against Dirkson."

"You've got his arrest record."

"I do?"

Cora shook her head. "You gotta make that sound less like a question, Chief. Try 'Yes, I do.' You got it from running his fingerprints. You got his fingerprints by having me hand him a metal clipboard with a photo attached in the guise of making an ID. A clever plan, Chief, and it worked, and that's how you knew Dirkson had been busted for drugs."

"I'll be damned."

"Now, on the strength of that, and the fact he fled, you ought to be able to get a search warrant for his house. Start with his computer. I think you'll find he's been ordering drugs by e-mail."

Chief Harper looked at her suspiciously. "Oh, you think that?"

Cora shrugged, the very picture of innocence. "Just a guess. But if you come across any coded messages, bring 'em to me. Then check out Raymond's laptop and see if he doesn't have the same ones."

"Why would he?"

"Why did he rent a house next to the Dirksons? Why did he have a wireless network adapter on his laptop? Do you suppose Raymond was tapping into their computer?"

"What makes you think that?"

Cora blew a smoke ring. "Just a hunch."

Chief Harper considered the smoke ring and he considered that. "So why did Jack Dirkson kill his wife?"

"He didn't like her," Cora said.

Harper scowled.

"Would you prefer 'How the hell should I know?'" Cora shrugged. "I would assume it had something to do with the fact that Jack and Daffy had just committed a murder together—Raymond's murder—and he was scared out of his mind she was going to slip up and give the game away."

"That's why he kept trying to shut her up when I questioned him?"

"No, I think that was part of the plan. If the two of them fingered Dennis, you might get suspicious. So the idea was for Daffy to feed you as much information as possible while Jack pretended he didn't want her to.

"Which is how Jack got Daffy to the church. Jack has Daffy call me, say she's got something important to tell me. As far as Daffy's concerned, she and Jack are just playing more of the game. She'll tell me she saw Dennis acting suspicious, but that Jack told her not to mention it.

"Jack has her call Aaron, too, because he's ready to frame Aaron for Daffy's murder. Jack frames Aaron because he thinks Dennis is in jail. Actually, Dennis got out in time to have killed Daffy, but Jack couldn't know that. Of course, Jack tells *Daffy* she's calling Aaron so her story will make the papers and really nail Dennis.

"Anyway, Jack and Daffy drive to the church in the microbus.